GNAMMA
BOOK FOUR OF
ABNER FORTIS, ISMC

P.A. Piatt

Theogony Books
Coinjock, NC

Copyright © 2021 by P.A. Piatt.

All rights reserved. No part of this publication may be reproduced, distributed or transmitted in any form or by any means, including photocopying, recording, or other electronic or mechanical methods, without the prior written permission of the publisher, except in the case of brief quotations embodied in critical reviews and certain other noncommercial uses permitted by copyright law. For permission requests, write to the publisher, addressed "Attention: Permissions Coordinator," at the address below.

Chris Kennedy/Theogony Books
1097 Waterlily Rd.
Coinjock, NC 27923
https://chriskennedypublishing.com/

Publisher's Note: This is a work of fiction. Names, characters, places, and incidents are a product of the author's imagination. Locales and public names are sometimes used for atmospheric purposes. Any resemblance to actual people, living or dead, or to businesses, companies, events, institutions, or locales is completely coincidental.

Cover Art and Design by Elartwyne Estole.

Ordering Information:
Quantity sales. Special discounts are available on quantity purchases by corporations, associations, and others. For details, contact the "Special Sales Department" at the address above.

Gnamma/P.A. Piatt -- 1st ed.
ISBN: 978-1648552519

Gnamma (ˈnamə)
Noun
1. (Australian) A hole or indent in solid rock where water collects.
2. (Australian) A planet with naturally occurring water.

* * *

One must not ask of a general "est-il habile?" ("Is he skillful?"), but rather "est-il heureux?" ("Is he lucky?")

Cardinal Mazarin, Chief Minister of France, 17th century

* * *

DINLI

DINLI has many meanings to a Space Marine. It is the unofficial motto of the International Space Marine Corps, and it stands for "Do It, Not Like It."

Every Space Marine recruit has DINLI drilled into their head from the moment they arrive at basic training. Whatever they're ordered to do, they don't have to like it, they just have to do it. Crawl through stinking tidal mud? DINLI. Run countless miles with heavy packs? DINLI. Endure brutal punishment for minor mistakes? DINLI.

DINLI also refers to the illicit hootch the Space Marines brew wherever they deploy. From jungle planets like Pada-Pada, to the water-covered planets of the Felder Reach, and even on the barren, boulder-strewn deserts of Balfan-48. It might be a violation of Fleet Regulations to brew it, but every Marine drinks DINLI, from the lowest private to the most senior general.

DINLI is also the name of the ISMC mascot, a scowling bulldog with a cigar clamped between its massive jaws.

Finally, DINLI is a general purpose expression about the grunt life. From announcing the birth of a new child to expressing disgust at receiving a freeze-dried ham and lima bean ration pack again, a Space Marine can expect one response from his comrades.

DINLI.

* * * * *

Prologue

The converted crew ship *Alharih* waited like an ambush predator in the cold darkness on the far side of the Maduro Jump Gate. Her sensor operator was alert for the telltale shimmer that warned of a vessel passing through the gate. Captain Mansoor leaned back in his control room chair and contemplated their situation.

Tensions aboard the pirate vessel were high. The crew had become bored and frustrated since their last score nearly eighteen months ago. Despite their new-found wealth, they needed action.

"We're filling orders like a bunch of damned grocery clerks!" one of them declared at an impromptu gathering on the mess deck the night before, and the crew roared their agreement. Mansoor was forced to accede to their demands or risk a knife to the throat while he slept. He was only the captain so long as he kept them happy. Some pirate customs remain unchanged, even in space.

Assaulting a ship traveling at jump speed was not for the faint of heart. Maneuvering a shuttle alongside the quarry required precision flying to avoid disaster. The boarding party had to force their way aboard and seize key ship control and engineering stations, a dangerous task even if the target crew hasn't fully recovered from the jump. It was a high risk, high reward operation that satisfied even the most hardcore adrenaline junkies among the crew.

"Captain! There it is!" the sensor operator announced. Mansoor studied his display for a long second before he keyed the mic on the general intercom circuit.

"Man the shuttle. Stand by for boarding operations."

He imagined the cheers as the crew ran for the shuttle and prepared for launch. One minute later Tench, the shuttle pilot, came onto the internal shuttle launch control circuit.

"*Alharih* this is Tench. The shuttle is manned and ready for launch. Two pilots plus forty boarders."

"This is *Alharih*, roger. Turning onto jump course and increasing speed."

Mansoor guided *Alharih* through the turn and pushed the throttles forward. It was critical that he closely parallel the course and speed of the target when it emerged from the jump gate to give the shuttle the best chance for a quick intercept. If he miscalculated the maneuver, they would end up in a tail chase and lose their prey. If the maneuvers took too long, the target crew would have time to recover and repel the attack. Of course, all of their efforts would be for naught if the target vessel collided with *Alharih* at jump speed. Then their problem would be one of simple survival.

"Here it comes!" the sensor operator said. A contact appeared on Mansoor's display, and for a heart-stopping moment the projected course lines of hunter and hunted converged and the collision alarm illuminated. He made a small course adjustment and the alarm cleared. The relative motion calculator dropped to zero as *Alharih* settled on a parallel course and speed.

"Shuttle, *Alharih*. You are cleared to launch. Target bears zero nine zero at two hundred meters."

"Roger. Opening hangar doors and extending the boom."

While Mansoor maneuvered *Alharih*, Tench had bled off the atmospheric pressure in the hangar, which saved critical minutes and allowed him to open the hangar doors as soon as they were ready.

"Doors open, boom is extended." Fifteen seconds later Tench's voice came over the external shuttle flight circuit. "Shuttle away."

Mansoor watched as the shuttle cursor crossed the distance between the ships and merged with the target.

"Contact." Tench's voice was tense as he reported touchdown. Powerful electromagnets anchored the shuttle to the other ship and an inflatable harness sealed any gaps. "Good seal." After a lengthy pause, "Hatch is breached. Assault team away."

For ten interminable minutes the circuit remained silent. Mansoor hated waiting to hear the results of the assault, but he knew it would do no good to pepper Tench with questions. The shuttle pilot only knew what the assault team leader told him.

"This is Tench. The target is secure. You're not gonna believe this."

Mansoor let out a deep breath. "What is it?"

"Nust just told me this is a Maltaani vessel." Enus Nust was the boarding party leader and overseer of prisoners they captured and sold into slavery.

"Maltaani? Is he sure?"

Nust's voice boomed over the circuit. "I'm sure. The bug-eyed bastards killed fourteen of my men."

"Any prisoners?"

"Nine, but one of them is pretty bad off; took a pulse rifle bolt to the chest."

There was a long silence before Tench spoke. "What do you want to do, Mansoor?"

Mansoor's mind raced.

What does one do with a ship full of alien technology?

"Do you think you can fly it, Tench?"

"I don't know. I'll have to go up to the bridge and see what's what."

"Do it and report back ASAP. Nust, secure the prisoners, but don't let your guys start stripping the ship until I give the order. I want to park this thing on ice next to the other one if we can. We just hit another mother lode, boys. A shipload of Maltaani technology should be worth a fortune."

* * * * *

Chapter One

First Lieutenant Abner Fortis, International Space Marine Corps, took a deep breath to calm his nerves as he paced backstage of the concert hall. He'd been on the road for a year giving speeches to encourage the citizenry of Terra Earth to buy war bonds and support the effort against the Maltaani, but he was always tense until he stepped into the spotlight.

Fortis stopped in front of a full-length mirror and checked his appearance for the hundredth time. What he saw pleased him.

The doctors at the Fleet hospital had abraded the facial scars from his fight with a mercenary on Eros-28 with careful precision. The scars were almost invisible, but Fortis was secretly pleased they weren't completely gone. He looked young for his age and the scars added a hint of hard service and experience to his appearance.

His dress uniform tunic fit perfectly; broad at the shoulders and narrow at the waist. The creases in his trousers were crisp and the crimson stripes on the seams were flawless. The *L'ordre de la Galanterie* hung around his neck on a blue and white ribbon. The medal was conspicuous in its own right and more so because it was Fortis' only medal. The president of the United Nations of Terra had awarded it to Fortis for his actions during his cherry drop on Pada-Pada. The medal gleamed with an internal luster and inspired both admiration and jealousy among his fellow Space Marines.

The only other adornment on his tunic was a badge with a blood red "9" pinned to his left breast. The badge signified his service with the ISMC Ninth Division, or "The Bloody Ninth" as it was known throughout the Corps. Five thousand Space Marines of Ninth Division had defeated a force of twenty-five thousand Maltaani during the Battle of Balfan-48, and Fortis was one of fewer than five hundred survivors. After the battle, the ISMC retired the divisional colors and authorized the survivors to wear the badge.

In place of the usual ceremonial officer's sword, Fortis carried a kukri in his sword belt. The brilliant red cordage wrapped around the handle of the weapon was pristine. ISMC tradition dictated that kukri were earned in combat and the red handle served notice to all who saw it that Fortis had killed an enemy with the wicked curved blade.

His shoes were traditional leather which Fortis shined to a mirror glow every night. He abhorred the patent leather shoes which many chose to wear with their uniforms. Fortis opined that a serious shine on leathers reflected more pride in appearance than the ersatz gleam of the plasticized footwear.

His dress uniform was a far cry from the utilities and lightweight body armor Fortis preferred to wear. Even after a year on tour he hadn't grown accustomed to the stiff formality of it. The public affairs manager assigned to Fortis called it his costume, and that was indeed how it felt when Fortis wore it.

Fortis had donned his costume and delivered his speech many times over the last year. In the beginning, he recited it word for word as it was written for him, but he slowly made changes as he became more comfortable in front of audiences until it became less speech and more conversation. The increase in war bond sales stifled any concerns with his changes.

He had agreed to the one-year assignment to give his wounds from the Battle of Balfan-48 time to heal. He'd lost his right leg below the knee and had been fitted with an osseointegrated prosthetic leg that was fused to his tibia and fibula. He controlled it with muscle commands and could wriggle his toes, roll his ankle, and everything he could do with his left leg. Today was his final performance, and he was anxious to finish it so he could rejoin the Corps.

A production assistant interrupted his reverie. "Lieutenant, you're next."

Fortis stepped aside as an older man supporting a sobbing woman passed him backstage. They were Gold Star parents whose daughter was killed when her hovercopter went down during a bug hunt on Shinto Bane. Their story was compelling, and Fortis' manager decided they made the perfect penultimate presentation for Fortis' finale. They took the crowd into a deep valley on an emotional rollercoaster which allowed Fortis to finish on a high note at dizzying, and hopefully generous, emotional heights.

"Fellow Citizens, it gives me great pleasure to introduce a true hero of the International Space Marine Corps and one of Terra Earth's favorite sons, First Lieutenant Abner Fortis."

Thunderous applause filled the meeting hall as Lieutenant Fortis entered from stage left and the spotlights found him. He acknowledged the reception with a wave and a smile as he crossed the stage to the lectern.

"Remember it's a smile of gratitude and not pleasure," his public relations manager had coached him. "And don't squint or shield your eyes."

Fortis carried a sheaf of notes in his left hand. After a year they were more prop than reference.

"Don't read from your notes. Think of your presentation like a performance," his manager told him. "The people have an image of their ideal hero. Your challenge is to fit that image."

When he reached the lectern, Fortis spread out his notes and scanned the crowd.

"Scan without seeing," he'd been taught. "Don't linger. Connect with the audience with split-second eye contact only."

After a few more seconds of applause, he smiled again and waved the people down into their seats. A brilliant blue holographic image of the ISMC logo appeared over the stage behind him. When the crowd settled, Fortis began.

"Thank you for your gracious welcome. It is my distinct honor and privilege to speak with you, my fellow citizens of Terra Earth."

A wave of applause washed across the room which Fortis greeted with another smile and nod. He glanced at his notes then looked across the audience again.

"I had a speech prepared—" he waved his notes, "—but I don't need a speech or a fancy holo show." Fortis pointed to the holograph and looked somewhere off stage. "Can we turn that off, please?" The holo disappeared. "Thank you."

With a self-conscious grin he stepped away from the lectern and began to move about the stage.

"There are some people who claim that I'm a war lover. They say that when I talk with you, I'm selling war."

Fortis paused as a murmur trickled through the audience.

"They couldn't be more wrong. I'm not selling war. What I'm selling is peace. The kind of peace paid for by concerned citizens like yourselves and Space Marines like me."

Heads nodded in the crowd. Fortis pointed to the ceiling.

"We are a spacefaring people, and our hopes have always been to enjoy peaceful relations with any intelligent species we might meet. Instead—" he paused and slowly looked over the crowd, "—we encountered the Maltaani."

Headshakes and grumbling from the crowd.

"The Maltaani are an aggressive and savage race. On Balfan-48 they attacked us without warning. They tortured and murdered the Space Marines unfortunate enough to be captured. They fight without mercy, and a Maltaani presence anywhere near Terra Earth poses a dire threat to the existence of the human race."

The crowd sat in stony silence as his warning weighed heavily on the room. He spent a few minutes describing the hell of Balfan-48, the terror of facing off against the Maltaani horde, and the irrepressible heroism of Space Marines like Private First Class Parrello and Lance Corporal Carrasco. He choked up when he spoke of the forty-five hundred Space Marines lost during the Battle of Balfan-48. He unconsciously touched the "9" on his chest when he did. His emotions were no performance and the crowd ate it up.

He went on to describe subsequent encounters between humans and Maltaani and how Maltaani expansionism threatened Terra Earth. He talked about the sacrifices made by Fleet personnel and Space Marines in defense of Terra Earth.

"It is incumbent upon all of us to do our part to protect our home planet. Don't let their sacrifices be in vain. The Space Marines are willing to fight and die if necessary. I'm asking you, my fellow citizens, to join us in the struggle to defend the human race. Terra Earth didn't start this war. We humans didn't want this war, but we will fight until final victory is ours."

He paused before delivering his final words.

"Terra Earth may be my home, but my destiny lies among the stars!"

The crowd roared as they leaped to their feet and applauded Fortis.

After a reception organized in honor of the most generous donors, Fortis changed into his utilities and zipped his dress uniform into a garment bag for safekeeping. His flight to ISMC headquarters in Kinshasa wasn't for another three hours, but he wanted to get started on his journey. The sooner he got to headquarters, the sooner he could get back to being a Space Marine.

After a final round of farewells with his manager and staff, Fortis caught a tram to the airport, checked in, and tried to look anonymous on a bench across from his gate. The speaking tour had brought him a fair amount of fame, and he had long since gotten used to the curious stares and doubletakes when people recognized him.

He finally boarded his flight and promptly fell asleep. Three hours later, he debarked into the familiar heat and humidity of Kinshasa.

It felt like home.

* * * * *

Chapter Two

It was after dark when Fortis checked into his hotel opposite the main gate to the ISMC headquarters. He had an appointment with the Junior Officer Assignments Division first thing the following morning, so he opted for a quick shower and an early bedtime.

The following morning, he grabbed a cup of coffee in the lobby and made the short walk to the ISMC Personnel building. He was twenty minutes early, but this was one appointment he didn't want to be late for.

"Lieutenant Fortis?" A balding major with a fleshy face and a too-tight uniform beckoned to him. "Follow me, please."

The major led him to a stuffy office. "Have a seat. I'll be right with you."

Fortis glanced around the room while the major, whose name was Innskeep according to the nameplate on his desk, scanned a thick file in front of him. Finally, the major closed the folder and squinted at Fortis.

"What exactly are you requesting, Lieutenant?"

"Assignment to an infantry company, either as a platoon leader or company XO. I've done both and I think—"

"Infantry is out of the question. You're not physically fit."

"Major, all I need is a physical fitness evaluation."

"It says here that your previous requests for a PFE have been denied."

"Yes, sir, they have. I believe those denials were made in error. My leg is one hundred percent, and I can exceed all the minimum standards required for duty in the infantry."

Major Innskeep rocked back in his chair and laced chubby fingers over his belly. "You want me to go against the medical advice of these doctors?"

"Not go against it, sir, put it to the test. None of those doctors have examined me in person. Schedule me for an evaluation and let me demonstrate what I can do."

"I'm sorry, Lieutenant. We're not in the business of testing the medical advice of Fleet doctors. Based on everything I see in your file, you're not fit for the infantry. Do you want to request a transfer to another branch?"

"Is there another branch that doesn't require physical fitness? Logistics? Personnel?" Fortis' eyes flicked to Innskeep's expansive waistline. The major's face reddened as he sat forward.

"Lieutenant, you would do well to remember that I hold your professional fate in my hands. I understand your frustration at being unable to serve in the infantry; I myself have experienced the frustration. That doesn't change the situation—I cannot approve an assignment to the infantry until the doctors clear you, and the doctors won't clear you without a satisfactory PFE."

"I don't have a satisfactory PFE because they won't schedule me for one, sir. That's the problem."

Major Innskeep spread his hands on his desk. "Scheduling PFE's is not my responsibility. I make assignments based on current qualifications. Right now, you're not qualified for infantry. When you get to your new assignment, your chain of command can assist you with this matter. My hands are tied."

There was a rap on the door and a pretty secretary poked her head in and waved an envelope. "Pardon the interruption, sir, but a courier just dropped this off for you. I think it has some relevance to Lieutenant Fortis' assignment."

The secretary closed the door behind her, and Major Innskeep tore open the envelope. His eyebrows went up as he read the enclosed letter.

"Do you know a Colonel Anders?"

"Yes, sir. I know Colonel Anders."

Innskeep handed the letter to Fortis. "It seems he wants you assigned to him. The Intelligence, Surveillance, and Reconnaissance Branch. ISR, for short."

Fortis read the letter.

From: Colonel Anders, Intelligence, Surveillance, and Reconnaissance (ISR) Branch Head

To: Major Innskeep, Junior Officer Assignments Division

Subj: 1ST LT ABNER FORTIS

1. It's come to my attention that 1st Lt. Abner Fortis has completed his special assignment and is available for orders. If possible, I would like to interview 1st Lt. Fortis for an opening in the ISR Branch.

2. Please instruct 1st Lt. Fortis to report to the ISMC intelligence headquarters building at 0800 hours tomorrow morning.

N. Anders
Colonel, ISMC

"You must be someone special to have a colonel requesting you by name." Innskeep held his hand out for the letter and tucked it into Fortis' file. "You have your orders, Lieutenant. Report to the intelligence headquarters building at 0800 tomorrow."

"Thank you, sir." Fortis stood and turned to leave.

"Oh, Lieutenant, one more thing." Fortis looked back and saw Innskeep had a derisive smile on his face. "If it doesn't work out with ISR, come see me. I might have something you're physically qualified for here in Personnel."

Fortis breathed a sigh of relief when he was back out on the sidewalk. Something about the headquarters building felt oppressive, and dealing with Major Innskeep left him uneasy. With the rest of the day to kill, he decided to tour the base on foot.

ISMC facilities were typically more utilitarian than Fleet facilities. There were no neatly mowed lawns or manicured flower gardens. Every square centimeter of open space was dedicated to supporting the ISMC mission, whether it was training, athletics, or research and development of new weapons and equipment. The far end of the base was dedicated to training new Space Marines, and that was where Fortis gravitated to.

He smiled as he read aloud the words carved into the stone archway that led to the training grounds: "It Takes Heat And Pressure To Make Diamonds." Fortis had experienced his share of heat and pressure during his time at ISMC Officer Basic School and the Advanced Infantry Officer course. The pace of training was aptly compared to drinking from a firehose, and Fortis' experience had been doubly difficult because he hadn't had the benefit of four years at the Fleet Academy to prepare.

Platoons of trainees jogged past, bellowing familiar cadences that were both humorous and mildly obscene. The chants helped keep the trainees in step, regulated their breathing, and fostered teamwork.

A ragged formation approached, and Fortis stopped to watch them. They were covered in dried mud and twigs that flaked off with every step. Each trainee wore a heavy pack and carried a pulse rifle at port arms. Their hoarse responses to the drill instructor's voice told Fortis they'd been having what the Corps described in typical understated fashion as "a bad day."

The formation drew abreast of Fortis, and the drill instructor ordered the platoon to halt. There was something familiar about the voice, but Fortis couldn't see him clearly through the formation.

"Right face!" ordered the drill instructor, and the trainees pivoted away from Fortis. The drill instructor walked around the formation and broke into a wide grin, which Fortis returned.

Sergeant Ystremski!

Ystremski threw up his best parade ground salute which Fortis returned, and then the pair exchanged a warm handshake.

"What the hell brings you back here, sir? Need some refresher training? Fall in at the back."

"No, thank you. It's time for orders. The clock ran out on the traveling dog-and-pony show. How are things here?"

"Good. Real good." One of the trainees shifted his feet and, somehow, Ystremski saw it even with his back turned. "Hey, pusbag! Lock it up!"

Fortis chuckled. "It looks like they're having a bad day."

"Every day is a bad day for these clowns. Hey, LT, do me a favor, would you? Say a little something to give them a boost. It's not often they meet a bona fide war hero."

Before Fortis could refuse, Ystremski addressed the platoon.

"Platoon, about face!" The platoon executed the command and faced Fortis and Ystremski. "At ease."

Fortis could almost hear sore muscles unwind as the platoon visibly relaxed.

"Listen up, ladies. This is Lieutenant Abner Fortis. Maybe you've heard of him; he led Ninth Division to victory against the Maltaani on Balfan-48."

Fortis saw surprise register on some of the faces in the formation.

"He saw you were having a bad day and asked me if he could say a few words to you. I told him you weren't worth the effort, but he insisted. Lieutenant?"

For a long second, Fortis drew a blank. The trainees stared at him as if they expected some great words of wisdom. Instead, they got a tongue-tied lieutenant.

"Okay, uh, I'm Lieutenant Fortis. If I led Ninth Division to victory, it was due to men like Sergeant Ystremski. Anyway, I know how you feel right now. Your backs ache, your legs are jelly, and your feet are throbbing. Those packs weigh a ton and you don't think you can run another meter." Wry smiles and nods broke out among the trainees. "I'm here to tell you that you can. You'll dig deep and find the strength to take another step and complete that next evolution, and then the next, and then the next. You'll withstand all the heat and pressure the drill instructors bring to bear, and you'll come out the other end as Space Marines. Remember, you don't have to like it, you just have to do it. DINLI!"

"DINLI!" the platoon roared back.

"Thanks, LT. I hope that keeps them going for the rest of the day."

"Happy to help."

"I gotta run, I have to get them cleaned up for chow. Why don't you come over for supper tonight?"

"Uh, I don't know. I have an early meeting with Anders tomorrow."

"C'mon, LT. My wife would love to meet you, and she's a dynamite cook."

"Your wife? You're married?"

Ystremski laughed. "Look me up in the base directory. 1900 sharp." He turned to the trainees. "Atten-*hut*! Right face! Forward at a double time, march!" He saluted Fortis. "See you at 1900."

Fortis stared, open-mouthed, and the platoon jogged away.

Ystremski is married?

* * * * *

Chapter Three

Fortis checked his reflection in the storm door of Number 534. Satisfied with what he saw, he pressed the doorbell.

Chaos erupted inside. A dog barked, children squealed, and footsteps thundered to the door. The door flew open, and three children confronted Fortis: twin girls of about five years old in matching pajamas and a male toddler in a diaper and T-shirt. A large mutt pushed its way through the kids and growled at Fortis.

"Don't open the door!" a woman shouted from somewhere in the back of the house. The girls giggled, and the toddler threw his arms up and ran toward their visitor. On instinct, Fortis reached down, and the dog snarled. He straightened and froze as the toddler threw his arms around one of the lieutenant's legs.

"Whoo! Whoo!" the child hooted.

"Petr, answer the door!" the woman shouted again, and Sergeant Ystremski appeared around the corner with a big smile on his face.

"Okay, all you monsters, let the poor man in," he told the kids.

The girls turned and disappeared inside, but the toddler maintained his grip on Fortis' leg while the dog growled and bared its teeth.

"Mongo, heel!"

The dog stopped growling and lowered its head, but its eyes never left Fortis.

Ystremski pushed the dog aside and pried the toddler loose.

"Some reception, Sergeant," Fortis said with a smile. "I haven't felt this welcome anywhere since we landed on Balfan-48."

Ystremski laughed. "Come on in; make yourself at home." He hefted the wriggling child under one arm. "This is Bull. Short for Bulldozer, or Cannibal. He's a hugger, as you might have noticed. The hound here is Mongo. Don't take the growling personal; he hates everyone." He stuck out his hand and the two men shook. "And stow that sergeant stuff. My house, my rules. When we're here my name is Petr."

"Abner."

Petr led the way down the hall into the kitchen, where an attractive woman in an apron stirred a steaming pot. Abner's mouth watered as the aromas hit his nose, and he couldn't help taking a deep breath.

"That smells fantastic!"

The woman smiled and wiped her hands on her apron.

"Something I whipped up for an honored guest." She surprised Abner with a kiss on the cheek and a warm hug. "I'm Tanya. My husband Petr is that rude man over there."

Petr had the toddler over his shoulder, and the child screamed with laughter as his father bounced him around.

"Hey, I got my hands full of monster!" He tipped his head toward Tanya and winked at Abner. "Now you know where he gets the hugging."

The twin girls were seated at a small table, and Petr gestured toward them. "Those are the twins, Milly and Dilly."

"Daddy!" they shrieked in unison.

"Whacky and Jacky?"

"No!"

"Let me see." Petr stoked his chin in an exaggerated thoughtful gesture. "Abby and Gabby?"

"Yes!" The girls broke into peals of laughter.

"Don't ask me to tell them apart," he told Abner.

Tanya took possession of Bull and waved to Abby and Gabby. "Come on, you three. Now that your father has you all wound up, it's time for bed."

"Good night!" the girls said in chorus. Bull made more hooting sounds and reached out for Abner, but Tanya held him tight.

"Good night," Abner replied.

The noise diminished as the trio went upstairs with their mother.

"I never pictured you with a wife, much less three kids," Abner said with a chuckle.

"*Five* kids. My oldest is upstairs studying for his Fleet Academy entrance exam and my second oldest is out on a date with her useless fuck of a boyfriend. The bun in the oven will make six."

"Wow." Abner held up the bag he was carrying. "I didn't know what to bring, so I brought wine. Red and white."

"Ah, perfect." Petr took the bag and set it on the counter. "Tanya's the one who knows which wine to drink with what food, so I'll leave it to her. Care for something stronger to whet your appetite?"

Tanya reappeared. "I got them into bed but they're demanding a story from the king storyteller. Your turn."

"I'm entertaining," Petr protested.

"Entertaining, my ass. You were about to break out that awful rotgut and start telling war stories before supper," Tanya scolded with playful seriousness. She gestured upstairs with a thumb. "March up there and do your duty, soldier."

Petr went down the hall toward the stairs while he protested over his shoulder, "I'm not a soldier, I'm a Space Marine!"

Abner and Tanya traded smiles.

"Is there anything I can do to help?" Abner asked.

Tanya pulled out a corkscrew and slid it across the counter. "Open the red and pour us a glass. I've got the rest under control."

Abner reached for the corkscrew, and Mongo growled.

"Mongo! Go lay down. Go on, get."

Mongo retreated from the kitchen, but he sat in the hall where he could watch Abner.

"That damn dog," Tanya smiled. "Petr insists we need a dog to protect the house."

"He's doing a good job."

"How about you uncork that wine?"

Abner did as asked while Tanya danced and whirled around the kitchen. She had several dishes in progress, and she juggled them all with practiced ease. One by one, Tanya plated the steaming food.

"Braised lamb, couscous, minted potatoes, wilted spinach, and a salad of bitter greens," she told Abner as he stared in amazement.

"Something you whipped up," he said, and she chuckled.

"Honored guest."

Petr returned to the kitchen, and the trio sat down to enjoy their meal. Abner couldn't remember his last home cooked meal, and it took a conscious effort to eat slowly.

"Tanya, this is really amazing," he said during a break for air. "I don't think I've ever eaten such delicious food."

"Better than pig squares?" Petr quipped, and Tanya gave him a playful slap.

Abner and Tanya drank wine while Petr opted for something stronger out of an anonymous decanter.

"It's not DINLI but it'll do in a pinch," he told Abner, and the younger man realized Petr was beginning to get drunk.

Tanya insisted on no shop talk at the table, so the two men tried to make small talk over their meal. There were uncomfortable silences whenever the conversation drifted to the Space Marines, and she shot a disapproving glance. Finally, they were finished.

Abner forced himself to refuse seconds, but he agreed to take some leftovers back to the hotel. He groaned with pleasure when

Tanya served strawberry cheesecake and coffee for dessert. When he was finished, he pushed his plate away, totally sated.

"That was incredible. Thank you so much."

Petr stood and began to clear the table. Abner tried to help, but Petr waved him away.

"She cooks, and I do the dishes," he announced in an overloud voice. "No guest of mine works in my house."

Tanya pointed to the back door. "Come on, Abner. Let's take our coffee outside on the patio and leave Petr to it."

"Yeah, leave the kitchen slave to his duty," Petr slurred.

Fortis followed Tanya outside, and they sat in plush patio chairs. For a long moment, neither one spoke.

"He loves you, you know," she said in a matter-of-fact voice.

Abner nodded. "I love him, too. I owe him my life."

She made a sound in her throat, like a stifled sob. "Don't take him away from me. Not yet."

"What?"

"Please. Don't take him away."

"I'm not taking anybody anywhere. I don't have the power to do that."

"Abner, I've been a Space Marine wife for a lot of years, and I've only heard Petr talk about one other man the way he talks about you. That was Gunny Hawkins."

Her words stunned Abner, and he struggled for a reply.

"Hawkins stood by Petr after he was busted down to private. Everyone else turned their backs on him, but not Hawkins. Hawkins is the one who convinced Petr to stay in the Corps. I hated him for it, but civilian life would have driven Petr mad."

"I had no idea."

She nodded. "I've finally got him a little domesticated again, and now you appear."

Abner started to rise. "I'm sorry, Tanya. If I'm disrupting your family life, I'll go."

"Sit down," she said a little too sharply. "I'm sorry. I don't mean it like that. I'm just scared of losing him again."

"Why? From what he told me, he's got at least two more years before he rotates to a deployable unit, and that's no guarantee that he'll go anywhere."

"I look at you, and I know you're headed downrange. Petr will follow you; all you have to do is ask."

Abner thought for a second. "Then I won't ask."

Petr picked that moment to join them on the patio.

"What are you two whispering about?" he asked with a half-drunk smile.

"Young Abner was trying to whisk me away to a distant planet," Tanya lied smoothly.

"Ah, betrayed!" Petr cried. He feigned a punch at Abner and sloshed his drink all over his pants. "Shit."

Tanya rolled her eyes and winked at Abner. "I'm going to take that as my cue to leave you two warhorses alone." She kissed Petr on the forehead. "Don't stay up too late, dear. The trainees start their day early." She gave Abner a knowing look. "Abner, it was nice to meet you. Good night."

When she was gone, Abner and Petr stared into the darkness and sipped their drinks in silence for several minutes. Finally, Petr spoke.

"How's your leg?"

"Good. Better than new, even. How's your ass?"

Petr snorted. "Never better." He raised his drink. "Here's to your leg and my ass."

Both men had been wounded during the Battle of Balfan-48. When Abner lost the lower half of his right leg to an enemy round, it was Petr's quick action that saved his life. Petr suffered serious burns across his back and buttocks after he threw himself over the wounded officer to protect him from a thermobaric drone strike.

"What's next for you?" Petr asked. "Your bond tour is over, right?"

"I gave my last speech yesterday."

"'Terra Earth may be my home, but my destiny is in the stars,'" quoted Petr in a comical voice.

"Shut up, dickhead. I didn't write it, I just had to recite it."

"DINLI."

"Yeah. DINLI."

"Seriously. Where are they sending you?"

"I haven't received orders yet. The doctors don't want to send me back to the infantry because of my leg. It needs more time, they say, but they haven't seen me running or lifting weights."

"You finished strength enhancements, right?"

"Level ten. Haven't been able to do the speed enhancements yet."

"You think they'll send you to mechs?"

"I really don't know. Honest." Fortis wanted to tell him about his encounter with Major Innskeep, but he didn't know where to start. "I'm supposed to meet with Colonel Anders in the ISR Branch tomorrow."

"Intel? Shit. Watch your back with those bastards."

"I don't know what the meeting is about. I haven't accepted orders anywhere yet."

"Well, whenever you find out, give ol' Sergeant Ystremski a call, would you? Pushing boots really sucks."

"Yeah, coming home to a beautiful family every night is terrible," Abner teased him.

"Man, don't start that shit." Petr threw back the last of his drink and set his glass down on the table with a bang. "The best part of my day is walking in that door and having the entire family go nuts. Even Tanya. Especially Tanya."

"Then what's the problem?"

Petr sighed. "It's the trainees. We're supposed to push them, to stress them and train them, and they fold. They're weak in mind and body, and they want to be officers?"

"That's why the Corps has guys like you, to train them up."

"I can't train quitters. How many quit when you came through?"

Abner thought for a second. "Two drops on request and two medicals. One of them rolled back and the other was disqualified."

"We've had forty drops from a company of a hundred already, and we're only halfway to graduation."

"Damn. DINLI."

"You want to know the worst part about it? The squirrels in Manpower are blaming the training cadre for the attrition rate. Apparently, we're too rough on the poor little lambs."

"Don't they understand?"

"Shit. The only thing those bean counters understand is bodies in billets. They've got us writing a report every time there's a drop. How the hell am I supposed to know why a candidate let the voice of defeat win the argument inside their head and talk them into quitting? I swear to God, some of these kids signed up thinking the ISMC was an extreme outdoor experience, a big team-building exercise."

Abner chuckled. "It is, kind of."

The two men sat in silence and stared at the night sky above. Finally, Petr wobbled to his feet.

"I gotta go to bed. Reveille's in a couple hours."

They shook hands at the front door.

"Petr, thank you for the invitation and a fantastic supper."

"The door is always open, Abner. And don't forget, when you find out where you're going, keep me in mind."

* * * * *

Chapter Four

Fortis woke early the following morning. After a brief set of calisthenics to get his heart started, he took a quick shower and slipped into his ISMC fatigues. He was glad for the comfortable anonymity they provided him after the attention his full dress uniform garnered. No medals or ribbons, just plain olive drab with his name tape and badge of rank.

He left the hotel and crossed the street to the base gate. After a routine ID check, he got directions to the intelligence headquarters building. It was two kilometers away, but Fortis had plenty of time and it felt good to stretch his legs. He traded salutes with other Space Marines as he walked, and it pleased him that there were no stares or doubletakes.

The ISMC intelligence headquarters was a squat, three-story building with plain lines and a forest of antennae and satellite dishes on the roof. A three-meter chain link fence with razor wire on top surrounded the building, and prominent signs warned of electronic surveillance, armed guards, and attack dogs. Fortis was fifteen minutes early, so he decided to walk around the building instead of waiting inside. He smiled as he read the stern warning signs; a squad of Space Marines could easily overwhelm the security measures and storm the building.

With four minutes to spare, he presented his ID to the guard at the gate and was waved to the front door. Inside, six sentries stood ready at a security checkpoint and watched as he showed his ID to the guard at the front desk.

"Who are you here to see?" the guard asked.

"Colonel Anders. He's expecting me."

The guard pointed to a security portal that led into the building. "Please proceed through to the scanner."

The guard at the security portal gestured to a retinal scanner. "Place your chin on the bar, focus on the crosshairs, and don't blink."

A blue beam scanned Fortis' eye. A second later the machine beeped, and a green light flashed.

"You're good to go, sir."

As Fortis passed through the portal an alarm sounded. The sentries raised their weapons to the low ready position. The lieutenant froze and slowly raised his hands.

"You have a weapon or any other large metal object?" the guard asked.

"No, I'm unarmed. I don't—" *My leg.* "I think your machine detected my osseointegrated leg."

The guard stared at him, uncomprehending.

"I have an artificial leg."

"Please remove your prosthesis for inspection."

Fortis chuckled. "I can't do that. It's fused to my tibia and fibula."

The guard gave him a puzzled look.

"Ask your men to lower their weapons and let me sit down, I'll show you."

"Lieutenant Fortis. Fortis, over here!" Colonel Anders waved from an open elevator door. "Gentlemen, please. The lieutenant is with me, let him pass."

After a long look, the guard nodded, and the sentries relaxed. A trickle of sweat ran down Fortis' spine as he lowered his hands.

"He needs a badge, sir," the guard announced. "Just a second."

Fortis wrote down his name, rank, and serial number in the visitor logbook and signed a disclaimer stating he would never talk to anyone about anything he learned while within intelligence headquarters. The guard passed him a bright orange clip-on badge with a "V" printed on it.

"Enjoy your visit, sir."

Anders ushered Fortis into the elevator with an apologetic smile.

"Sorry about that. Sometimes we take ourselves too seriously." He pulled a key out of his pocket, inserted it into the elevator control panel, and pressed his thumb to a sensor pad next to the keyhole. After a brief second, the elevator began to descend. Fortis watched all this in silence. Somehow, he knew this wasn't the time or place to ask questions, so he simply nodded.

Anders chuckled as the elevator doors slid open. "Welcome to the Puzzle Palace."

Fortis followed Anders into a large room full of cubicles bordered along three walls by glassed-in offices. It looked exactly like the office complex of the biodome engineering firm where Fortis had nearly been imprisoned after university before he escaped to the Space Marines. He shuddered.

Anders paused at an office marked, "Intelligence Surveillance Reconnaissance (ISR) Branch Head," entered a series of numbers on a keypad next to the door and held the door open for Fortis.

"Come on in, have a seat. Can I get you a drink?"

"No, thank you, sir."

Fortis sat in a chair in front of the desk while Anders slipped in behind it. He waited for Anders to speak.

"You look good, Abner. Fit. How's the leg?"

"Great. It took a little getting used to but now I don't even notice."

"Excellent. Too bad for you the ISMC doesn't agree."

"Sir?"

"The doctors won't release you back to full duty with the infantry."

It surprised Fortis to hear Anders knew of his struggles to return to the infantry. He shook his head. "I just have to show them that I can do everything the job requires."

"Hard to do if they won't give you a chance."

"Colonel, with all due respect, how do you know all this?" He tried to keep his voice level, but it was obvious Anders sensed his suspicion.

"Relax, Abner. I haven't been spying on you. I'm just keeping tabs on your progress."

"I only want to get back to the infantry and do my duty."

Anders made a dismissive gesture. "You can do much better than the infantry. *Much* better. Here in ISR, for example."

Fortis didn't know how to respond. He didn't want to damage the cordial relationship that had grown between him and Anders, but the last thing he wanted was to man one of those cubicles and never get back to the infantry.

"Colonel, I'm sorry, but I'm not an intel type. I joined the ISMC to avoid driving a desk."

"We do a lot more than drive desks in the ISR Branch."

Fortis stayed silent.

"Promotions for infantry officers have stalled since the disappearance of the *Imperio*. The ISMC has failed to recruit enough new officers to replace the missing cadets, even with the direct accession program like the one you came through. They can't promote anyone without replacements. Some platoon commanders are a year overdue for promotion, and company commanders are no better off."

"I don't worry too much about that stuff, sir."

"You should. What do you think is going to happen when the situation stabilizes?"

"I don't know."

Anders made a flushing sound and swirled his hand downward. "All those lieutenants who've been stuck as platoon commanders for three years or more will get replaced by the new officers. A few will be promoted to replace company commanders, who will also be flushed out. It's a pyramid, Abner, and the numbers get pared down every step of the way up. What do you think they'll do to a first lieutenant with an artificial leg who can't get a chance to prove that he's fit for duty?"

Fortis looked away to blink back the sudden tears of frustration that threatened to spill over his cheeks. Anders was right, and Fortis knew it, but he hadn't realized his situation was so bleak; the whole world had moved on without him while he was giving speeches and selling war bonds.

"Why are you helping me?"

Anders paused for a second as if debating what to say. "I'm not offering you anything but a chance to serve, Abner. I believe you have the makings of a remarkable officer. It would be a big mistake if the ISMC tossed you aside because of a shortsighted personnel policy or career chauvinism." The colonel flashed him a mirthless smile.

"I enjoy rubbing the noses of the higher-ups in the shit they've been serving the rest of us for a long time. You've got them spinning because they're afraid of you. You didn't spend four years at Fleet Academy learning which asses to kiss and how to kiss them. After a few short months at Officer Basic School and Advanced Infantry Officer training, you've outperformed the best the academy has produced for a generation. You're a first lieutenant but you've already won *L'ordre de la Galanterie* and earned the right to carry a crimson kukri.

"There are generals who haven't won any medals or done anything noteworthy their entire careers. They think all there is to being a Space Marine is nuking bug holes and looking good in a dress uniform. They sit on thrones earned through political connections and longevity. I enjoy watching them squirm on their fat asses."

Anders' response puzzled Fortis. "You went to Fleet Academy, sir."

"I did. I played their game and did all the right things. I was a 'promising young officer,' as they say. Then I wasn't. I was shuttled off to intelligence, and I realized the whole system is a game. I played badly, and I lost."

"What happened?"

Anders gave Fortis an enigmatic smile. "That's a story for another time."

Fortis had regained his composure, and he looked Anders in the eye.

"No desk?"

"Only if you need somewhere to put your feet up."

"Okay, Colonel. What's the job?"

"First things first, you need to meet a team that I'm forming for an upcoming mission. If there are any problems or personality clashes, I need to know about them now. After that, you'll be fully briefed about the mission with the rest of the team."

"I'm ready to go right now, sir."

"Not so fast. I've got to cross some Ts and dot some Is with personnel to get your orders sorted out and assemble the rest of the team. Which reminds me, is there anyone you'd like to bring onto the team with you? Sergeant Ystremski, perhaps?"

Fortis flashed back to his conversation with Tanya the previous evening. *Don't take him away from me.* "Hmm, no. I saw him last night, and I think he needs more time with his family."

"Fair enough."

"Can you tell me about the team, Colonel?"

"I can't tell you their names just yet, but it's a mix of Space Marines, Fleet personnel, and civilian contractors. You'd be in command."

"Civilians?"

"Yes. We frequently employ civilian contractors. They have certain technical skills that are unavailable anywhere else. But don't worry, they've undergone the same strength and speed enhancements that you have, and they have operational experience."

"That's a lot of horsepower. What kind of mission is this, sir?"

"Let's just say that I like to keep my options open. Like the sign says, this is the ISR Branch, and that's what we do. If one of my teams is faced with a situation that requires, ah, direct action, then I want them to be capable of doing so. The mission is a basic reconnaissance mission. That's all I can tell you for now."

"Can I have some time to think this over?"

Anders shrugged. "Take all the time you want but understand that I need an officer now. Your assignment to Public Affairs has ended, so you're vulnerable to whatever idiotic plan the folks in Personnel come up with. Did you know that Captain Reese is now Major Reese, and he's a member of the task force charged with managing the manpower crisis?"

"What? How did—" Fortis shook his head. "Never mind."

Captain Timothy Reese had been Fortis' first company commander and then Second Battalion Administrative Officer, and he'd been fired from both jobs due to performance failures for which he blamed Fortis. The last Fortis had heard, Reese was cashiered from the commanding general's staff and sent back to Terra Earth in disgrace. Now he was back, newly promoted, and in position to screw with Fortis. Again.

Fortis sighed. *I can't catch a break.* "I guess I'm in."

"You guess?"

"No. I don't guess. I'm in."

Colonel Anders stood and extended his hand. "Welcome to ISR, Lieutenant Fortis. I'm happy to have you."

* * * * *

Chapter Five

After his meeting with Anders, Fortis ate lunch in the base chow hall where he hoped to catch sight of Sergeant Ystremski. He drew a few stares when other Space Marines read his nametape or recognized his face, and he was glad to escape back to his hotel room.

He changed his clothes and went to the hotel exercise room to work out. Like most hotel workout rooms, the weight machines were inadequate for a Space Marine with level ten strength enhancement. There was a rack of dumbbells, but they were too light as well. If he wanted to lift weights, he'd have to go to the weight room on the base. Fortis hadn't begun the speed enhancements due to his leg injury, so he decided to run a few kilometers on the treadmill. It was boring to run in place for long distance, but he needed the time to think.

While he ran, Fortis thought back to his meeting with Anders. He remembered Tanya's plea and the look of frustration on Ystremski's face as he talked about his current duties. His thoughts turned to the last year and the grind of the war bond tour, which led him to memories of the Battle of Balfan-48. With every step he ran, he dove further into his memories—past Balfan-48 to the desperate struggle with the Kuiper Knights on Eros-28, to the fighting on Pa-da-Pada—all the way back to the fateful day he met Captain Reese on the tarmac to catch the shuttle to the Fleet flagship *Atlas*.

The faces of the dead floated in front of him, and he struggled to remember their names.

Time doesn't heal all wounds. It just helps you forget the pain.

When he finally slowed and stopped the treadmill, Fortis was shocked to see another person in the exercise room. He'd been so deep into his thoughts that she had entered unnoticed. From the looks of things, she had been exercising for several minutes.

Exhausted, he draped a towel over his head and sat down on a vacant bench. His breathing slowed, and he wiped the sweat from his face and neck. The woman, an attractive blonde with brilliant blue eyes and a firm, taut body, smiled at him from the leg machine.

"I hope I didn't bother you," she said. "It looked like you were on another planet."

Fortis chuckled. "I was, actually. Sorry about that, I didn't mean to keep the treadmill for so long."

"I don't mind," she said as she began another set of leg presses. "I don't run on leg day anyway."

He stopped at the water cooler for a drink, and her voice stopped him as he reached for the door.

"Do I know you from somewhere? You look very familiar."

The woman's question sounded exactly like a pick-up line, but he didn't sense any sort of suggestion.

"I don't think so. I'm sure I'd remember meeting someone like you."

Over the course of the war bond tour, Fortis had been approached by women, and some men, who were attracted to the idea of sex with a war hero. In the beginning, he welcomed the attention and indulged himself. Much to his surprise, the novelty of sex with many willing partners quickly wore off, and he soon began declining their offers. Fortis' manager invented a girl-back-home story for him to use as his excuse, and he spent many nights alone as the tour continued.

She snapped her fingers. "The holovision. You're the guy from the news, the soldier."

"I'm a Space Marine, and yes, I've been in the news."

"I knew it. I never forget a face." She beamed at him. "I've been exercising next to a hero and didn't even realize it."

Fortis' cheeks flushed, and he flashed an embarrassed smile. "I'm not a hero, but I served with some."

She stood and walked over to him. Fortis couldn't help but stare at her body as she moved. The Lycra workout suit she wore hugged her curvaceous shape, and it left enough to the imagination to be titillating. Her smile was like a beam of bright white light, and he was captivated by it. He felt a sudden irrepressible attraction to her.

She extended a slender hand. "I'm Idoia. Ida, for short."

"Abner."

Her touch was like an electric shock, and Abner held it for a beat too long.

"That's a beautiful name," he blurted, and his neck and face burned.

"Thank you. It's Spanish."

Abner stood mute as he bathed in her nearness, and she gave him a knowing smile.

"Abner, can I ask a favor of you?"

"Anything."

Ida motioned to the weight bench. "I want to do some bench presses, but the machine doesn't go high enough. Would you spot me a set or two on free weights? It won't take long, I promise."

"Sure."

Ida put a bar on the rack and they added iron plates to each side simultaneously to keep it balanced. As Fortis retrieved another set of plates from the wall rack, he glanced at the maximum weight setting on the bench press machine and saw "150 KG" stamped on the side.

A hundred and fifty kilos isn't enough for her?

An alarm went off in his head, and time stopped as everything happened at once.

Fortis caught his reflection in a wall mirror. He saw Ida behind him, her lips drawn back in a snarl and a weight bar raised over her head. He whirled and got his left arm up in time to absorb the heavy blow she had aimed at the back of his head. His split second of confusion became an instinctive somersault away from his attacker, and he rolled to his feet between a weight machine and the wall. His left arm was numb, so he flexed his hand to bring it back to life.

Ida followed him as he tried to escape her assault, but she couldn't swing the iron bar in the narrow space around the machine. Instead, she thrust it forward like a spear. Fortis twisted and turned to avoid being jabbed by the blunt weapon. She growled with every thrust, and spittle flew from her mouth.

Fortis timed her next thrust and grabbed the bar with his right hand, but she jerked it away.

What the hell is going on?

He cast about for a weapon of his own, but there was nothing handy in the corner where he'd taken cover.

Her next lunge was aimed at his head. Fortis ducked away and danced out of the corner, slipping along the wall behind a rowing machine next to another rack of dumbbells and plates. Ida was right behind him, and a sharp pain exploded through his body as she poked him in the kidneys with her iron pike. Fortis went down on one knee and grabbed at his back while Ida cackled and raised the bar overhead to deliver a killing blow.

At the last second, Fortis dove forward under her strike and put all his weight behind a punch deep into her solar plexus. Ida's breath whooshed out as she staggered back, gasping for air. He tried to follow her, but she held onto the iron bar and jabbed at his face while she fought to catch her breath. He retreated to the weight rack and grabbed a ten-kilo dumbbell.

"Catch, bitch."

Fortis hurled the weight with all his strength, and Ida squealed as she dove out of the way. The heavy missile hit the mirrored wall and shards of razor-sharp glass rained down around her. He grabbed another barbell and heaved it at her, but she poked it aside, and it clanged into the rowing machine.

Ida charged before Fortis could grab another barbell, forcing him to retreat further along the wall. His left arm still throbbed but feeling and movement had returned. He stumbled over a basket of stability balls, and Ida slashed at the air where his head had been a moment before. Fortis threw a couple of the rubber balls at her to cover his movement as he leaped toward the open space in the center of the room. She batted the balls away with the weight bar, but the momentary delay gave him time to get to his feet next to the bench with the loaded bar.

He grabbed the bar and kicked the bench over. The weights crashed to the floor. Fortis chuckled as he brandished his own iron weapon.

Ida spun hers like a majorette twirling a baton, and Fortis got a sinking feeling in his chest.

She's strength enhanced, and trained to fight, too.

He recognized that his best chance to fend off her attacks was to stay among the various machines and walls so Ida couldn't wind up. The kidney poke hurt like hell, but if she got real momentum behind a strike with her iron bar, it could be fatal.

Fortis ducked another sweeping blow aimed at his head and barely got out of the way of a sweep at his knees. Ida's bar whirred as she spun and twirled, only pausing her motion to lash out at him. Her bar whooshed past his face again, but before she could follow up with a low strike, Fortis sprang forward with his own attack. He thrust his bar forward in a textbook bayonet attack, and the blunt end of his bar hit Ida square in the chest. A pained look of surprise crossed her face as she parried the blow. The bar spun out of Fortis' hands and smashed another set of mirrors.

He backed away as she came at him again, but there was no speed behind her movements. Blood trickled from the corner of her mouth and her breathing became a ragged wheeze. Fortis knew he'd done some real damage with his strike to her chest. She feinted high and swung low, and her bar struck Fortis on his prosthesis. He didn't feel any pain, but the vibration traveled up his leg and into his hips. He chanced a look down but didn't see any damage.

She snarled and bloody bubbles collected on her chin as she leered at him. "That's right, you one-legged fucker. I'm gonna smash your leg and then I'm gonna smash—"

She attacked before she finished her sentence, but her ruse didn't fool Fortis. He sidestepped and ducked behind the lat pulldown machine. He grabbed the rope handle as he circled around and used it as a flail to whip Ida across the back. She screamed in pain and whirled to defend herself, but Fortis had already moved out of range.

The combatants glared at each other through the machine as they calculated their next moves. The shock of Ida's surprise attack had worn off, and Fortis was determined to finish the fight.

He glanced toward the door and took a step in that direction. As he hoped, she circled to block him. Now she had her back to the door, and the weights he'd kicked free from the bench littered the floor behind him.

Ida scowled. "There's no escape."

Fortis spun around and grabbed two ten-kilo plates from the pile. He threw them in rapid succession like frisbees. The first one missed, but Ida was too slow to dodge the second, and it smashed into her knee. She howled and staggered back. He grabbed two more plates.

Ida dropped her bar and lurched for the door. The move surprised Fortis, and, for a moment, he only stared. He snapped out of his shock and hurled a plate at the retreating assassin. It caught her between the shoulder blades and knocked her into a cart full of towels and spray bottles next to the door, and she went down in a heap. He waited, but she didn't move.

Fortis retrieved the bar from where Ida had dropped it and cautiously approached her body. He poked at her foot, but she didn't respond. He stepped closer and jabbed at her buttocks, still no reaction. He breathed a deep sigh of relief and poked her shoulder to roll her over.

Ida attacked.

She blinded Fortis with a shot of cleaning chemicals from one of the spray bottles. A handful of towels thrown in his face further confused him. Ida jumped to her feet as he stumbled backward and blindly parried with the iron bar. His eyes burned, and the sharp smell of cleaning chemicals stole his breath.

A kick hit Fortis above his left ear, and stars exploded in his head. He wobbled and almost fell as the world lurched one way and then the other. He heard Ida move in for another attack, but Fortis was able to get his left arm up in time to block it. Pain shot up to his shoulder when her foot pounded the same spot as the weight bar, and his arm went numb again. He dropped the iron bar and lurched backward.

A torrent of tears poured down his cheeks, and Fortis caught sight of his assailant through blurry eyes. Ida coughed and thick, dark blood spilled over her chin and stained her bodysuit. It was clear to Fortis that she was still a serious threat even though grievously injured, and he had to go on the offensive to survive.

He lunged forward and threw a straight right punch at her nose. His fist connected. Ida took a step back as her hands went to her face, and Fortis followed up with a kick to her groin with his osseointegrated right leg. Ida let out a guttural scream as she went down to her knees and clutched at her injured crotch. Bloody vomit spewed from her mouth, and her body spasmed as she fought for breath.

Fortis bent down to pick up the iron bar, and a wave of dizziness sent him sprawling. Ida groaned as she struggled to her feet. She clutched her stomach in a bent-over shuffle as she staggered toward the door, and he had the momentary thought to let her go.

But Fortis forced himself to get up. He picked up a kettle ball weight and stumbled after her.

Ida reached the opaque glass door of the workout room, and she struggled to turn the handle. Fortis got behind her and swung the kettle ball with all his remaining strength. The weight hit her in the back of the head with a wet thud, and the murderous woman pitched forward. The glass door exploded under the impact of her body, and she sprawled through it into the hallway. He kicked his way through the wreckage of the door and stood over her. Her body twitched. Fortis raised the weight as high as he could and slammed it down on her head. He heard a *pop* as her skull collapsed.

The floor lurched under his feet as a wave of vertigo scrambled his brain. He collapsed forward and fell to the floor.

Who is she?

* * * * *

Chapter Six

Colonel Anders arrived on the heels of the medics and police. He insisted they move Fortis to a furniture storeroom down the hall. The injured lieutenant slumped in a lounge chair and winced as the medic probed his cuts for glass shards.

"We should stay clear of the crime scene investigators," he told Fortis. "There will be plenty of time for you to give them a statement later."

Fortis tried to talk to Anders, but the colonel glanced at the medic and waved away his questions. "Let's get you fixed up and then we'll talk."

Finally, the medic dabbed antibacterial cream on Fortis' cuts and straightened.

"Lieutenant, I don't think any of your wounds need stitches, but you should get evaluated for a concussion. Do you want me to call an ambulance?"

"That won't be necessary, thank you," Anders interjected.

The medic shrugged, packed up his trauma kit, and pulled the door shut behind him as he left.

"Did I miss something, Colonel? Why all the secrecy?"

"Until we get more clarity about the attempt on your life, it's better that we keep our information to ourselves. That medic could be anybody."

"The *medic?*"

"Abner, you're part of the intelligence world now. Anyone is a potential source of information, whether they know it or not. He could make an off-hand remark about this situation to stranger in a bar that completes a puzzle."

There was a rap on the door and a female staff sergeant poked her head in and handed Anders a file folder. "Pardon the interruption, Colonel, but the rapid DNA scan results are back."

The colonel looked over the document inside the folder before he passed it to Fortis. "As we suspected."

Fortis looked at the document. It was a one-page profile of Idoia Guerra, with a blurry picture affixed to the top. The information stunned him.

"Excuse me, Lieutenant, I need to draw some blood." The sergeant produced a phlebotomy kit and reached for his arm. "Standard toxicology screen."

Fortis glanced at Anders, who nodded.

"Her name was Idoia Guerra. Also known as 'La Química,'" Colonel Anders said. "The Chemist."

"I don't understand. She was a chemist?"

"No, La Química was her alias. She specialized in killing her targets with poison."

"Ida was an assassin?"

"Yes, and a good one, too. She is suspected in a dozen murders over the last decade, but law enforcement couldn't get a solid lead on her. For a long time, they weren't even sure she existed."

"Lieutenant, did you smell anything unusual during your, ah, encounter with her?" the sergeant asked as she snapped a piece of surgical tubing tight on Fortis' bicep. "Perhaps a strange sensation?"

"She clobbered me with a weight bar and kicked me in the head, those were strange sensations."

"No, sir, not like that." She smiled. "A feeling or sensation that might have been chemically induced."

Fortis thought for a second. "You know, when we first shook hands I had this crazy urge to have sex with her. I mean, well, having sex isn't a strange sensation," he stammered. "It's just—ah crap, I'm sorry, it's hard to explain."

"No apologies necessary, LT." The sergeant removed the needle and taped a piece of gauze over the puncture. "You're all set." She gathered her gear and headed for the door. "I'll have the results ASAP, Colonel."

"Thank you."

Once she was gone, Fortis gave Anders a quizzical look. "Who would send an assassin after me? I'm just a Space Marine."

"That's a very good question, and one Guerra might have answered if we'd gotten the chance to ask her," Anders said with a disapproving tone.

"Are you blaming her death on me, Colonel?"

Anders shrugged. "I saw the security footage. She was flat on the floor when you smashed her head. Who else is there to blame?'

"She was trying to kill me."

"Nevertheless, we can't gather much intelligence from a dead woman."

"What now? I go to jail for defending myself against an assassin?"

"Hardly. Fortunately, this hotel is part of the greater military reservation, so we have jurisdiction here. There won't be any local law enforcement involvement, and we have some influence with the military police. You won't suffer any repercussions."

Fortis blinked and tried to wipe the fog from his brain. He head felt like the kick had shaken something loose. Anders' words reverberated as if he was shouting down a long hallway. The beginnings of a massive headache sprouted just behind his eyes, and he suddenly felt very tired.

"Come on, Abner." Anders stood and helped Fortis to his feet. "Let's get you to the hospital and get your head checked."

* * *

Three hours later, Fortis was cleared to leave the hospital. After a battery of tests and scans, the doctor didn't find any evidence of lasting damage to his head or body.

"You're going to have quite a headache, but it will subside." The doctor handed Fortis a pill bottle. "These are a mild painkiller and sedative combined; they will ease the pain and help you sleep. Your left arm is going to be sore for a while, but the bruising should disappear within a week. That was some gym accident."

Fortis grunted but didn't answer. After Anders' warning, Fortis was reluctant to talk to anyone about the assassination attempt. His headache had blossomed into a full-blown migraine, but the fog in his head was gone.

Anders led Fortis to a waiting vehicle.

"I had all your things collected from your room," he told Fortis. "I hope you don't mind. I moved you into our team building for security reasons. We can talk freely there."

The vehicle stopped in front of a plain brick building that had been a hangar in a previous life. The armed guards recognized Anders and waved them through. Fortis followed Anders inside. They passed through a small foyer and into a main hallway with three doors: left, right, and center.

Anders gestured to the left. "Chow hall, weight room, briefing theater, offices, etc." He pointed to the right. "Berthing. Everyone gets their own room, yours is the first one on the left." He pushed through the double doors directly in front of them into a cavernous space with a thirty-meter roof and cement floor. "This is the hangar. We can build full-scale target mockups, sand tables, and whatever else it takes to ensure mission success." He pointed to a door with FIRING RANGE painted in bright red letters.

"That door leads to an underground firing range. Handguns only. We don't do a lot of long-range shooting in our line of work, but I can arrange time on a rifle range if you have the need."

Fortis tried to take it all in as he followed Anders from place to place. The team building was an incredible facility. And it was completely deserted.

"Where is everybody?" he asked as Anders led him down the hall toward the offices.

"The kitchen staff is hard at work. This building is for mission planning and preparation," Anders said as he pushed open a door marked COMMANDING OFFICER. "You're not the only show in town. Everyone else is deployed or training elsewhere."

Anders' office had the usual desk and visitor chairs, but there was room for a large map table and an area arranged with plush chairs and a sofa.

"This is my office, but I don't spend much time here," Anders said as they settled into the chairs. "After a mission is proposed, and the team goes into isolation, I stay away until they're ready to brief their mission plan."

"Why?"

"I don't want to influence the planning process. The operators we bring in are the best at what they do, and they're more than capable of developing a tailored mission plan they can execute. If I'm there, it might bias their planning."

"Colonel, are you sure I'm the right guy for this job? You talk about mission plans and operators, but I only have the minimum level of training for a Space Marine Infantry Officer."

Anders smiled. "That attitude is exactly why you're here, Abner. You see, this job isn't considered career-enhancing for an officer. Promotion boards only see that an officer has been assigned here. Their specific duties are secret. It's a dead spot in a career path because you can't talk about what you do here, now or ever. Still, many mediocre officers imagine they can reignite fading promotion prospects by coming here, and personnel is happy to send them."

"You said your operators are the best at what they do?"

"They are. The officers are another story."

"Thanks."

Anders chuckled. "Don't take it personally, Fortis. You're a completely different animal than they are. Hell, I've had captains and majors who couldn't plan their way from their racks to the chow hall and back, and they weren't smart enough to recognize it. They get sidelined and assigned to coordinate support or whatever other excuse the teams come up with to leave them behind and out of the way. That won't happen to you."

Fortis was still skeptical, but the shift in the conversation was uncomfortable. He didn't like to talk about himself, and Anders' complete confidence in him made Fortis uneasy. Anders seemed to sense it.

"We'll get to the team and the mission when the time is right." He pulled a data tablet from his pocket. "While you were being treated in the hospital, I thought of some possible answers to your question about who might send an assassin after you. In no particular order, these are some possibilities.

"First off, it could be a case of mistaken identity. I think this is the least likely possibility. An assassin like La Química doesn't make a mistake like that, especially not after she verified your identity.

"Second, it could be someone who is envious or angry at your success."

Fortis laughed. "Really? Who would do that? That sounds crazy."

"People have murdered for less, Abner. For example, Major Timothy Reese comes from a prominent family, and you've embarrassed him twice, once as company commander and once as battalion administrative officer. Then you were hailed as a war hero on a global war bond tour. Is it possible he is angry enough to want you dead?

"Another possibility is the Kuiper Knights. Although they don't have a presence here on Terra Earth, you broke up their plans to take over Eros-28 and killed a number of their brotherhood in the process. It's difficult to say whether they're angry enough to spend the money on a contract with La Química, but it's not impossible."

Fortis thought back to Mikel Chive, the leader of the Kuiper Knights on Eros-28, moments after he slashed the mercenary open from crotch to throat with his kukri. Cold fingers tickled his spine, and he gave an involuntary shudder.

"There's always a chance it was a random weirdo, some anti-war type with a bone to pick with the ISMC. I'd rank this right next to mistaken identity, though; very low probability.

"Finally, and the most likely in my opinion, is a person or persons who lost a lot of money, power, or both when you destroyed the Galactic Resource Conglomerate's test tube soldier project on Pada-Pada. Someone like Dexter Beck, perhaps."

Beck had been the GRC project manager for their precision-crafted soldier project, or "test tubes" as the clones were called, when Fortis and his Space Marines destroyed his project. Beck was also a witness for the prosecution during Fortis' subsequent court-martial.

"The GRC?" Fortis shook his head. "I don't know, Colonel. That seems pretty unlikely."

"Abner, when the news about what happened on Pada-Pada broke, the GRC stock price plummeted. People lost trillions of credits and more than one investor was financially ruined. The conglomerate lost several defense contracts over the incident, and they have not yet fully recovered."

"What about what we did on Eros-28? We saved the GRC from the Kuiper Knights."

"You certainly did, but you have to remember that the GRC is a massive organization with many different interests. It's not necessarily someone from the GRC. Some very important people inside the government lost a lot of money, power, and prestige as well."

"Colonel, you think someone inside the government paid La Química to kill me?"

Anders threw up his hands. "Based on what I know about you and the impact your actions have had, that's the most likely place to search for a suspect."

His data tablet beeped, and the colonel answered the alert.

"Ah, good. Your toxicology screening is complete. No poisons, but the lab detected a synthetic pheromone. Looks like La Química distracted you with it to get close enough to use the weight bar."

"I should have seen it coming."

"Nonsense, Abner. You had no reason to think she was anything but a friendly, attractive young woman."

Just then, Fortis' stomach gave a loud growl, and his face reddened.

"Excuse me, Colonel."

Anders smiled. "It's been a long time since lunch, Abner. Let's head down to the chow hall and get supper. I think you'll like the food here."

Colonel Anders was correct; Lieutenant Fortis did like the food. It wasn't as good as Tanya Ystremski's cooking, but it was the best he'd eaten in an ISMC dining facility. Anders and Fortis had the dining area all to themselves, and they sat at a table far from the service line.

"What's the plan for me now, sir? What should I do until the rest of the team gets here?"

"Rest. Eat. Exercise. Whatever you want, as long as you don't leave this building. It's only for a couple days. The rest of your team will be here in forty-eight hours. Do you want a masseuse to work on that shoulder for you?"

Fortis rotated his left arm and resisted the urge to groan. "I'll be okay. A hot shower and a light workout should loosen it up."

When they were done, Fortis accompanied Anders to the foyer. The colonel paused and patted him on the shoulder.

"Take it easy, Abner. Enjoy the break. Once the rest of the team gets here, there won't be any time off until mission complete."

* * * * *

Chapter Seven

For the next two days, Fortis explored the empty building while he waited for his team. He discovered a therapy tub next to the weight room, and he spent several hours soaking out the aches from his fight with Idoia Guerra. There was a deep purple-black bruise on his left shoulder and a perfect plum-colored circle on his back where she'd poked with the weight bar.

The weight room was a pleasant surprise. It was equipped with weights and machines built for heavy lifting. Fortis took full advantage of the opportunity. He had completed the course of strength enhancement to level ten while he was on the war bond tour, but most of the facilities available on the road were inadequate for him to fully train. He lifted to muscle exhaustion twice a day and reveled in the euphoria of the endorphin rush every time.

There were also high-tech treadmills and stair-steppers, but he chose to run laps around the cavernous hangar instead. He did some footwork drills while he ran to help train and strengthen his leg. The starts, stops, and quick changes in direction trained muscles that the machines couldn't, and he pushed his osseointegrated leg as hard as he could, with satisfactory results.

On the morning of the third day, Fortis had just completed a long run and was in the middle of cooldown laps when the door of the hangar banged open, and a massive man walked in.

"Honey, I'm home!" he announced in a booming Australian accent as he dropped a duffle bag onto the concrete floor. The newcomer, a bald black man with muscles that bulged through his T-shirt, didn't acknowledge Fortis. Instead, he took a deep breath and let it out with an exaggerated sigh of satisfaction.

"Smells like home cookin,'" he said to no one.

The door banged open again, and an Asian man with a long black ponytail entered. His physique was a miniaturized version of the first man, and he likewise dumped a duffle bag on the floor.

"Son of a bitch, don't tell me I'm saddled with you again, Bender," he said to the bigger man.

Bender shook his head. "I don't believe it, mate. How am I supposed to operate if I have to carry a pogue like you?"

The two laughed and bro-hugged.

Fortis was unsure whether to approach and introduce himself or not. They settled the matter when they hoisted their duffle bags and disappeared back into the foyer.

Maybe they're on another team?

He finished his cooldown laps and headed for his room. When he entered the hall where his room was located, he discovered Bender, the Asian man, and another individual in the middle of an animated discussion further down the passageway. They glanced at Fortis but turned back to their conversation when he opened his door.

After a quick shower, Fortis made his way to the chow hall. He discovered the trio together at a remote table, heads bent together over their meals. There were two additional people, a gray-haired man and a petite blonde woman, seated at separate tables. He exchanged nods with the man as he sat down at an empty table and ate quickly. There was an occasional burst of laughter from the three men at the other table, but otherwise the room was quiet.

Fortis finished his meal and returned to his room. There was a note taped to his door.

Team meeting 1900 in the briefing theater.

He checked the time and saw it was ten minutes until 1900, so he decided to head over to the briefing theater.

Can't be late for the first meeting.

Fortis entered the theater and saw the trio of men were already there, as were the man and woman he had seen in the chow hall. He took a seat in the rear and sat back to wait for the meeting to start.

Right on time, Colonel Anders entered the room, trailed by a short, dark-haired woman who slipped into a seat in front of Fortis.

"You all know who I am, so let's find out who you are," Anders said. "We'll start up here." He pointed to the trio. "Name and specialty."

The large black man stood. "They call me Bender. I'm a weapons specialist and a combat engineer."

The Asian man with the ponytail was next. "I'm Bugs." He gestured to Bender. "I'm a better combat engineer than this lug, and I'm a medic."

The third man of the group smiled and gave a little wave. "I'm known as Cheese and I'm a communications technician and intelligence specialist."

The blonde woman said, "I'm an electronics specialist and my friends call me Tweak."

The gray-haired man was next. "My name is Cujo, and I'm a pilot. If you can build it, I can fly it. I'm a lover not a fighter."

The introductions continued, and Fortis suddenly realized he had no nickname or special training. His mouth went dry and his palms began to sweat.

The dark-haired woman in front of Fortis stood. "My name is Lou and I'm a linguist and a microcomputer technologist. I'm also a medic."

Fortis stood. "My name is Abner Fortis, and I don't have a particular specialty."

One of the trio chortled, and Cujo did a double-take.

"Are you sure he's ready for this, Colonel?" Bender asked.

Anders stepped forward. "Mr. Fortis specializes in command and control, and he is in command of this mission."

Fortis felt like a little kid whose big brother stuck up for him, and his face grew hot.

Anders continued. "A long time ago, a Cardinal Mazarin in France said the question to ask of generals isn't 'Is he skillful?' The question to ask is 'Is he lucky?' I can assure all of you that Mr. Fortis is both skillful and lucky."

"Lucky it is," Bender replied. "Welcome aboard, Lucky."

Everyone laughed, and the tension in the room evaporated.

"You're now designated Team X5D1," Anders snapped, and the room became serious again. "Ground rules for this mission are as follows: this is a covert mission. You'll wear civilian clothes, and you will not use military ranks or civilian titles. From this point on, you will have no contact with anyone outside this room except as the mission requires. No spouses, no sweethearts, no old military buddies.

"This mission consists of three phases. First, you'll be issued some specialized equipment and do some familiarity training with it. Phase Two is mission planning. Phase Three is mission execution. Phase One begins tomorrow morning. Any questions?"

Bugs stood. "When do we find out what the mission is, Colonel? It would be nice to know where we're going and what we're doing."

"Bugs, this mission is extraordinarily sensitive for a number of reasons. I'm sorry, but I'm not authorized to brief you on specific details at this time. When I receive authorization, you will move into the mission planning phase."

Fortis sensed something odd about Anders' response to Bugs, and a thought flashed through his mind. *He's nervous.*

"Any others?"

The team was clearly experienced enough to know they would only get non-answers from the colonel so there was no point asking for more details.

"Okay, then. Reveille is at 0500 for breakfast. At 0600, muster in the hangar for gear issue." Anders looked around the room one more time. "That's it then. Dismissed."

Fortis waited by the door for the team members to file past him and shook their hands in turn. Bender was the last in line, and he paused to let the others exit the briefing room. Bender's hand swallowed Fortis'.

"Lucky, I didn't mean anything by my question about your readiness for this mission. You wouldn't be here if you weren't."

"No offense taken, Bender. I realize what it must look like to a room full of experienced operators to have a relative cherry in command."

Bender leaned close and lowered his voice. "I recognized you right away, LT. I'm a master gunnery sergeant myself."

"Your secret is safe with me, Bender," Fortis replied with a wink.

The two men chuckled and headed for their rooms.

"What do you make of all this, Lucky? I've been doing intel missions for a while, and this is the first time it's ever gone down like this."

Fortis wondered how far he could trust Bender, and he decided to keep his opinions to himself for now.

"I don't know. It seems odd, but I guess the colonel knows what he's doing."

They arrived at Fortis' room. "Have a good night, Bender. I'll see you bright and early for chow."

Bender laughed as he walked away. "Right. Chow. Good night."

*****

Chapter Eight

Fists hammered on Fortis' door and jerked him from a deep sleep.

"Lucky, let's go!" Bender bellowed from the passageway. "It's PT time."

Fortis checked the time. 0400.

He stumbled to the door and looked out.

"You're an hour early. It's only 0400. Reveille's not for another hour."

"Come on, sleepy head. Time to rise and shine with the daily dozen."

The daily dozen was a standard group of exercises prescribed by the ISMC to maintain peak fitness. Since most Space Marine infantrymen were now strength and speed enhanced, the practice had begun to wane except among old school Marines like Bender.

Bugs and Cheese pounded on the other doors, and soon the hall was filled with their bleary-eyed team members.

"You've got thirty seconds to fall out into the hangar, dressed and ready to exercise," Bender announced. "This team does everything together, starting now."

"If I tell you to go fuck yourself, do I have to be there?" asked Cujo, and everyone laughed. Even Bender cracked a brilliant white smile.

"Yuck it up, old timer. In twenty seconds, I'll drag you over there, and you'll be exercising in your boxer shorts."

Once the team was lined up, Bender led them through the calisthenics. The workout got Fortis' blood pumping, but he saw Tweak struggling to keep up. He moved next to her and paced his movements to match hers.

As the group progressed from one exercise to the next, he watched her form and offered advice.

"You got this. Steady breathing and controlled motion," he told her. "Do as many as you can and then one more."

By the time they were finished, Tweak's face was a blotchy red and sweat gleamed on her face and neck, but she was smiling.

"Thanks, Lucky. I wasn't sure I was gonna make it," she gasped. "I'm not cut out for this shit."

"You did fine. It takes a little getting used to, but you'll be knocking them out in no time."

"Ten minutes for showers," Bender announced as he led the group back to the dorm. "Muster here in the hall to go to chow. Together."

Nine minutes and forty seconds later, Fortis stepped into the hall and found the team waiting. It became clear that the rest of the team knew what to expect from Bender, who had assumed an active leadership role.

Am I the only newbie on this team?

The team filed through the serving line and gathered around two tables Bender pushed together. Fortis ended up between Cheese and Lou. He turned his attention to Lou.

"You said you were a linguist, Lou. What languages do you speak?"

"I speak English, of course. The common tongue, two dialects of Chinese, French, some German, Spanish."

Fortis nodded as she recited the list.

"And Maltaani."

The last stunned him.

"You speak Maltaani? How? I mean, how did you learn Maltaani?"

She waved for him to keep his voice low.

"I was assigned to interrogate the Maltaani soldier captured during the Battle of Balfan-48," she said with a knowing smile.

"Fuck You Too," Fortis said.

"Aardvark, as we like to call him. It fits their naming conventions better than Fuck You Too."

"I wondered what happened to him. How did you come to work with him?"

"I served as an interpreter under Colonel Anders when he was a captain, so when he needed someone to work with Aardvark, he offered me the job. It turns out Maltaani is similar to our common tongue. They're a lot like us, you know."

"Yeah, I remember thinking that same thing," Fortis said.

"Aardvark remembers you."

"Really? I hardly had anything to do with him."

"He asked about you during our first session."

"Huh. Where is he now?"

"He's been repatriated back to his own kind. Aardvark was a low-ranking conscript of little intelligence value. We learned everything we could about the Maltaani race from him, and there was no reason to hold him any longer."

Bender interrupted them. "Eat up, ladies. We're due in the hangar in thirty minutes."

Just then, Colonel Anders entered the chow hall, went through the line, and joined the team.

"Good morning. You're all up early this morning," he said.

"Looks like you slept in again, Colonel," Cheese said.

"Yeah, well, some of us need more than thirty minutes of sleep to function. If you must know, I was up all night ensuring that you would receive the proper gear this morning."

"You should have been here for PT, sir," Bender replied. "Nothing like the daily dozen to wake up a tired body."

"Sorry I missed it. Maybe next time."

"Yes, sir."

Anders looked at Fortis. "The supply sergeant and her team are putting the gear out right now; they should be done in twenty minutes or so. Do you have any plans for the team between now and then?"

Fortis glanced at Bender, who shrugged.

"We were about to go back to our rooms for a few minutes before we mustered up in the hangar, sir. With your permission, of course."

"It's your team, Lucky. Do whatever you want, just don't be late."

The team rose, deposited their dishes on a cart by the door, and headed for their dorm.

"Pump and dump and be back out here in fifteen," Bender instructed.

After their break, the team joined up and proceeded to the hangar. There they found a row of tables with stacks of gear labeled for each team member. A supply sergeant with a no-nonsense look on her face stood next to Colonel Anders.

"Team, this is Sergeant Dunham, our logistics sergeant. She will issue you the gear you'll need for the mission. Sergeant."

Sergeant Dunham stepped forward. "Good morning. The equipment you're about to receive is extreme cold weather, or ECW, gear. It is vital that you follow my instructions step by step. The ECW is a layered system that functions together to protect the user, and every layer must be worn properly.

"The first layer is a body suit specially fitted for you based on laser photometrics collected as you passed through the entryway. It's a snug fit, and it's designed to wick moisture away from your body and reflect body heat back. Embedded in the body suit are over a thousand temperature sensors. These report body temperatures to the control system which uses them to maintain suit temperatures within a preset range.

"The next layer is the power supply, worn as a vest. The ECW is powered by body heat and the vest senses core body temperature. Finally, the external layer is ice resistant and puncture proof coveralls. On the left sleeve is a system status display which includes a heat map of the user's body, generated by the body suit sensors. As long as the body suit, vest, and coveralls are in physical contact, data and temperature orders can be transmitted between the layers.

"Next to the suits you'll find matching boots, gloves, and a hood. They must be zipped securely to the coveralls around your ankles, wrists, and neck. Please put them on now."

"The final piece of ECW gear is the helmet. It is designed to keep your head warm, protect against injury, and it is the heart of the system. The visor has a heads-up tactical display, and the helmet allows for hands-free communications. Around the bottom of the helmet is what we call the scarf, which is zipped to the coveralls. The zipper is how the helmet interfaces with the suit, and it must be securely fastened.

"The ECW can also be worn in lieu of a space suit. The atmosphere where you're going isn't toxic in the short term, but you don't want to breathe it without your helmet or your lungs will freeze, and you will die slowly and in great pain. Does anyone have any questions about the ECW?"

Bugs raised his hand. "The fingers on these gloves are awfully bulky. How are we supposed to fire a pulse rifle with them on?"

"The short answer is, you don't," Colonel Anders replied. "At the temperatures you'll be operating in, pulse rifle performance is unreliable. You will be issued ballistic sidearms with modified trigger guards instead. Any other questions?"

The team exchanged glances and shook their heads.

"Good. Get your suits on and get down to the firing range."

The team spent the rest of the day on the firing range learning how to shoot while wearing the ECW. After they all demonstrated the ability to hit the target, Bender introduced basic tactical movement into the training. The Space Marines paired up with the civilians and practiced moving and shooting in twos and then threes. Of the group, Cujo was the worst shot and the most careless with his weapon.

"I told you, I'm a lover not a fighter," he said as Bender took his pistol away. "I hate guns."

Bender ended training with Fortis' concurrence once he was satisfied with the team's performance. "Head up to the hangar and get these suits off. We're done for the day."

* * * * *

Chapter Nine

At nine o'clock the next morning, Fortis and the team waited in the briefing theater for Colonel Anders to arrive. The mood in the room was subdued, and even Bugs and Cheese were quiet.

Colonel Anders entered and went straight to the computer terminal. His face was fixed in a scowl, and he didn't offer his typical greeting. After a few keystrokes, a holograph of an anonymous planetary system appeared.

"The system you see in the holo behind me is called The Menard, named after the astrophysicist who discovered it. Much like Menard himself, the system is cold and inhospitable and little is known about it. The Survey Service conducted a basic data collection mission through the system, and all they found were frozen rocks. The Menard is one of those systems that defy scientific explanation. It is a cluster of desolate planets two hundred and fifty million kilometers from the nearest star, clinging together at the edge of known space.

"During the Battle of Balfan-48, the Maltaani easily jammed our command-and-control circuits, which nearly led to our defeat. Since that battle, there has been renewed interest in non-traditional communications systems and frequencies. A lab assistant experimenting with a very low frequency, or VLF, system discovered this signal."

Anders tapped the keyboard and Fortis heard a beep over the speakers. A few seconds later, the beep was repeated.

"In real time, it sounds like a random signal or an anomaly, but when she sped it up, this is what she heard."

The colonel hit another key and the beeps became a recognizable pattern. Three short beeps, three long beeps, three short beeps.

"SOS," Tweak said. "International distress signal."

"Precisely." Anders entered another command and The Menard holo zoomed in on the largest body in the system.

"As soon as the signal was authenticated, we dispatched a survey drone and it followed the signal to this planet, designated Menard-Kev. It's the largest planet in the cluster, large enough to have an atmosphere, even if it is extremely cold. There's also a dense layer of ice crystals and clouds that shroud the planet, so it's almost totally dark, too."

"*That's* where we're going?" Bugs asked. "A space icicle? Why?"

"The Law of Space obligates us to assist stricken vessels and investigate distress signals, regardless of where they come from."

Fortis sat forward in his seat. "I think Bugs' question is why us? Why not send a Fleet vessel to investigate?"

"The Menard is on the far side of the Maduro Jump Gate."

Lou and Cujo gasped, and Cheese swore.

"That's Maltaani space," Tweak said.

"Technically, no. Not exactly," Anders replied. "As you know, since the Battle of Balfan-48, there haven't been any major engagements between our races. It seems that neither side wants to replicate the carnage of Balfan-48. Still, we don't have a formal ceasefire or truce agreement, which means there is no Maltaani space, only contested space."

Cujo raised his hand. "Colonel, a Notice to Spacefarers from the UNT Navigation Bureau put the Maduro Gate off limits."

Anders nodded. "Which explains the need for secrecy surrounding this mission and the requirement for a team like you. If we send a Fleet vessel to investigate, it won't remain secret for long. And if the Maltaani detect a Fleet vessel in that sector, it might spark a renewal of hostilities.

"As for why a team like you, the distress call may be an actual call for help, but there are other possibilities we have to consider. What if the signal is bait for an ambush? Perhaps the Maltaani want us to probe the area so they can conduct a surprise attack or seize a vessel or two. Maybe it's an undiscovered alien race which would benefit from a resumption of hostilities between humans and the Maltaani. Perhaps the signal is an anomaly. After all, for every gain we make in our understanding of deep space, we discover more that we don't understand.

"In short, there are many possibilities. Regardless of what it is, your mission isn't to sit around and what-if this thing. It's your mission to travel to Menard-Kev and investigate the signal.

"You have forty-eight hours to develop a plan for how you will accomplish that mission. The mission start point is this building and the only limitation on your planning is that you must proceed in complete secrecy. If you have specialized equipment requirements, submit them when you brief your plan. Any questions?"

The team exchanged glances but remained silent.

"All right then, I'll see you back here in forty-eight hours."

With that, Colonel Anders left. The door closed behind him, and the tension in the room evaporated.

"What's eating him?" Cheese asked.

"Somebody missed his nap," Bugs answered.

Bender spoke up, "Lock it up, ladies. We have a lot of work to do in the next forty-eight hours. Lucky, you're in charge. How do you want to work this?"

Fortis thought for a second. "I think we should start with a timeline of the mission and then break it down into specific steps and work out the details." He stood and went to the rolling dry erase board standing on one side of the stage. One the left-hand side he made a big dot and wrote "Terra Earth" and on the right side he made another dot labeled "Menard-Kev." He connected the dots with a horizontal line.

"Mission timeline," he said.

"You left off the part where we come home, Lucky," Cheese noted.

Fortis chuckled. "Okay. Half our mission timeline."

"The movement from here to the civilian spaceport should be easy enough," Tweak said. "Find the nearest tram station and hop on."

Bender stood up and rubbed his hands together. "True, but we can't go all at once. People see a group like us and they start to wonder where we're going."

"That includes the trip up to the Terra Earth Jump Gate," Cujo added. "We can't have everyone hanging around trying to ignore each other."

"Good, good." Fortis made two notes on the board, "Travel separately" and "Schedules." "We need schedules for the spaceport tram and the jump gate shuttle."

"I'll get them," Lou said.

"Lucky, I think you and I should travel together first," Cujo said. "We won't find a vessel willing to take us to The Menard at the jump gate."

"Why not?"

"We need a captain who's willing to bend a few rules, and they don't hang around the TEJG. Our best bet is a vessel fresh out of salvage orbit with owners who are looking to make a quick credit. We'll find them on the Moon at the Salvage Orbit Management Office. You and I can go there while the rest of the team assembles on the TEJG. Once we hire a vessel we can pick them up, load our gear, and be gone before anyone has time to ask questions."

Fortis and Bender exchanged looks and nodded. Fortis added notes to the white board.

"Speaking of gear, does anyone have special gear requirements?"

Cujo raised his hand. "We need a twenty-man shuttle, which means we need a vessel with a boom to launch and recover it."

"Twenty man?"

"Yeah, twenty man. It will help disguise the size of our team and it won't add that much to the cost of hiring a ship."

Tweak said, "I'll work with Cheese to make a list of the equipment we'll need to triangulate the signal once we get close to our objective. I don't think it will be high tech or hard to find, but I don't want to get there and discover the ship we hired can't copy ELF."

Fortis scribbled on the board. "How about you, Bugs? Any medical gear or explosives?"

"I'll pack a standard trauma kit and an extra satchel of ointments and medicine to treat extreme cold injuries. Bender, do you think we'll need some boom-boom?"

Bender shrugged his massive shoulders. "It won't hurt to bring some basics. We'll need cutting torches, too."

Fortis stopped writing and looked up. "What are the torches for?"

"If this signal is legit, we might have to cut our way into a wrecked spacecraft."

"While we're spending the colonel's money, we ought to bring a thermal scanner, too. We can use it to locate survivors, if there are any."

"What about body bags?" Fortis asked.

"No way. If we bring bodies back, we'll have to go through quarantine. That will blow our cover, so no bodies. If the UNT wants to send a recovery team, that's their choice."

The discussion went on like that for another two hours. One team member would pose a question or suggest a solution and the group would examine it through the lens of their knowledge and experience. It pleased Fortis to watch the team work together without any egos or hurt feelings when their ideas were dissected and rejected. Bender was clearly the alpha of the group, but he deferred to Fortis and the others seemed willing to follow his lead.

Eventually, the conversation waned, and Fortis decided it was time to break.

"We'll stop here for now. We've got twenty minutes until lunch. We'll muster back here at 1300 to continue."

The team filed out of the briefing theater, and Bender stopped Fortis.

"Do you trust me enough now to tell me what you think of all this, Lucky?" The massive man gave him a slight smile.

Fortis chuckled. "Yeah, I do. I don't know Anders all that well except that he was the battalion intel officer when I was a platoon leader. I get the sense that he's conflicted about this mission, but I can't put my finger on exactly what the conflict is."

"Huh. It's interesting to hear you say that because that's exactly how I feel about it. I don't think he's told us everything, and it's getting to him."

"I might try to get in to see him after we finish for the day to update him on our progress. Maybe I can check his pulse and see what's up."

"I dunno, mate. He can be pretty close-mouthed when he wants to be." Bender gestured toward the door. "C'mon, we can't leave Bugs and Cheese unsupervised for too long."

* * *

After lunch and a brief break that Bender called a "pause for the cause," the team returned to the briefing theater and continued planning the mission. When they finished, Fortis flipped the white board around to the blank side.

"Let's do it again."

The team went through the entire mission again. Fortis questioned team members about details outside their purview. He asked Lou about medical supplies and had Cheese describe how Fortis and Cujo would go about hiring a ship and captain. Bugs and Cujo took turns answering questions about the communications gear Tweak was requesting, and Tweak explained why Bender wanted cutting torches. When team members got details wrong, they received good-natured ribbing from the rest, but it was apparent to Fortis that they had all paid close attention during the first planning session.

All the pieces of the plan fit together until the mission arrived in orbit around Menard-Kev. Colonel Anders' lecture about the meaning of the distress signal hadn't gone unnoticed, but there was little specific planning they could do until they were on site.

Finally, the team settled on two contingency plans. If the distress call was legitimate, they would locate the source and deal with whatever conditions existed there. If it was an ambush, they would fight their way out and escape back through the Maduro Gate.

There was a spirited debate about personnel assignments if an orbit-to-surface movement was required. At least one of the team had to remain aboard the ship with their gear. Cheese was the obvious choice.

"Aw, come on," he complained. "You can't expect me to stay behind and let you guys have all the fun, can you?"

"Cheese, we need you up there to watch our backs," Fortis told him. "You're a communications specialist and a scary looking dude, too. Somebody has to make sure the captain doesn't get cold feet and decide that half a payday is good enough."

Bender clapped Cheese on the shoulder with one of his giant paws. "Don't worry, little brother. If there's any shooting and looting to be done, I'll make sure you get in on it. Besides, you don't like the cold anyway."

After they completed their second full run through the mission plan and discussed a long list of what-ifs, Fortis called a halt.

"I think we've done a solid job thus far. Tomorrow morning we'll reconvene and walk through it. Tomorrow afternoon we'll draw up the final operational plan and requirements list for Colonel Anders. I'm assuming that at some point he'll want the whole thing briefed, too. Good work everyone and thank you."

Lou volunteered to remain behind and transcribe the notes Fortis had written on the white board, and the rest of the team headed for the dorms. Bender and the other two Space Marines planned to hit the weight room, and Fortis wanted to join them, but he ran into Colonel Anders in the foyer.

"Colonel, do you have a few minutes?"

"Sure, follow me."

The trio of Space Marines waved and joked as the colonel led Fortis back to his office. They sat in the same chairs as Fortis' first visit to the office.

"What's on your mind?"

"Nothing in particular. I want to update you on where we are with mission planning. We've made good progress toward a final operational plan, which is a credit to the professionalism of the team. They work well together."

"Excellent. I'm happy to hear that. You'll be able to submit your plan on time?"

"No doubt."

"Good." Anders studied Fortis closely. "Is that all you wanted to talk about?"

Fortis shifted in his seat. Times like this made him wonder if Anders could read his mind.

"Not exactly, sir. You see, some of the team members have expressed the feeling that there's something more to all this that we're not being told."

"Some of the team being Bender?"

Anders' deduction startled Fortis.

How does he know?

"Yes sir, Bender is one of them."

"And you."

Fortis nodded.

"Bender is an outstanding operator with a lot of experience, which is why I selected him for this mission. His problem is that he has a lot of experience, which makes him skeptical toward anyone not on his team. The intelligence community hasn't always taken good care of their operators. Being wary isn't a bad thing, until it affects one's ability to follow orders and solve problems."

"Sir, I didn't mean to imply that Bender is a problem—"

"I understand. If I thought he was, he'd be gone. What I'm trying to say is, listen to what he has to say, but do your own thinking."

"I have, Colonel, and I have to admit, I sensed the same thing before I talked to Bender."

Anders sighed and massaged the bridge of his nose between thumb and forefinger.

"This mission does not enjoy unanimous support among the members of the Grand Council Intelligence Committee. Some of them don't want it to happen at all."

"But the Law of Space requires us to investigate distress signals."

"It does, but it doesn't specify what constitutes an investigation. There has been a proposal put forth by a committee member to request the president declare that our analysis of the signal is investigation enough. Since we cannot determine whether the signal is authentic through simple analysis it must be an anomaly and we are therefore relieved of the obligation to investigate further."

"That's outrageous! How can they do that?"

"It's pure politics. The Council is made up of lawyers. They're capable of anything. At the other end of the spectrum, some committee members whose interests are closely aligned with certain military industrial activities want to send in Third Division to investigate and probably provoke the Maltaani at the same time. They view what happened on Balfan-48 as an opportunity to generate sales, and they'd love to see more of it. Third Division is conveniently deployed and could be there in short order."

"Bastards." Fortis' face flushed as he remembered the desperate struggle for survival against the overwhelming Maltaani force on Balfan-48.

"Again, lawyers. In the middle of the madness are guys like me who acknowledge our obligation to properly investigate and want to do so without provoking a renewal of hostilities with the Maltaani."

"You should have just sent us without telling anyone."

"Eh, tempting, but ultimately a bad idea. Transparency is one of the principles that bind the member nations of the UNT together. If we keep secrets from each other, the alliance will cease to function properly, and it will fail."

"Even in an emergency like this?"

"Is this an emergency? We detected this signal purely by chance on an obsolete frequency band. How old is the signal? It may have begun transmitting a hundred years ago and we've only now discovered it. An automated beacon could transmit almost indefinitely as long as the vessel's reactor is operational."

"What happened to the drone you sent?"

Anders threw up his hands. "Another mystery of Menard-Kev. The last communication we had with it was just prior to atmospheric penetration."

Fortis sat silently and absorbed all the information Anders had given him.

"We're between a rock and a hard place on this one and time is becoming a factor. The longer we wait to launch the mission, the greater the probability that it will be scrubbed. In fact, I was told this afternoon that you will be required to listen for an abort signal every day, even after you enter orbit around Menard-Kev."

"I'll have the operational plan and requirements list in your hands tomorrow afternoon, sir."

"Excellent."

After a pregnant pause, Anders stood and walked to the door, and Fortis followed.

"I don't need to tell you not to share what we discussed here, do I?"

Fortis shook his head.

"The team needs to go on this mission with absolute confidence in the chain of command. If they suspect they won't receive complete support, they might hesitate at a crucial moment."

"I understand, sir. Not a word to anyone."

"Good." Anders opened the door. "I'm looking forward to reading your plan, Lucky."

* * * * *

Chapter Ten

After his discussion with Colonel Anders, Fortis joined the other Space Marines in the weight room. Even though Fortis had received the maximum strength enhancement, they lifted weights far in excess of what he could handle. They showered him with good-natured barbs, which Fortis gratefully endured. One thing he'd learned during his brief time in the ISMC was that the troops saved their best jokes and insults for the officers they liked.

"Anders have anything to say?" Bender spat through gritted teeth as he bench-pressed a bar loaded with over two times his body weight.

"Not really." The lie came too smoothly, but Fortis recalled Anders' warning. He was glad the weights distracted Bender, because he felt the falsehood all over his face. "He said time is becoming a factor, which is ratcheting up the pressure on him." At least that much was true and more innocuous than the rest of the story, so Fortis was comfortable sharing it with the trio.

Cheese and Bugs guided the bar down with a *clang* and Bender sat up. "I guess we should turn in our plan as soon as possible then. You want to have a session tonight?"

"No. Lou is going to drop off the rough draft based on our work today, and I'll spend tonight going over it. We'll hit it hard again tomorrow morning. If everyone is satisfied, we can give it to the colonel tomorrow afternoon."

"Where does it go from here?" Bender asked as Cheese took his turn on the bench. "Is there a general in the loop?"

"I don't know. It's got to go somewhere, because I don't think the colonel has the authority to launch a mission like this."

"Don't be too sure," Bugs said from his end of the bar. "The universe is littered with the bodies of Space Marines who ran into colonels with too much authority."

Cheese finished his set and stood up. Bender patted the weight bench. "C'mon, Lucky, show us what you're made of."

Fortis did some quick math. The bar was loaded to the maximum he'd ever attempted, and he hesitated before sliding under it.

"DINLI," he grunted as he pushed the bar up and then lowered it to his chest.

"DINLI," the trio echoed.

* * *

After supper, Lou came to Fortis' room to deliver the draft operational plan.

"Thanks, Lou. I appreciate the quick turnaround on this."

"No worries. You did all the work. I just plugged in your notes." She turned to go.

"Hey, Lou, can I ask you a question? If you have time, I mean."

"I'm not going anywhere. What can I do for you?"

"I'm curious about your work with Fuck You Too…er, Aardvark. What are they like? The Maltaani, I mean."

"That's an interesting question." She gestured to an empty chair. "Do you mind?"

Fortis waved her into the chair and sat down opposite her.

"My tasking was to communicate with Aardvark and extract as much intelligence from him as possible. I was only partially successful. I learned his language, but he had little useful knowledge about their capabilities or tactics."

Fortis snorted. "As I recall, their main tactic was to charge forward. The way humans used to fight each other a thousand years ago."

"It's funny you say that because a number of military historians made the same observation. It turns out that the Maltaani don't have much experience with warfighting because they rarely war amongst themselves. Other than that, they're quite similar to us in a lot of ways. In fact—"

Lou stopped herself, and Fortis sat silent and waited for her to continue. When she didn't, he prompted her. "In fact what, Lou?"

Lou took a deep breath and let it out slowly. "There's a theory in the scientific community that the Maltaani *are* human, or closely related to us."

"What?"

"Yeah, I know. It sounds crazy. I reacted the same way when I first heard it. But when I put together all we know about them, it started to make sense."

"This I gotta hear."

"Are you sure? It gets convoluted and much of it is still theoretical."

"I'm very sure."

"Hmm, okay. The first piece of the puzzle is navigation. When humans first explored the space around Terra Earth, we navigated by the stars. Even in the farthest reaches of our solar system we could always rely on star sights to know where we were at. Then we developed radio beacons, satellite systems, and the other technologies we use today. With me so far?"

Fortis nodded.

"The second piece is time. Our ancestors learned to tell time by observing the same stars they used to navigate by. Telling time is a precise science now, but it all started when our ancestors observed patterns of celestial movement in the sky.

"The third piece is our discovery and use of space warps at the jump gates. When we jump through a warp gate, clocks stop keeping time for an unspecified period. We assume it's only seconds because that's what we experience, but without a way to measure we don't truly know. It could be hours or even days."

"Where do the Maltaani fit into this?"

"I'm getting there. Now, when we emerge on the other side of a warp, how do we know where we are? Without a known star system to observe, we're essentially lost. We dealt with this by establishing the jump gate beacon system, which tells us where we are relative to the transmitter. In reality, we have no idea where we are. Make sense?"

"Yes."

"We don't know where we're at, and because the clocks stop in the warp, we don't know *when*, either." She smiled broadly. "Here comes the fun part. What if a vessel full of pilgrims looking to colonize a new planet passed through a warp and got 'lost,' for lack of a better term? Is it possible those colonists could end up a million years in the past relative to Terra Earth time?"

"Sure, I guess."

"That's the theory about the Maltaani. A group of humans passed through a warp, got lost, and discovered a habitable planet where they thrived. As generations passed, they evolved different physical characteristics than their Terran cousins. Their language and customs evolved as well, and the story of their origin faded from memory. They developed similar technology because our brains and physiology are similar. Their spacecraft look familiar because we share a basic body shape and because we developed space flight in a nearly identical fashion. The Maltaani are our cousins, many times removed."

Lou's statements stunned Fortis. "Are you nuts? You think the Maltaani are *human*?"

"Well, it could be that humans are Maltaani who got lost and colonized Terra Earth. The origin story works either way. It's the chicken and egg causality dilemma, but does it matter which way it goes?"

Fortis thought for a long second. "Everything you just told me is supposition and speculation. Just because they look like us doesn't make them human. What hard evidence do you have for any of this?"

"We did some comparison analysis between common human languages and the Maltaani vocabulary I learned from Aardvark, and there was an eighty-five percent correlation between Latin and Maltaani. Eighty-five percent is way beyond random chance and leads to one conclusion: the languages have a common origin.

"We also collected samples from Aardvark for molecular analysis. Hair, skin cells, blood, etc. Guess what we found?"

Fortis shrugged.

"In double-blind testing, his DNA profile was ninety-nine-point six percent identical to a nominal human profile. That's only one tenth of one percent less than Neanderthals, who existed alongside modern humans early in our history. A number of factors could account for the differences between the races including solar radiation levels, gravity, and other environmental conditions on their home planet."

Fortis flashed back to his brief encounter with Aardvark after the Maltaani was captured during the Battle of Balfan-48. He had felt a stirring deep inside when they locked eyes, and now he understood it was the recognition of a fellow human.

"Why have I not heard about any of this before? We've been at war with the Maltaani for a year."

"That's above my paygrade, but if I had to guess, I'd say it was probably power and greed. Lots of money to be made preparing to fight the Maltaani, you know. There's also no reason to assume that they're interested in a happy family reunion with their long-lost cousins, either. Aardvark didn't have much to say on the topic; he seemed as surprised by us as we were of him."

"You said we repatriated him. We had to make contact with them, right?"

"Hmm, not exactly. We found a common frequency for him to talk with them. We agreed to release him in an escape pod from a Fleet frigate at a prearranged time and place. The frigate delivered him as promised, but we've heard nothing since."

"This is incredible."

"It certainly helps explain the security around this mission."

Fortis almost commented but stopped short when he realized he was perilously close to breaching his agreement with Anders. He settled for a nod.

"Anyway, sir, you've got the draft of our operational plan. Let me know what changes you want made, and I'll get them turned around as soon as I can. It's becoming a time crunch?"

"Yeah. I think the sooner we leave the better. I appreciate your efforts."

Lou left, and Fortis spent a long time staring into the distance as the Battle of Balfan-48 replayed in his mind's eye.

They're human?

* * * * *

Chapter Eleven

After the daily dozen and breakfast the following morning, Fortis went back to his room and spent an hour scouring the draft plan. Everything they had talked about was in there, along with an extensive requirements list. He noted a couple areas he thought needed more granularity, but overall, the plan was satisfactory.

Fortis made it to the briefing theater with seconds to spare and earned a glare from Bender as he hustled to the front of the room.

"Sorry I'm late, but I wanted to make sure we had the best possible product to work with this morning. Thanks to Lou, we do."

For the next three hours, the team went over their plan in careful detail. As Fortis expected, there were no major changes to the outbound journey. What happened after they arrived at Menard-Kev was still contingent on what they discovered there, so they detailed the two main probabilities.

When they finished, Fortis called a pause for the cause and lunch.

"We'll take an extra hour break after lunch to give Lou time to make these changes, then we'll read through it one more time," Fortis told the team.

Lou spoke up. "If it's all the same to you, Lucky, I'll work through lunch."

"Are you sure? There's no rush; our plan isn't due to Anders until tomorrow morning."

"The sooner we get it turned in, the sooner we leave, and the sooner these apes let me sleep in. I didn't sign up to do exercises before the sun comes up."

The team laughed.

"You heard her; be back here after lunch."

They reconvened, and Lou had final drafts for everyone to mark up. They went through the plan line-by-line, and, when they were done, the team agreed that it was a workable plan with a high probability of success. Lou corrected two typographical errors and printed out the final copy, which Fortis signed.

"Hang loose while I deliver this to the colonel," Fortis told the team. He took the plan to the colonel's office and rapped on the door.

"Enter."

"Colonel, here's our final plan." Anders' eyebrows went up as Fortis handed him the signed document.

"You're early. Are you sure this is complete?"

"Yes, sir. As complete as we can make it. The trip to Menard-Kev is straightforward. We planned on two major contingencies once we're on site and left enough flexibility for unforeseen eventualities."

"Thanks. How soon can you brief it?"

"Whenever you want, sir."

"Very well. I'll be in touch."

Two hours later, the communicator in Fortis' room buzzed. It was Colonel Anders.

"Assemble the team in the briefing theater in fifteen minutes for the mission brief. Clean clothes, no PT gear. We have a VIP coming."

Fortis ran from room to room and notified the team. They assembled in the hall and proceeded to the theater with a few minutes to spare.

"Who's the VIP?" Cheese asked.

"The colonel didn't say," Fortis replied. "My guess is his boss, maybe a few staffers."

The team gathered as instructed and waited for Colonel Anders. A few minutes past the appointed time, they heard the hangar doors open and close and vehicle doors slam. Seconds later, Colonel Anders entered the room with two Fleet admirals and an ISMC general Fortis didn't recognize. A gaggle of suits followed, and, in the middle, was a tall, silver-haired woman Fortis *did* recognize. Briega Volanda, UNT Minister of Defense.

Shit!

The group was barely seated when Colonel Anders pointed to him.

"You may begin."

Fortis cleared his throat. "Our mission is to proceed to Menard-Kev and investigate the source of a distress signal received via an extremely low frequency, or ELF, transmission."

As he spoke, several of the suits scribbled furiously, and he wondered if they planned to transcribe everything he said.

"This is a clandestine mission and there are to be no connections to the UNT government or military. All travel and operations will be conducted outside official channels without specific authorization."

Fortis wondered how far into the details he should get when briefing the MoD, but he saw she held a copy of the plan and decided more was better.

"The first stage of the mission is personnel movement from this building to the Terra Earth Jump Gate, or TEJG. When ordered, our mission pilot, Cujo, and I will take the public tram to the civilian spaceport and book flights to the TEJG for further transfer to the Salvage Orbit Management Office on the Moon."

"Why the SOMO?" One of the staffers, a pinch-faced man with an elaborate combover, waved his pen.

"Sir, we need to hire a captain who's willing to take our team and a load of gear to an undisclosed location in distant space for an unspecified reason. Our cover story is that we are a wildcat mineral survey crew, but there's no way to know if he will believe it or not. The kinds of captains who would accept such a charter don't operate from the TEJG. There are too many people with an interest in what happens there, including the sky marshals. People on SOMO are more likely to mind their own business."

Combover clicked his pen. "Proceed."

"At staggered intervals between eight and twelve hours, the rest of the team will follow and assemble on the TEJG. Cheese is our cargo master. He will travel last and is responsible for transporting the gear to the TEJG. The team will avoid being seen together until the last possible moment when Cujo and I arrive to collect them and our gear. We expect to be underway before curiosities are aroused.

"We estimate the vessel will cost between four and five million credits to hire and another two million for a shuttle to transport us to the surface of Menard-Kev and back into orbit."

"Seven million credits?" Combover sounded incredulous. "Why so much?"

Cujo spoke up. "Sir, a mission like this won't be cheap. No captain is going to risk his license, his freedom, and maybe his life for peanuts. Even with a convincing cover story, there's a large element of risk involved. Another factor is price inflation due to the rumor mill. If we offer five hundred thousand credits and get no takers, our only option is to increase our price. Captains talk. By their way of thinking, if we're willing to pay five hundred thousand, we'd be willing to pay a million, then two million, and so on. If we offer two million up front and two million upon our return, it should head off a bidding war."

Combover clicked his pen again, and Fortis continued.

"Once we hire the vessel, we will contact the team on the TEJG, pick them up at one of the transit gates, and be on our way. At that point, we will make our first coded status report to Colonel Anders.

"We estimate the trip will take between six and eight days. Once we—"

"Six to eight days?" Combover brandished his pen again. "A transit of that length shouldn't take more than four."

"If we take a direct route, you'd be correct. However, we decided to make the trip in three legs to throw off anyone who might attempt to track us. We're not going to jump through the TEJG for the same reason."

"Do you think it's really necessary? This mission *is* time sensitive."

"Yes, sir, we understand the time element, but the need for secrecy is paramount. Or so we've been instructed."

Click. Click.

"Once we arrive in the vicinity of Menard-Kev, the vessel will go into orbit, and we'll transmit another status report. We will deploy drones to evaluate the location of the signal and collect whatever intelligence is available, which we expect will take no more than twelve hours. After we analyze the intelligence, we'll proceed to the surface and locate the transmitter, leaving Cheese aboard the mothership for coordination and communication."

"What's your plan if you encounter a hostile force?"

Combover didn't have to say "Maltaani" for Fortis to understand the question.

"Our intention is to avoid contact with anyone by minimizing transmissions, especially communications. If we cross paths with hostiles, our plan is to run. We'll have personal sidearms, but the ship will be unarmed."

"And if you're captured?" *Click, click.*

"Sir, we've assessed the risk of capture to be very low. If it happens, we'll stick to our cover story and get word back here as soon as possible. Given the recent lack of hostilities between us and the Maltaani, I believe we'll be more at risk from pirates, or even slavers."

Combover returned to scribbling, and Fortis continued.

"At this point, the operational plan becomes flexible and depends on the conditions on the surface. If we find a crashed vessel with no survivors, we will silence the distress signal, gather whatever information we can about the ship and crew, and leave. If we discover survivors, we'll fall back on our cover story and bring them out with us. Unless we find sensitive or dangerous technology or cargo, we will leave the wreck as we find it."

"At what point will you make the mission go/no-go decision?"

Fortis looked at Anders, who sat forward and spoke up.

"The go/no-go decision will be made when we receive final authority to launch the mission. After that, the operation will proceed as planned unless there is a casualty to the ship or a major change in prevailing conditions."

Combover and Minister Volanda exchanged glances but seemed to accept the colonel's answer.

"Before departure, we will report our status and commence our return voyage using an indirect return route. When we arrive at the TEJG, I will pay the captain the balance of his fee after all onboard navigation system memories are wiped clean by our electronics expert."

"Is it wise to carry that much money on the mission?"

"If the captain knows the other half of his fee is with me on Menard-Kev he'll be less likely to abandon us on the surface if trouble develops. We'll also leave Cheese aboard as further insurance against such an occurrence."

"Is that all, Mr., eh…" Minister Volanda asked Fortis.

"Lucky, ma'am. And yes, that's our plan."

She turned to Anders. "Colonel, could we have use of the room for a few minutes?"

Anders stood and waved at the team. "We'll be in the lobby if you need us, Minister."

They stood around the foyer and Fortis took a deep breath. He discovered the back of his shirt was wet with sweat. Bender slapped him on the shoulder with a meaty hand.

"Good job, Lucky."

"Man, that dude with the hair was driving me crazy with that pen," Bugs said.

Anders laughed. "That 'dude' is the Under Secretary for Defense Affairs and Finance. He's the one who will approve the funds for this mission…who *might* approve the funds, if the MoD authorizes it."

"I'd love to be a fly on the wall in there," Tweak said with a wry smile. "Even a tiny bug."

"You didn't!" Cujo exclaimed.

"No, I didn't. But I wish I had."

Just then, one of the suits stuck his head through the lobby door.

"Colonel Anders, they'd like to see you."

"Stay loose," Anders told the team as he headed for the briefing theater. Ten minutes later, he returned.

"Bring them in, Lucky."

The team followed Anders back into the briefing theater and took their seats. Minister Volanda was standing at the podium, so Fortis sat next to the colonel.

The minister spoke.

"You have been selected for a critically important mission to an extremely sensitive region of deep space. Even if you succeed in your mission objectives, the mission will be a failure if you are identified as agents of the UNT or the Ministry of Defense. Under no circumstances will you allow yourselves to be detained by a law enforcement organization or military forces, and, if you are, you will not be interrogated. That is not negotiable.

"Colonel Anders has assured me that this team possesses the skills necessary to successfully complete this mission. This mission is approved as briefed. I wish you the best of luck and a safe return."

Minister Volanda strode to the door and her gaggle of suits jumped to their feet and followed. A few seconds after she was gone, the rumble of the hangar doors announced her departure from the facility.

"Any questions?" Colonel Anders asked.

Fortis stood. "Sir, I need some clarity on the minister's remarks. She said we are not to be detained by law enforcement or military forces. Does that mean we are supposed to use deadly force against our own people?"

"You are to use whatever means available to avoid capture," Anders replied. "I can't tell you to use deadly force without knowing the situation. Besides, that would be an illegal order. It's up to you to decide what is appropriate."

It was a non-answer, but Fortis knew he wouldn't get anything more from Anders. "My other question is about not being interrogated if we are captured."

"If this mission fails and capture is imminent, we expect full unit closure."

Anders and Fortis locked eyes, and he understood.

Suicide.

"Any other questions?" Anders looked around the room. "No?" He gestured to Fortis. "Let's get this show on the road."

* * * * *

Chapter Twelve

Fortis and Cujo left the team building less than thirty minutes after Minister Volanda approved the mission. The trip to the Terra Earth Jump Gate was uneventful and Cujo led the way to the lunar shuttle gate. As he boarded the shuttle and searched for his seat, Fortis saw his fellow passengers looking at him intently.

They were a rough-looking lot with plenty of tattoos and angry scowls. He even saw one heavily tattooed man with the distinctive dueling scars of the Kuiper Knights, the pseudo-religious organized crime cult he had battled on Eros-28. He flashed back to Colonel Anders' theory that the Knights might be behind Idoia Guerra's assassination attempt and goose pimples tickled his spine.

Cujo sensed his unease and chuckled as they slid into their seats. "This is nothing. Wait until you see the guys at the SOMO."

There was a bump as the shuttle disengaged from the docking port, and the passengers surged against their harnesses when the gravity from the TEJG ceased. The cabin lights dimmed, and a startled Fortis looked around.

"You need to relax, Lucky. Try to get some sleep; we'll be lucky to find decent accommodations at the SOMO."

"One of the passengers is a Kuiper Knight. I've had my share of trouble with them."

Cujo shook his head. "That guy's not a Kuiper Knight. The UNT wouldn't permit a Kuiper Knight to be on the TEJG. My guess is that he's fresh out of prison. His tattoos tell me that he was owned by the Knights on the incarceration station, but he's not a Knight."

Fortis slumped down in his seat. "Everybody on this shuttle eyeballed me like they knew me."

"They probably do. You're famous. 'My destiny lies among the stars' and all that, remember?"

"Dammit. You think they saw that?"

"Who didn't? Relax. It's too late to do anything about it now. When we get to SOMO, don't take any shit from anyone, but don't start any, either."

With that, Cujo twisted in his seat and got as comfortable as he could. Fortis reclined and stared at the ceiling of the shuttle cabin while sleep eluded him, and the operational plan ran repeatedly through his mind.

Fortis woke with a start and saw Cujo standing over him.

"We're here. Come on."

The gray-haired pilot led a groggy Fortis off the shuttle and into SOMO. The arrival area was dirty and run down, and crowds of shady characters mobbed together as they competed to shout the loudest. The smell of unwashed bodies and industrial fumes of all kinds almost overwhelmed Fortis, and he coughed and wiped his eyes.

"Stay close and keep one hand on your money belt," Cujo cautioned Fortis. "Even if someone bumps you, don't let go."

As if on cue, a large, grimy faced man with rings in his earlobes and septum slammed into Fortis and knocked him into the crowd.

"Hey! Watch where you're going!" he growled.

Fortis felt anonymous hands grasping at his belt as the crowd pushed him away, but when he turned to confront the thieves, all he saw was a faceless mass of humanity. He turned back around to face the man who shoved him, but he had disappeared.

"See what I mean? Now, come on." Cujo grabbed Fortis by the shoulder and dragged him out of the arrival area and into a relatively calm passageway.

"The parasites and predators hang around the arrival lounge and wait for nice, clean-cut folks like yourself. They know you're looking to make some kind of underhanded deal and you don't have friends here."

"I should have sent Bender on this leg."

"Nah. He would have started a brawl, and we'd both be locked up. Don't worry about it; you're doing fine."

"How do you know all this?" Fortis asked as he followed Cujo.

"I didn't always fly for Anders," the pilot replied with a wink. "I made a lot of money flying out of here before the sky marshals caught up with me." He stopped and jerked his head toward an unmarked door. "Buy me a beer, and I'll tell you all about it."

"It's a little early for a beer. Shouldn't we be looking for a captain?"

Fortis followed Cujo through the door and stopped. The interior was lit by flickering sconces and a few candles scattered on tables throughout the room. Along the far wall, a jazz quartet played a muted free-form tune that covered a hundred hushed conversations.

"Where do you think we're going to find one?" Cujo gestured to an empty table. "Have a seat and order some drinks, I'm going to say hello to an old friend." He wended his way across the room and greeted an enormous fat man who occupied a lot of space at the bar.

Fortis slipped into the booth and looked around. Nobody paid any attention to their arrival, and he was glad for the dim atmosphere. He hadn't considered how his public exposure might impact their mission, and he regretted the oversight.

"What can I get ya, hon?" A plump waitress in a too-tight sequined outfit and a wildly colored hairdo placed cocktail napkins in front of Fortis and the seat next to him.

"Two beers, please."

"Draft okay? It's all we have."

"Draft is fine."

"You look a little lost, sweetie."

Fortis felt his face flush. "Ha, no, I'm not lost. Just waiting for my friend."

"Hmm, okay. If you want something, anything, just let me know. I'm Charlotte."

Charlotte walked toward the bar with an exaggerated wiggle. Fortis contemplated her backside and the word *anything*.

"I see you've met Charlotte," Cujo said as he slid into the booth next to Fortis.

"You know her?"

"Everyone knows Charlotte." Cujo smiled as she returned with a tray bearing their beers. "Charlotte, my love. It's been too long."

Her fleshy face lit up when she recognized the pilot. "Cujo! My goodness, I thought you'd forgotten all about me. Give Momma Charlotte a hug."

She set the tray on the table and buried Cujo's face in her fleshy bosom. Cujo gasped when she let him up for air.

"Whoa, Momma. I sure did miss your hugs. Have you met my friend Lucky?"

She reached for Fortis and gave him the same suffocating treatment.

"Lucky, you say?"

"Nice to meet you, ma'am," Fortis stammered.

"Did you hear that? Ma'am, he says." She tossed her hair and thrust out a hip. "I'm not your mother, boy, but I'll be your momma."

Cujo and Charlotte laughed at Fortis' apparent distress before she gave them a finger wave.

"Gotta go, boys. Lots of thirsty men in here today." She fluttered her eyes at Fortis. "See you around, Lucky."

Cujo quaffed half his beer and wiped his mouth with the back of his hand. "What's the matter, you've never touched a boob before?"

The tips of Fortis' ears glowed. "No. I mean, yeah, of course. It was just unexpected, that's all."

The pilot laughed. "Don't let her fool you, mate. Charlotte will steal your breath and your money at the same time. You gotta watch that one."

Fortis caught sight of the waitress at the other side of the room rubbing up on two well-dressed men. Charlotte laughed as she walked away from the table. She smiled and winked when she caught Fortis staring.

Cujo drained the rest of his beer. "Drink up, Lucky. We're going to meet a captain and look over his ship."

They headed for the door, and Cujo made a detour, intercepting Charlotte along the way.

"Here you go, love, that's for the beers," he said as he handed her some credits. He slapped her buttocks and smiled. "That's for the hug."

Fortis could only smile as he passed the waitress and followed Cujo outside.

"Where to now?"

"Down to the hangars. Captain's name is Stoat. He's got a ship he just claimed from salvage and he's looking to make some quick cash."

"He just claimed it? Is it spaceworthy?"

"That's what we're going to find out." Cujo stopped him with a hand on his chest. "One small detail. We don't work together. You hired me to help broker a charter, but that's it, understand?"

"Okay, but why?"

"Because I don't plan to fly for Anders forever, and if these guys found out what I've been doing, I'd be lucky to land a mate's job on an ore train."

Cujo threw open a set of double doors, and the noise and heat of the industrial area beyond engulfed Fortis. Blinding spots of light marked where welders were busy attaching metal to metal, and grinders showered the area with orange sparks. Everywhere Fortis looked, grimy workers moved around the area with loads of sheet metal and tools.

"Watch out, dummy!" someone shouted behind him, and Fortis turned and ducked as a large metal beam swung past his head. He sidestepped, and his foot knocked over a section of pipe propped up on a crate.

"What the fuck?" demanded the welder ready to begin cutting on the pipe. "Watch what the hell you're doing, idiot!"

Cujo grabbed Fortis by the sleeve and pulled him out of the way. "This way, Lucky. Follow me and watch your step."

The pair picked their way through the area until they arrived at a narrow walkway secured by a chain strung across it. A sign overhead read "Salvage Claim Dock One. Authorized Personnel Only."

Cujo ducked under the chain and held it up for Fortis. "This is it. Coming?"

The walkway was actually a long metal gangplank suspended by wires above a dank-smelling pool of oil and twisted metal. Fortis lurched sideways and almost tumbled into the morass. He teetered on the edge of disaster for a long moment before Cujo got a hand under his arm and pulled him back.

"Damn, Lucky, you didn't even have a whole beer and you're stumbling around."

They reached the end of the gangplank and climbed back down onto the steel deck. Fortis looked up and saw a squat, boxy spacecraft parked next to the hangar doors.

The ship had black scorch marks around the engine exhaust ports, and patches along the fuselage told a tale of long, hard service. On the side, Fortis saw a faded image painted on the hull. When he looked closer, he saw it was a fire-breathing dragon with wings outstretched and iron bombs gripped in curved talons.

"She's a *Baxter*-class Atmospheric Light Bomber," Cujo said. "Or rather, she was." He banged on the hull. "Anybody home?"

An emaciated man appeared in the hatch. He was dressed in filthy sleeveless coveralls and his arms were covered in grease and elaborate tattoos.

"Whaddya want?"

"Are you Stoat?"

"Who's asking?"

"My name's Cujo. The fat man sent me. He said you might be looking for a charter."

"He did, did he? Huh." The man wiped at the grease on his hands with a dirty rag and threw it on the deck. "I'm Stoat. Come aboard."

Stoat disappeared inside the spacecraft, and Cujo led Fortis up the boarding ladder. They climbed inside and found Stoat seated in what appeared to be the messing compartment.

"Grab a seat, and welcome aboard *Dragon's Breath*."

* * * * *

Chapter Thirteen

"What's all this about a charter?"

"My companion Mr. Lucky wants to charter a captain and ship, and he hired me to help him find one. The fat man said you might be interested."

Stoat eyeballed Cujo for a long second and frowned. "Middlemen get in the way, soak up the profits."

Cujo started to get up. "We can look elsewhere."

"Oh, sit down," Stoat growled. "You won't find another ship ready to launch, and you know it, or you wouldn't be here at SO-MO." He turned to Fortis. "What's the job?"

"I lead a team of wildcat mineral surveyors. We need a ship to transport us and our gear to a certain location and stand by until our survey is complete. We'll also need a twenty-person shuttle to take us to the surface for three, maybe four days, tops."

"What location? Do you have a star chart?"

Fortis tapped his temple with forefinger. "It's all up here. I'll tell you everything you need to know when you need to know. You'll get the first leg when we're underway."

Stoat turned to Cujo. "Is this pup playing with me?"

Cujo shrugged. "That's the job. I told him when he hired me that it would be difficult to find a captain who would sail under such strict secrecy."

"It's not the secrecy." Stoat turned back to Fortis. "It's not the secrecy, you see. I can keep a secret, but I'm the captain. The captain should know where he's headed."

"I can't take the risk of our destination getting out," Fortis replied. "There's too much at stake."

"How big is your team?"

"There are seven of us. Well, six, plus Cujo if he agrees to come along to pilot the shuttle."

Stoat scratched his whiskered chin. "Five million credits."

"Two point five," Fortis countered without hesitation.

"Two point five? I have a crew to pay, and expenses. Four point five."

"Two million even."

Stoat gaped at Fortis and then turned to Cujo. "Does this pup know how negotiations work?"

"I'm not a pup, and I know a highball bid when I hear one. Three million credits for two weeks work is good money, even after you pay your crew."

"So now it's three million?"

Fortis nodded. "Final offer. Half now, half when we get back."

Stoat looked at Cujo, who shrugged. He held out his hand to Fortis. "Three million it is. Let me show you what you're getting for your money."

Fortis reached out to shake hands and then withdrew it.

"Three million for your ship *and* a twenty-man shuttle."

Stoat snorted in disbelief, but he didn't take his hand back.

"You'll get your shuttle, Mr. Lucky."

The two men shook, then the gaunt captain led Fortis and Cujo forward to the cockpit.

"As your agent so astutely observed, *Dragon's Breath* was indeed a *Baxter*-class Light Atmospheric Bomber, or LAB. She's totally demilitarized; all the bomb racks and pulse cannons have been removed and their hatches welded shut. What's left is a somewhat slow but powerful craft." Stoat patted the helm. "She can haul you, your team, and however much gear you need to carry and have still plenty of power to spare."

Stoat headed back the way they came.

"The staterooms port and starboard are for crew use," he said walking past closed doors. "The two bunkrooms here and here are available for your use." Stoat opened a door and stood aside as Fortis peered inside. The space was cramped, with two bunks stacked on either side, but it looked clean.

"Not first class, but it beats a bedroll on the mess deck."

They continued aft, past the table they had negotiated the charter in, and through a heavy hatch into an open space fitted out like a hangar.

"This is where the bomb racks used to be. Below them were the bomb bay doors."

Fortis saw scars where something had been cut from the overhead and hastily painted over. A pair of heavy-duty booms were mounted either end of the space, over the former bomb bay doors.

"You told me the hatches were welded shut. Did that include these doors?"

Stoat smiled. "They were welded shut, but I opened them again. I can handle a lot of cargo with those booms. I can also launch and recover a shuttle."

The captain led them through another hatch into a cramped space with two large tanks on either side of the ship.

"Fleet Command decided that the LAB payload wasn't heavy enough so they removed the potable water tanks and added more bomb storage. I heard it made the crews unhappy," he said with a chuckle. "And smelly, too. Anyway, I located these tanks at the breaker's yard and put them back in, so water's not a problem. I also installed a gravi-sim system." Stoat stamped the deck. "*Dragon's Breath* is a little on the small side for an upgrade like that, but I'm too old to be bouncing off the bulkheads. Besides, zero gravity makes my acid reflux flare up."

The trio returned to the mess decks.

"That's the tour. The rest of the ship is engineering and auxiliary spaces which are off limits to passengers. Speaking of passengers, when will your team arrive?"

"They will meet us at the TEJG sometime within the next forty-eight hours," Fortis replied.

Stoat sucked air between his yellowed teeth. "The TEJG will be tricky. I don't have the best reputation over there."

"Who does?" Cujo replied. "You have forty-eight hours and three million reasons to figure it out."

"Hmm. Speaking of three million, we agreed to half now."

Fortis shook his head. "When *Dragon's Breath* is underway from the TEJG with my team and our gear aboard, not before."

"But I have expenses," Stoat protested.

"You said she was ready to sail. 'You won't find another ship ready to launch,' you said. Remember?"

Cujo laughed. "The pup's got you there, Captain."

"Bah! All right! Half when we're underway from the TEJG." He waved a thick finger at Fortis. "Don't be late, Mr. Lucky, or you won't be lucky for long."

They exchanged communicator numbers before Fortis and Cujo made the perilous journey back across the suspended gangway.

"What do you think?" Fortis asked when they stopped in the relative safety of the industrial area.

"I think you drove a hard bargain, and you were smart to hold the money back. It wouldn't be the first time a captain took half and disappeared."

"Now what?"

"Now, you go back to TEJG and wait for the team. I'm going to stay here and keep an eye on Stoat. Contact me when you're ready for pick up, and I'll tell Stoat that I'm hitching a ride with him."

"Why don't I stay here with you and we can both ride over?"

Cujo smiled. "Lucky, you don't have the look for SOMO. You don't have any tattoos or piercings, and the doctors did too good a job on the scars on your cheeks. I'm sorry, but you don't fit in here and you'll draw unwelcome attention. Besides, we're not friends, remember? You hired me to find a charter. I found it and now we're strangers again."

Fortis frowned, but nodded his understanding.

"Okay, you're right. I'll catch the next shuttle to the TEJG. As soon as the rest of the team arrives, I'll call."

Cujo walked with Fortis to the departure area, which was only slightly less crowded than the arrival area. Fortis kept a tight grip on his money belt, but he didn't detect any attempts to relieve him of it.

"Go find the team," Cujo said before Fortis climbed the shuttle boarding ramp. "I'm going to find Charlotte."

* * * * *

Chapter Fourteen

The trip back to the TEJG went smoothly. Fortis found Bugs and Tweak waiting for him at the lunar shuttle gate. The trio settled into a booth in a small coffee lounge to talk.

"Anders pushed us out the door almost before you and Cujo caught the shuttle," Tweak said. "The rest of the team will be here on the next shuttle in nine hours."

"So much for clandestine," Fortis said.

"I guess something changed, because he sent the logistics sergeant out with the mission requirements list and ordered her to report back ASAP. Did you have any luck with a ship?"

"Yes, we did. She's a converted Light Atmospheric Bomber called *Dragon's Breath*."

"A *Baxter*?" Bugs asked.

"Yeah, why?"

"*Baxters* are old and slow, and they rattled like hell when they were new. Can she take a warp jump?"

"I didn't think to ask, but Cujo didn't say anything."

Tweak looked around. "Speaking of Cujo, where's he at?"

"He stayed on SOMO to keep an eye on our captain."

Tweak and Bugs exchanged a knowing look. "Charlotte," they said in unison.

"Did I miss something?"

"Charlotte is Cujo's ex-wife, or double ex-wife, since they've been married twice."

"What? Are you kidding me?"

"No, no joke."

Fortis shook his head. "I've been played."

"It could be worse, Lucky. At least you don't have to sit over there and watch him make a fool of himself again."

Fortis fought to suppress a yawn. "I could use some shuteye. Any idea where I can get a room?"

"No rooms here," Tweak said. "Not unless you're part of a conglomerate crew. You can get a sleeping pod at the transient quarters, though."

Fortis found the transient quarters and paid for twelve hours, which was the minimum increment available for a sleeping pod. The pods were large tubes equipped with eye masks, headphones, and holographic porn on demand. They were stacked five-high along a narrow hallway, and the setup reminded Fortis of his family mausoleum on Terra Earth.

He climbed a rolling ladder to get up to his pod and slid in feet first. After he arranged for a courtesy wake up call, Fortis set the alarm on his communicator, found a mellow channel on the headphones, and donned the eye mask.

Fortis was deep in a highly erotic dream that featured Charlotte's fleshy backside when his communicator dragged him back to the conscious world.

"H'lo?"

"Lucky, it's Bugs. Wake up and get down here to Cargo Dock Five. We've got trouble."

"What?"

"Just move! Cargo Dock Five."

The call ended and, disoriented, Fortis banged his head on the top of the sleeping pod when he tried to sit up.

Shit. I'm in a pod.

He opened the pod door and swung himself down to the deck. As he walked down the long hallway to the exit, he rubbed the new knot forming on his forehead.

Cargo Dock Five wasn't far from the transient quarters, and, when he arrived, he found Bender, Bugs, Cheese, Tweak, and Lou in a standoff with a dozen sky marshals over several cargo pallets. The sky marshals held their stun batons at the ready, and Cheese had a large scorch mark on the side of his face.

"There he is," Bender announced when he caught sight of Fortis.

"What's the problem?" Fortis asked the sky marshal wearing bright red sergeant stripes.

"We attempted to inspect this cargo, and that man assaulted us," the sergeant replied, pointing at Cheese. "After we subdued him, these others got involved."

"The cargo is marked FFT, meathead," Cheese said. "Eff. Eff. Tee. For Further Transfer. That means it doesn't require inspection."

"We have the authority to inspect any and all cargo passing through the Terra Earth Jump Gate," the sergeant replied. "That includes cargo marked FFT."

"It's under hermetic seal. If you break that, it has to be repacked and resealed, at great expense."

The sergeant shrugged. "That's not my problem."

Bender had to put a massive arm around Cheese's chest to stop the smaller man from lunging forward.

"Sergeant, can we step away and talk for a moment?" Fortis asked. "My team won't do anything if your men won't. We can figure this out."

The sergeant nodded, and the pair moved several meters away.

Fortis looked around, but there was no one in earshot.

"Sergeant, these pallets are a high-priority ISMC cargo that has to arrive at its destination sealed in the original packing materials. I apologize for the behavior of my team, but we're in a time crunch right now. If we have to take the time to unpack and repack all this stuff, our entire mission will fail." He poked at his communicator until he found Anders' number. "You can reach Colonel Anders, the mission commander, at that number. Tell him Lucky gave you his number and explain the situation. He'll arrange for whatever clearances you need to let us pass."

Fortis knew the call to Anders would infuriate the colonel, but there was no easy solution to their predicament. Even if the team were able to fight off a dozen sky marshals, there were probably a hundred more on the TEJG, and there was nowhere for the team to run.

"Lucky? That your name now, LT?"

Fortis studied the other man for a long second before he recognized him. "Private Trapp?"

"First Platoon, Foxtrot Two/Nine," the sky marshal replied cracking a wide grin.

Fortis chuckled as they shook hands. "What the hell are you doing here?"

"Ah, well, after Pada-Pada, I got sent to another company, but it wasn't the same. The sky marshals were hiring, and here I am. What are you up to? I saw you on the holovision. Nice speech."

"Ha, yeah thanks. I'm doing odd jobs for the ISMC while they decide if I'm fit for full duty." He gestured to his leg. "Lost my leg on Balfan-48."

"Yeah, I remember reading about that. Good luck." Trapp looked back at the team and the sky marshals gathered around the pallets. "You and your people are free to go, LT." He gave Fortis a sheepish grin. "We don't really care what you're transporting, as long as it's FFT. It's been another slow day in a month of slow days here on TEJG."

Fortis clapped Trapp on the shoulder as they walked back to the cargo. "Hop a shuttle over to SOMO. It looks like there would be plenty for you to do over there."

"Fuck no," Trapp replied. "We'd need an army to clean that place up."

The tension between the groups disappeared when they saw Fortis and Trapp smiling and talking.

"You're cleared to proceed," Trapp said. "Just make sure these pallets remain sealed until they're off the jump gate."

Fortis and Trapp shook hands again and then the sergeant led his sky marshals away from the cargo dock.

"What did you say to him?" Bender asked.

"I didn't have to say anything," Fortis replied. "We served together on Pada-Pada."

"He recognized you?"

"Yeah, but I don't think it will be a problem. He didn't seem interested in what we're doing; he told me they just wanted to inspect because they were bored and looking for something to do. How's your face, Cheese?"

"It's killing me," Bugs quipped.

"Are you going to stand around gasbagging all day or are you going to get that stuff loaded?" Cujo had approached the group unseen. "Let's go, we're over at Cargo Dock Three."

"Did you have fun on your honeymoon?" Fortis asked the pilot as they guided their pallets to the waiting *Dragon's Breath*.

Cujo chuckled. "I was watching Stoat, sir. Charlotte was just a pleasant diversion."

Fortis stopped the pallet jack. "Your private life is your business, but anything that happens on this mission is my business. Including ex-wives."

"Okay, Lucky, I hear you. I'm sorry, but I just can't stay away from her."

They pushed the pallet into motion again.

"You're the lucky one, Cujo," Lou said.

"Lucky she hasn't shot his ass or married him again," Cheese added.

They arrived at Cargo Dock Three and found Stoat and two unsavory looking characters waiting for them.

"Get that stuff loaded up and let's get out of here," Stoat urged by way of introduction. "Crab and Munk will show you where to stow it."

Cujo, Fortis, and Stoat stood off to one side as the team wrestled the pallets onto *Dragon's Breath*.

"Is she ready to go?"

Stoat nodded. "She's ready, and so am I." He cast a furtive look around the dock area. "I hate this damn place."

"Lucky, I picked up a pallet of rations on SOMO," Cujo said. "Prepackaged military surplus, but it's better than starving."

Bender came back down to the dock and said, "Everything is secured. We're ready to go."

Stoat practically ran up the ramp. "Mount up, let's go."

The team assembled on the mess deck and awaited the launch. Finally, Stoat's voice crackled over the intercom.

"Lucky, I need you in the cockpit. The jump gate launch master has asked for our destination."

Fortis went forward and gave Stoat a string of numbers and letters from memory. "Those are the coordinates of our first turn."

"At least now I know where I'm going," the captain grumbled before he radioed the jump gate.

Satisfied with their response, the launch master cleared *Dragon's Breath* for launch and the boxy craft slipped out of her berth. The sudden loss of centrifugal gravity caught Fortis by surprise, and he bumped up against the cockpit ceiling.

Stoat pointed to the empty seat next to him. "Sit here and belt in, we have a financial matter to discuss."

Earlier, Fortis had taken one point five million credits from his money belt and tucked it into his pocket, he withdrew it now and handed it to Stoat. The captain grunted with satisfaction and stuffed it deep into his grease-stained tunic.

"You've got yourself a charter, Mr. Lucky."

* * * * *

Chapter Fifteen

Fortis rejoined the team on the mess decks, but before he could say anything Tweak held a forefinger over her lips. She pressed a button on a small box in front her and a red light went on.

"Okay, you can talk now."

"What the hell is that?"

"Just a little something I threw together to make sure nobody can listen in on our conversations."

"I'm impressed."

"Learned this lesson on a freighter bound for a mining colony once. The captain overheard our plan and tried to double-cross us."

"They're still looking for him," Bender said, and they chuckled.

"Is it safe to talk now?"

Tweak nodded. "As long as that red light is on, you're good to go."

"All right, here's where we're at. I gave Stoat the first set of coordinates along with half his fee. I have to transmit our first status report to Anders and then we wait. Did all the gear make it in good shape?"

"Sergeant Dunham couldn't lay her hands on the drones in time. Otherwise, we're good to go," Cheese replied. "Except for those goons on TEJG, there were no problems moving the stuff."

"I think we should have someone stand watch on the gear," Bugs said. "The guys on this ship look a little shady to me."

"Good idea. Bender, set up a rotation."

"Will do. Six of us can cover four hour shifts without too much trouble."

Fortis shook his head. "Seven. Put me in the rotation, too."

"I already had. I wasn't counting me," Bender replied with an amused smile.

"How many crew are there? I saw Munk and Crab, and Stoat of course."

Cujo spoke up. "Stoat told me there are six total. Him, two cargo masters, and three engineers."

"Huh. Not many to run a ship this size."

"Fewer mouths to feed, fewer pockets to fill."

"Yeah, I guess. Okay, unless anyone has anything else, I need to report to Anders. Tweak, show me the way to the comms gear."

Tweak stopped Fortis in the passageway and leaned in close to his ear. "Cheese and I put together a bigger version of our little box to stifle comms from the ship. It's set up in the cargo area along with our own comms gear. We can't have the crew of this ship sending messages to anyone else."

"Won't they notice jamming?"

"It's not exactly jamming. The ship's system will send the message, but it won't go anywhere."

"Good idea."

"It might be better if we keep that between us, at least for now."

"Really? Why?"

"I trust our guys to keep a secret, but I don't trust them to keep their mouths shut. All it takes is one careless comment and the whole thing goes to crap."

"Who else knows?"

"Just you, me, and Cheese."

Fortis nodded. "Mum's the word."

The pair continued to the cargo area, where Tweak showed Fortis how to enter the prearranged signal to indicate the mission was proceeding smoothly. He included a brief description of Stoat and *Dragon's Breath* along with an ETA to orbit around Menard-Kev. He pressed the encrypt button, and, when the light on the keyboard changed from red to green, he hit the transmit button. Two seconds later, the light changed back to red, and the message was gone.

"Thanks for the help, Tweak."

"No problem, Lucky." While he'd been working on the message she had created a nest out of the bags with their ECW gear. She settled into it and pulled out a data tablet. "I've got the first watch."

Fortis returned to the mess deck, slid into an empty table, and waved Bender over. He checked for the red light on Tweak's invention before he spoke.

"The message is sent. Next turn in twenty-seven hours."

"Don't be surprised if it's sooner than that," Bender replied.

"What do you mean?"

"Remember how that finance guy reacted when you said it would take six to eight days to get to Menard-Kev? I'm surprised the suits didn't insist we change the mission timeline right then."

"They'd better do it soon or we'll be too far along."

Just then, Fortis' communicator beeped. It was Tweak.

"Hey, Lucky, we just got a message from Anders."

After they decoded the message, Fortis saw it was a new set of track coordinates. The original waypoint remained the same, but the others showed a direct path to the Maduro Jump Gate and Menard-Kev.

"That answers that," Bender said.

"Doesn't hurt my feelings at all," Cheese added with a theatrical stretch that tickled Lou's ear. "This crate is already too small."

She swatted his hand away. "I can't wait to get into that suit and escape your body odor."

"That's man musk, baby. It's got all the stuff Mother Nature gives virile men to attract fertile women."

Lou rolled her eyes and slugged him on the shoulder. The rest of the team laughed.

Bender banged the table with a meaty fist. "All right, enough grab-assing. Based on this new track, we'll be there two days earlier than planned. If you have equipment checks to do, get them done now. Lucky?"

"Cujo, I want to take a look at the shuttle and get your take on it."

"The shuttle is the best part about this mission. No worries there."

"How do you know?"

"I flew it into the cradle," Cujo replied as they climbed into the now-crowded hangar. "I wasn't banging Charlotte the *whole* time I was over there. You wanted a twenty-person shuttle, but we got a twenty-four."

Fortis was surprised to see the shuttle was sleek and shiny, practically brand new.

"How old is this thing?"

"I don't know. All the identification plates are gone."

"It's stolen."

"The word 'stolen' makes people nervous. It came from SOMO, so let's call it salvage." Cujo opened the hatch and beckoned to Fortis. "Check it out."

The interior was as clean as the exterior. There were no scratches or scuff marks, and the passenger harnesses were still fastened and covered in their original plastic.

"This thing is brand new. Where did you get it?"

"Lucky, you wanted a shuttle, so I got a shuttle. What difference does it make where it came from?"

"What if the owner of this thing had come looking for it, or if those sky marshals had discovered it? Do you think it would have made a difference where it came from then?"

"I get the feeling you don't approve of my methods."

"Not when you jeopardize the mission."

Cujo shook his head. "This is why I don't like having a military officer in command. Nothing personal, mind you, but it's a whole different mindset here in the intelligence world. We don't have quartermasters who supply us with everything we need when we hand them a signed requisition." He pointed to the shuttle. "Do you think Anders or Combover would have given us the money to *buy* this thing? Hell no! It's bad enough we had to hire a third-rate heap to get us where we're going; I'm not going to trust my life to a piece of shit shuttle that has to punch through the atmosphere, land, and return to orbit, all in one piece.

"Out here in the clandestine world, we have to scratch and claw for everything we get. If I see an opportunity to get an advantage and the risk is reasonable, I do it; no questions asked. I admit, I should have told you about my plans for Charlotte, but grabbing this thing? No, sir. I won't apologize, and I don't feel guilty about it."

After a long moment of silence, Fortis smiled. "It *is* a nice shuttle."

"Damn right it is. The GRC…er…the previous owners did a good job taking care of it for us."

"Okay, so it can do what we need it to do?"

"Absolutely. The shields are one hundred percent, so atmospheric entry shouldn't be a problem. It's got retractable wings which means we can glide and not just fall like a dropship. It also means we can land on wheels or skis. That's important, because from what I've heard Menard-Kev is covered with ice, and if we burn in like a dropship, we might get trapped in ice. It also means that almost anyone can fly it. Both Cheese and Lou have flight training and could take over if something happens to me."

"Cheese is supposed to remain here when we land."

"That's true, but *Dragon's Breath* is equipped with escape pods. He could ride to the surface if he had to. It wouldn't be my first choice, but it's an option."

"What about comms?"

"The shuttle has the standard suite of hailing and emergency freqs. Too public for our purposes. When Tweak gets off shift, she and Cheese are going to install a custom setup so we can have some privacy."

Over the next three hours, Fortis gained a new appreciation for the pilot as they explored the shuttle. Cujo knew a great deal about the craft and the intricacies of the power plant, flight control surfaces, and electronics. He peppered his lecture with anecdotes and lessons learned, and it became clear to Fortis that Cujo had thousands of flight hours as well as experience with countless emergencies.

"She's not sexy like a star fighter or a hovercopter, but for stability and reliability, I'll take her any time."

"What did Stoat say when you showed up with a brand new GRC shuttle?"

"Stoat's a weasel who was happy to pay me a finder's fee to locate the shuttle he agreed to provide."

"He paid you to get the shuttle for us?"

"You and the team are supposed to be just another contract to me, remember? I wasn't going to do it for free."

They shared a laugh and then Cujo grew serious.

"While we're talking about Stoat, let me give you some advice. I don't personally know him, but I know his breed. Space is littered with dead explorers and prospectors who discovered too late that you can hire a captain like Stoat, but you can't buy his loyalty. He will stab you in the back and steal everything you have without breaking a sweat."

"Do you think he'll betray us?"

"Probably not. He'd lose out on one point five million credits if he did. It's hard to say what his crew might do, but I have the feeling they won't get paid until Stoat gets all the money. That said, you might want to offer him a bonus when we arrive in Menard-Kev orbit, just to keep him in your pocket."

"How much?"

"Five hundred thousand ought to do it. Make sure his crew overhears you, so they know what's at stake, too."

* * * * *

Chapter Sixteen

Twenty-two hours later, Fortis found Stoat dozing in his cockpit chair.

"I've got our next waypoint, Captain."

The bleary-eyed captain entered the coordinates and then sat up when the graphic display revealed their destination.

"The Maduro Jump Gate?"

"Is that a problem?"

"Yeah, it is. You can spin whatever fables you want about mineral surveys, but I know who you are. There's a war on and Space Marines headed through the Maduro Jump Gate into Maltaani space spells trouble I didn't sign up for."

"What trouble? We're on an unarmed vessel bound for a distant planet to conduct a mineral survey."

"In case you haven't noticed, *Dragon's Breath* is a converted bomber. The Maltaani know what a bomber looks like, and they're not going to wait to find out whether we're armed before they vaporize us."

"We jump through the gate nice and quiet, get in and out, and we're gone before anyone knows we were there."

Stoat snorted. "You're not a good liar, Lieutenant. You can't wish away a war."

"My name is Lucky, and I'm not trying to. There haven't been any major engagements with the Maltaani for over a year, and there's no reason to think that will change now, even if they detect us. Which they won't, as long as we're not broadcasting."

Stoat squinted as he eyed Fortis, and he could almost hear the wheels turn in the captain's head.

"Penetrating a non-war war zone is going to cost you extra."

Fortis shook his head. "No, it won't. We agreed on three million credits. You got half to take us where we want to go and you'll get the other half when you bring us back."

"My crew won't be happy to hear we're transporting Space Marines," Stoat sneered. "But don't worry, Lieutenant, your secret is safe with me."

"And yours is safe with me."

"What secret is that?"

"That we paid you five million credits for this charter."

"Five million? That's ridiculous!"

"It won't sound so ridiculous on the other side of the Maduro Gate. In fact, a less trustworthy crew might start asking hard questions of their captain if they heard they were being shorted."

Stoat shook his head. "I knew you were trouble the moment I laid eyes on you." He tapped his navigation screen. "Sixteen hours to the Maduro Jump Gate. *Lucky*."

* * *

The term "jump gate" was inaccurate, as there were no physical gates for spacecraft to pass through. When a new space warp was discovered, the UNT installed a jump gate beacon nearby to transmit a signal that spacefarers used to navigate through unfamiliar space. Some of the jump gates, like the TEJG, became elaborate affairs with cargo handling and storage, repair docks, and even rest and recreation facilities. Others, like the Maduro Jump Gate, were unmanned spacecraft that merely transmitted their beacon through the jump gate and relayed communications through the warp. A ship only had to plot the position of the warp relative to the jump gate, achieve the proper angle and speed, and pass through the warp. As long as travelers tracked the beacon, they could guide themselves back.

A warp jump affected everyone differently. Some people experienced no ill effects, while others suffered headaches, nausea, and in some very rare cases, death. Medical science hadn't yet discovered how to predict a person's resistance to the forces involved, so every warp jump was potentially fatal. All the passengers could do was strap in and wait.

The harnesses on the mess decks were as old and dilapidated as the rest of *Dragon's Breath*, so the team decided to weather the warp gate jump strapped into the seats in the shuttle. Cujo joined Stoat in the cockpit to observe the jump. Fortis transmitted the prearranged signal to Anders reporting their arrival at the jump gate and then he joined the others.

Stoat gave a theatrical and completely unnecessary countdown as the ship approached the jump and then time stood still. Some people described warp jumping as floating in a warm pool of water. Fortis felt like he was suspended in cold gelatin. His skin became clammy, his senses dulled, and his mind became muddled. He was grateful his body spared him the nausea most people experienced.

Nobody knew how long a jump lasted since clocks stopped working, but Fortis only experienced the symptoms for several seconds. The cold sticky feeling subsided, and his mental fog began to clear.

"We're through," Stoat announced.

Fortis took a few seconds to clear his head. He heard Cheese and Bender laughing, and when he turned around, he saw Bugs had vomited on his shirt.

"Not only did he get sick, but he missed the bag," Cheese crowed.

"I hate warp jumping," Bugs said with a groan.

Fortis unbuckled his harness and headed for the cockpit. Two unfamiliar crewmembers stared at him as he passed through the mess deck, and they didn't acknowledge his nod.

When he got to the cockpit, Cujo and Stoat welcomed him with big smiles.

"Looks like you fared well through the jump," Cujo said.

"No problems for me. Stoat, I have our next waypoint."

Stoat punched in the numbers and scowled when Menard-Kev appeared on his display.

"What the hell is *that*?"

"That's our destination."

"Why?"

"Minerals. Precious metals. Wealth beyond imagination."

"I hope you brought warm clothes, because that place is going to be a cold sonofabitch."

Fortis chuckled. "We'll be burning thousand-credit bills to stay warm soon enough."

Stoat rolled his eyes. "Whatever you say, Lucky. We'll be in orbit in fourteen hours."

Fortis returned to the cargo area, where he found Bender on watch over their gear.

"I got back on watch as soon as I could and I found a couple of Stoat's guys in here."

"Did they mess with anything?"

"I dunno. It doesn't look like it, but I can't tell for sure."

"Looking for a quick buck, probably."

"They left as soon as I came in, emptyhanded, so I don't think they stole anything."

Fortis looked over the comms gear, but as far as he could tell, it was unchanged. He entered the message indicating they were through the jump gate and hit the transmit button. The signal would travel back through the warp, get boosted by the jump gate, and transmitted to Anders on Terra Earth.

Just then, Tweak entered the space with her privacy box in hand. She held it up to show Fortis and Bender that the light was red before she spoke.

"I told you I've been blocking the comms from this ship." The two men nodded. "Well, I can't decrypt the messages, so I decided to add a data logging function to track how often the ship sends messages. I didn't expect much from it, so I didn't check it until just now. Someone on this ship has sent twenty-two messages since we left TEJG."

Fortis' eyebrows shot up. "Twenty-two? Are you sure?"

"I'm sure. This tub isn't equipped with P2P, either."

P2P, or point-to-point terminals, were circuits installed on many space-going craft that permitted crewmembers to send and receive text, voice, and video messages from other terminals in space or back home on Terra Earth. For a vessel like *Dragon's Breath*, without crew access to the unlimited communications of P2P, twenty-two was an incredible number of messages.

"Can you tell who they were intended for?"

"No. Like I said, I can't decrypt them, but almost all of the messages appear to be the same. The same characters in sets of five repeated six times."

"It's a good thing we've been blocking them," Bender interjected. "A kid with a home electronics kit could have tracked us all the way from SOMO."

"Maybe that's the point," Fortis replied. "Maybe somebody is trying to track us."

"Who? Nobody knows we're here."

"Stoat recognized me back at SOMO, and he doesn't buy the wildcat mineral survey crew story, either. He had plenty of time to set something up before we left."

The trio pondered the situation in silence.

"What do you want to do, boss?"

"We're here. Can you think of a reason we shouldn't continue on mission?"

"Not right now, but we have to keep a close eye on Stoat and his crew. We need to brief the others, too. If there's a double-cross in the works, it's going to happen quick."

"Maybe we should act first," the massive master gunnery sergeant said.

"Hold on a second. Stoat is a sleazy bottom-feeder, but we don't have a reason to take over his ship, do we? What do we have, some inexplicable messages?"

Tweak and Bender exchanged glances before the electronics expert spoke.

"Lucky, we have to let Cheese in on this. He's going to be up here while we're down on the surface. In fact, we might want to leave someone else with him."

"Who?"

"Lou, maybe."

"Eh, I don't think so," Bender said. "I mean, we're talking six on two if they make a move while we're on the surface. Lou's a tough lady, but I'd feel better if I knew Cheese and Bugs were watching our backs. Stoat and his crew might think twice if they're faced with a couple strapping Space Marines. They tend to have a certain deterrent effect."

Tweak shrugged. "Fair point.

"How do we explain the change of plan?"

"We don't," Bender said. "Right before we launch the shuttle, tell Bugs he's staying behind to support Cheese. He'll be pissed, but he'll get over it. DINLI. Eliminates the chance of an accidental leak and Stoat won't have a chance to betray us."

Fortis turned to Tweak. "What do you think?"

"As far as planning on the fly goes, it's not bad. Personally, I think five people on the surface of Menard-Kev will be three too many anyway."

"You do?"

"Yeah, I do. I think we're going to find some freeze-dried astronauts who managed to activate their emergency beacon before they died fifty years ago and the reactor just hasn't shut down yet."

"Maybe we should leave you here too, then."

"Not a chance. I'm going."

"Why?"

"What if I'm wrong?"

* * * * *

Chapter Seventeen

Thirteen hours later, Fortis was ordering the team to load their gear onto the shuttle. At the last second, he had them load several cases of pig squares.

"Just in case," he told Lou when she gave him a curious glance.

Bender pulled him aside by the hatch.

"Bugs bitched a little, but he understands why we need him to stay here with Cheese. He's going to make up a story, so go along with it. Also, Tweak told me her gear logged three more transmissions since we talked."

"Huh. I wonder if they're expecting a response?"

"Too late to worry about that now."

"True. Okay, I'm going to the cockpit to talk to Stoat and observe our approach. Once we're in orbit I have to send an arrival message to Anders, then we should be ready to go."

"Okay, boss, I'll meet you in the hangar."

Fortis found Stoat and Cujo in the cockpit, so he unfolded the flight engineer's seat and squatted between them.

"Everything okay?"

"So far," Stoat replied. "As soon as I get a good read on this planet's rotation, we'll settle into orbit, then you and your team can launch the shuttle."

"We're not all going," Fortis said. Stoat gave a momentary twitch, but he didn't otherwise react. "Two members of my team will remain here."

"Two?" Cujo turned and gave Fortis a puzzled look. "We—I mean, you told me I was carrying five passengers to the surface."

"Four or five, what difference does it make?" Fortis shot Cujo a look, but the pilot had turned back to the control panel. "You're being paid to fly the shuttle, not take a head count."

"No difference, really. I just don't like when plans change without warning."

The trio lapsed into silence as the minutes ticked away. Stoat reached up and tapped one of the digital readouts.

"Lucky, this is the range indicator. It's measured in kilometers. When it gets to zero, we'll be at the correct altitude to maneuver into orbit."

Finally, the range readout approached zero, and Stoat flipped several switches as he grasped the joystick in front of him. The pitch and yaw indicators rolled as the captain guided *Dragon's Breath* into orbit, and Fortis watched the range indicator begin to climb.

"Did we miss it?"

Cujo chuckled as he stood up. "Not hardly. Captain Stoat just maneuvered the ship into perfect orbit."

"But the range is increasing."

"We can't maintain a geosynchronous orbit because the planet's rotation is too unstable, so we're forced to use a traditional orbit. The range will increase until we reach the apogee of our orbit, then it'll decrease until we reach perigee. At that point, we'll launch the shuttle." Cujo motioned toward the cockpit door. "Speaking of the shuttle, we should prepare for launch, unless you want to go around again."

Cujo stopped Fortis in the passageway that led back to the hangar. "Why did you decide to change the plan? Who is staying behind?"

"Bender and I talked about Stoat and his crew, and I decided to leave more horsepower than just Cheese. Bugs is going to stay behind with him."

"Stoat's not going to do anything to risk one point five million credits."

"It's not just Stoat I'm worried about. I don't want the team to be at the mercy of complete strangers while we're on the surface."

Cujo shook his head. "It's your call, but I think it's unnecessary."

Bender had the team loaded and strapped in by the time Fortis and Cujo arrived at the shuttle. Crab and Munk were stationed in the boom control room overlooking the hangar, but neither responded when Cujo waved.

"We have a good lock on the distress signal. Comm checks with Cheese and Bugs are complete," Tweak reported. "I'll try them again once we're underway and again after we hit atmosphere."

"Shit! I almost forgot." Fortis jumped up out of his seat. "I have to signal Anders."

"Better hurry," Cujo said. "We'll be at perigee soon."

Cheese and Bugs looked up sharply when Fortis entered the cargo area. Both men had their hands inside equipment bags on the deck next to them.

"Don't shoot. I need to call Anders," Fortis told them.

He punched in the coded signal to report their arrival at Menard-Kev and the launch of the shuttle. The lights on the comms set confirmed transmission, and he jumped up.

"I don't think we'll be gone long," he told the Space Marines. "If there's anything worth looking at, maybe we can make another shuttle run before we leave."

When he got back to the hangar, Stoat was there, along with two of his other crewmen.

"All set, Mr. Lucky?"

"Yes, we are." Fortis dug into his pocket and produced a wad of credits. "In recognition of the outstanding job you've done bringing us here, here's a five hundred thousand credit bonus for you and your crew."

Stoat stared at Fortis for a long second before he reached out for the bills. His crew stared at the bankroll with palpable greed, and their eyes didn't leave it until Stoat tucked it into his tunic.

"That's very generous of you. I'll be sure to give each of my crew their fair share." His eyes narrowed for a split second before his face broke into a wide grin. "The pleasure girls on SOMO are going to be very happy when we get back."

Fortis climbed aboard the shuttle and locked the hatch behind him.

"We good?" Bender asked.

"Yep. I sent the message to Anders and gave Stoat a nice bonus in front of his crew. Maybe that will cause some dissent in their ranks, or at least distract them for the next few hours."

Cujo's voice boomed over the intercom. "Ladies and gentlemen, welcome aboard Cujo Airlines. Buckle up and get ready, because punching through the atmosphere might get a little bumpy. Stand by for launch."

Fortis heard a clunk as the booms engaged the shuttle, and then a loud whine as the bomb bay doors opened. There was no sensation of movement, but, a few minutes later, Cujo came back on over the intercom.

"We're away, folks. Atmospheric entry in two minutes."

Fortis discovered he was white knuckling his arm rests, and he forced himself to relax. He looked up and saw Lou staring at him with an amused look on her face.

"Relax, Lucky. Cujo can be a screwup, but he's an excellent pilot."

The shuttle began to shake as the craft encountered the outer layers of Menard-Kev's atmosphere. The cabin temperature became noticeably warmer, and the lights blinked on and off every time the craft bounced. A low rumble developed under Fortis' feet, and he felt the deck vibrate as the rumble grew louder.

Suddenly, all the noise and vibration ceased, the cabin lights steadied, and the temperature dropped.

"We're in," Cujo announced. "I'd turn the camera view on, but there's not much to see without any daylight."

Tweak fiddled with her gear. "I've got a lock on the emergency beacon, and I sent the line of bearing to the cockpit nav computer."

"What about *Dragon's Breath*?"

"I'm trying them now. It might take me a minute to find a freq that can burn through the atmosphere."

Cujo came over the intercom again. "Lucky, come up to the cockpit and take a look at this."

Bender followed Fortis forward and squeezed in behind the two men. Cujo pointed to a topographic image on the heads-up display.

"This is what the surface looks like. It's mostly flat, but there's a prominent ridgeline on a north-south axis about twenty klicks from our target. That green line is the bearing Tweak sent for the beacon, and it points straight at that huge lump."

Fortis saw a large, oblong geographic feature and a second, smaller one close by. "Any idea what that is?"

"The shuttle isn't equipped with scanners. All I can do is map it with the lasers. Whatever it is, it's huge. It's at least three hundred meters high and a thousand meters long, and the smaller one is a hundred high and about four hundred meters long."

Bender whistled. "Meteorites?"

"I think a meteorite that big would have left a huge crater."

"I don't think meteorites send out emergency beacons," Cujo quipped. "What's really strange is this area here." He used a cursor to indicate an area near the largest lump. "This looks like a prepared landing area. It's smooth, and this line is too straight to be natural."

"You think someone else has landed here?"

"I get paid to fly, not think, but, if I had to guess, I would say yes. I don't know what the wind or snow conditions are like here, but it looks like a cleared runway to me."

Cujo piloted the shuttle in a large loop around the strange formation and runway, but they didn't detect any other features. The green line of bearing pointed at the largest lump the entire time.

"If it is a runway, it doesn't look like anyone's home unless they're hiding. We can do a touch-and-go and see what happens."

Fortis nodded. "Yeah, let's do that. If we don't provoke a response, I guess we'll land."

"Buckle up, boys," Cujo said. "This is where the job gets fun."

Fortis and Bender returned to their seats and cinched their harnesses.

"Check your straps. Cujo's about to do some aerobatics."

Tweak and Lou groaned as they tightened their seatbelts. "He's not going to crash this crate into a mountain, is he?"

Bender laughed. "Nah, just a touch-and-go to test a landing strip."

Fortis felt the shuttle roll as Cujo steered them around to line up on the runway and there was a slight bump when the shuttle skis touched down. After several seconds, the craft lifted off again.

"No reaction from the surface, and the strip felt solid," Cujo reported over the intercom. "This one's for keeps."

The landing was routine. The skis touched down and the engines roared as Cujo applied reverse thrust to slow them down, and then everything was silent.

"Welcome to Menard-Kev."

* * * * *

Chapter Eighteen

"The outside temperature is a balmy minus one hundred and fifty degrees Celsius," Cujo told the team as they donned their ECW gear. "The wind is blowing ninety kilometers an hour. Zip up tight because at this temperature you won't even feel it burn."

Once they were dressed, the group buddy-checked each other to ensure everything was secure. Cujo's warning was a stark reminder of how hostile the environment was and how fragile they were in comparison. They all carried their ballistic pistols, and Lou carried the thermal scanner as well.

Fortis stood by the hatch, looked back at the group, and flashed them a thumb's up. He received four in return, and he turned his attention to the access hatch. He twisted the locking mechanism, the hatch popped open, and he stepped out onto the access ramp. The wind buffeted him and plucked at his ECW gear, but he was warm inside the suit. He descended the ramp with slow, careful steps while he got used to the sensation of wearing his helmet.

The surface of Menard-Kev was frozen solid, and Fortis felt it crunch underfoot as he walked. Whenever he stopped moving, ice crystals collected on the windward side of his suit.

Fortis waited for the rest of the team at the bottom of the ramp. He switched displays on his visor to achieve the best image. He settled on a combination of low light and infrared, and he adjusted the resolution to give him the sharpest image. Finally, all five team members stood together next to the shuttle.

"Everybody all set?" After a chorus of yesses, he said, "Tweak, take point and guide us to the beacon."

Tweak set off toward the lump looming over the shuttle, followed by Fortis, Lou, Cujo, and Bender. The hardpacked ice made for easy going, and it wasn't long before they arrived at the enormous ice-covered structure. Fortis got an eerie feeling as he stood next to the frozen monolith.

"This is it," Tweak said. "The signal is coming from somewhere inside there."

"This doesn't make sense," Cujo said. "The beacon is buried inside a snowball?"

"Hey, check this out." Lou held up the thermal scanner she was carrying. "This thing might be frozen on the outside, but it's warm on the inside."

They took turns viewing the thermal scanner display. Lou was right. The outside was a frozen shell that showed as white, but the inside was a soft orange color, indicating heat.

"Looks like you're right, Cujo. The beacon is buried in there somewhere."

"How are we supposed to dig it out?"

"We don't have to," Bender said. While the others were looking through the thermal scanner, he had followed what appeared to be a walkway around the side. "I found a hatch."

The team gathered around and examined his discovery. There was a hole chipped through a meter-thick crust of ice, and, at the back of the hole, Fortis saw a hatch, which was askew, as if the structure it was attached was leaning to one side.

"It looks like a standard spacecraft access hatch," Cujo said.

"It is, but someone made sure it couldn't be opened." Bender pointed to a thick metal bar crudely welded across the hatch.

"Can you cut those welds?" Fortis asked.

"Yeah, but I'll have to get the cutting unit from the shuttle. Stand by, I'll be right back."

"Lou, go with him," Fortis ordered.

The hulking Space Marine and his much smaller companion disappeared into the near darkness. Tweak hunched her back against the wind and adjusted her portable comms set.

"The atmosphere is playing hell with our signal, Lucky. This unit doesn't have the power to burn through the scatter, and Cheese and Bugs are cutting in and out."

"When you get through, tell them what we found and let them know we might be out of contact for a while."

"Will do."

"Hey, Lucky, do you think it's a good idea to cut this hatch open?" Cujo leaned in and inspected the bar. "Somebody obviously doesn't want whatever's inside to get out."

"Maybe they're trying to keep us out."

"Yeah, I don't know. I'm not a fan of releasing a bunch of bugs. I vote we err on the side of caution."

"The thermal scanner doesn't show any movement, at least around the hatch," Tweak injected.

Just then, Bender and Lou reappeared.

"Here's the cutting unit. Stand back." Bender pointed the torch at the weld and the cutting unit flared to life. He touched the flame to the doorframe side of the weld. Slag sizzled as it dripped into the snow. When he finished, Bender stood back and gestured to the door.

"It's all yours."

"I'll get it." Tweak stepped forward and grasped the locking handle. She looked back at Fortis, who nodded.

"Do it."

Tweak turned the handle and the hatch popped open. Warm, humid air poured out and turned into an instant ice shower when it collided with the frigid outside air. Fortis drew his pistol and stepped through the hatch onto the slanted deck. What he saw inside left him speechless.

He stood in a cavernous hangar or cargo handling area inside a spacecraft of incredible size. The space was at least fifty meters across and twenty meters tall, and despite the tilted deck, Fortis imagined rows of ISMC mechs or hovercopters parked inside.

"Wow."

The rest of the team followed Fortis inside, secured the hatch, and stood in awe of what they saw.

"This is unbelievable."

"What the hell is this place?"

"Look familiar, Lucky?" Bender rumbled.

"I see it, but I don't believe it." Fortis looked at the deck and recognized the lines used by squadron personnel to jockey aircraft within the tight confines of a full hangar. "This looks like the hangar on a Fleet spacecraft."

"This whole ice mountain is a Fleet spacecraft?" Cujo couldn't hide the incredulity in his voice.

"I didn't say that." Fortis crossed to the nearest bulkhead and tested an access hatch. It opened easily. "Let's take a look around."

The team followed Fortis down a narrow passageway that twisted and turned for fifty meters. He paused at random intervals and opened doors and hatches to investigate the spaces beyond, but most appeared to be stripped clean. The few spaces that weren't empty had papers strewn around the decks, but he saw no equipment or other materials.

"Where's the transmitter?" Fortis asked Tweak.

Before she could answer, they heard a loud bang at the far end of the passageway, and Fortis caught a glimpse of movement as someone or something dodged out of sight.

"Runner," Fortis said as he gave chase. He pointed to a hatch on a nearby bulkhead. "Bender, cut him off!"

By the time Fortis got to the far end of the passageway, his quarry was nowhere to be found. Fortis stopped and listened, and he heard faint sounds of movement in the distance. The faint sounds became shouting, and he wasn't sure if it was coming from the voice circuit or the outside environment.

Over the circuit, Bender grunted and said, "Got you!" and the shouting ceased.

By the time Fortis got back to the group, the other four team members were gathered around a figure spread eagled on the hangar deck. He saw it was a young woman with matted brown hair and shabby coveralls. Her face was streaked with dirt and sweat, and her hands were filthy.

"She ran all the way back here before I could catch her," Bender reported.

"Who is she?" Fortis asked.

"Those are Fleet coveralls," Lou said. "The name tape and rank insignia have been torn off, but those are definitely Fleet issue."

"What's a Fleet sailor doing here?" Tweak asked.

Fortis pulled off his helmet. "Why don't you ask her?" He'd seen her eyelids flutter, and he prodded the woman's foot with his boot. "She's awake."

The young woman suddenly came to life and tried to scramble away, but she wound up wrapped in Bender's massive arms.

"Take it easy, it's okay," Fortis said. "We're friends."

The woman looked from person to person in wide-eyed fear. Lou removed her helmet and knelt next to the frightened sailor.

"It's all right, sweetie," the operator crooned. "You're okay. Nobody's going to hurt you. We're friends."

The panic in the sailor's face gave way to confusion as she sank back to the deck.

"W-who are you?" she asked in a tiny voice.

"We'll get to that," Fortis said. "Let's start with you. Who are you?"

"I'm Auxiliary Technician Third Class Ludana Vidic."

"And you're a Fleet sailor?"

Vidic nodded.

"This is your ship?"

"Of course. Fleet Academy Training Vessel *Imperio.*"

The team gasped.

"*This* is *Imperio*?" Fortis croaked. Suddenly, he realized why everything had seemed so familiar. *Imperio* was the sister ship to *Atlas*, the flagship of the ISMC Ninth Division that Fortis had deployed on a year earlier.

"You're missing!" Cujo exclaimed.

Vidic nodded. "We've been trapped here for two and a half years."

"But how? I mean, how did you come to be here, on this planet?"

"We came through the Maduro Jump Gate and were attacked by slavers. They took over the ship and forced the captain to bring her here. We've been here ever since."

"Slavers? There are three thousand people on this ship. How did they capture three thousand people?"

Vidic squirmed, and Fortis saw that she was uncomfortable with their questions. She stuck out her chin in an expression of defiance.

"I've answered enough of your questions. Now it's my turn. Who are you?"

"We're here to investigate a distress signal detected coming from your ship."

Vidic's face brightened. "You're here to rescue us?"

"Yeah, something like that. How many of you are there?"

"We mustered thirteen hundred and sixty-four after the last cull."

"Cull?"

Her face tightened into a fierce scowl. "Yeah. Every so often the slavers come back and take off a group of people. Sometimes a dozen, sometimes a hundred."

"Where do they take them?"

"Wherever slave labor is needed, I guess. Asteroid mines, terraforming—" Her voice caught in her throat. "Pleasure ships."

Tweak groaned.

Vidic looked around the darkened hangar. "We need to move."

"Is there someone else here?"

"It's better if we don't make too much noise. Come on."

Vidic got to her feet and used a small light on her belt to guide them to a door on the near bulkhead. She entered and the team followed.

Inside, they found a small office. The desks were pushed together with blankets piled on top, and empty ration packs littered the deck. The team members piled their helmets on a vacant desk and the lights illuminated the space.

"This is your place?" asked Lou. "You live here?"

Vidic shrugged. "Sometimes. I hide out in here when the slavers come back."

"How often do they come back?"

"Hold on a second," Fortis interjected. "Let's go back to the beginning and let Ludana tell us her story." He unfolded a chair, sat down, and motioned at Vidic. "If that's okay with you?"

* * * * *

Chapter Nineteen

"My name is Ludana Vidic, and I'm an Auxiliary Technician Third Class here on the Fleet Academy Training Vessel *Imperio*. Two and a half years ago, we passed through the Maduro Jump Gate and slavers captured the ship. They were waiting for us, and before the ship could recover from the jump they were aboard.

"The captain got on the general intercom system and ordered all crew, Fleet Academy staff, and cadets to muster by department in the hangars. Thirty minutes later, when the muster was incomplete, the slavers killed ten ships' officers."

"Monsters," Tweak breathed.

"Worse than monsters," Vidic replied. "After the muster was complete, the Fleet Academy instructors and most of *Imperio*'s officers were segregated into Hangar Six. At least four hundred people." Her voice wavered and caught in her throat. She squeezed her eyes shut for a long moment, and when she opened them, a tear leaked down her cheek.

"They dogged down the interior hatches and opened the hangar doors. They airlocked all of them."

The team reacted with shock and revulsion. Lou drew a ragged breath, and Bender cursed under his breath. Fortis' stomach lurched at the image of four hundred people fighting to breathe in the vacuum of space while their blood boiled, and they froze simultaneously.

"Worse than monsters," Tweak echoed.

"After that, they forced the senior male cadets into Hangar Four and threatened to airlock them if we didn't follow orders. The captain brought *Imperio* here and managed to deorbit without cracking up, but the engines were damaged by the impact. That's when the slavers held the first cull."

"That's when they take people away?" Cujo asked.

Vidic nodded. "They hauled away a bunch of cadets and put the rest of us to work stripping the ship of everything that wasn't welded down."

"How many slavers are there? Why didn't you fight back?" Bender asked.

"They put the captain and the remaining officers in Hangar Six to 'clean up,'" Vidic said, making air quotes. "When the space was clean, the slavers opened the outer doors and let them freeze to death. After that, there was no resistance. Besides, we don't have any weapons. *Imperio* is a training vessel, remember?"

"There are thirteen hundred of you still here?" asked Fortis.

"Thirteen hundred and sixty-four."

Vidic's voice cracked, her face contorted, and she burst into tears. Lou took the younger woman in her arms and made soothing noises as Vidic sobbed into her shoulder.

Fortis motioned to Bender. "Let's take a walk and give them a minute. Tweak, you come too so we can call *Dragon's Breath*. Cujo, stay here and keep your eyes open."

The trio grabbed their helmets and headed for the outside hatch.

"When we get outside, tell Cheese and Bugs that we found a crash and we're exploring, but nothing else, okay? I don't want to take the chance that Stoat and his guys might overhear what's going on down here."

When they got outside, Tweak walked a short distance away and Bender turned to Fortis.

"What are you thinking, boss?"

"I have no idea what to think. This is incredible, and if I wasn't here to see it, I wouldn't believe it."

"It's one hell of a story, that's for sure."

"Colonel Anders is going to lose his mind when he hears about this one."

Bender guffawed, Fortis chuckled, and soon both men were laughing at the thought of Anders' reaction to their discovery.

"What are you laughing about?" Tweak asked when she rejoined them.

"Colonel Anders," Bender sputtered.

"Lucky, Cheese and Bugs acknowledged our message. Everything is quiet on *Dragon's Breath* right now."

"Good."

"So, what have you decided?"

Fortis threw up his hands. "I don't know where to start. We can't rescue them. If we packed people in, we might fit three hundred people on *Dragon's Breath*. With a twenty-person shuttle, that's fifteen round trips. I don't know if we have the fuel for that."

"We can't leave them here. What if the slavers come back?" Tweak protested.

"What if they do? What if the slavers return and discover three hundred people missing? What do you think they'll do to these kids then?"

"Damn. I didn't think about that. Nothing but terrible choices."

"Yeah, no kidding."

"DINLI," Bender intoned.

"DINLI, indeed." Fortis turned for the hatch. "C'mon, let's get back inside."

They returned to Vidic's office and found Cujo standing watch outside with his pistol drawn.

"What's going on?" Fortis asked.

Cujo tipped his head at the door. "I'll let her tell you."

"Is something wrong?" he asked Lou when they reentered the office.

Lou nudged Vidic. "Tell him."

"Some of the cadets have been collaborating with the slavers. They basically act like jailers when the slavers aren't here."

"*What?*"

"They're awful. They control the food and decide who lives in what berthing compartments. Sometimes they throw some of us in the brig when we argue. The slavers call them the Cadre, and they gave them a comm set. When the slavers show up, the Cadre help round everyone up and take muster."

Bender slammed a massive fist into his other palm. "Let's crush those fuckers."

Fortis held up his hands. "We'll deal with the traitors when we get back home. Right now, I need to explain what's going to happen."

"Okay." Vidic's voice was heavy with suspicion.

"We can't take any of you with us right now."

The petty officer's eyes widened in shock and her mouth fell open.

"I know it's hard to understand, but let me explain. Our ship is too small to take everyone. What happens if the slavers return and notice a bunch of you are missing?"

"What if they come back and take more away?"

"You said they don't hesitate to kill. If they find out someone else has been here and taken some of their prisoners away, they might decide to cut their losses and kill everyone. Even if they didn't figure it out on their own, do you think the collaborators will keep it a secret?"

Vidic's face fell. "No, I guess not."

Fortis put his hands on her shoulders and looked directly into her eyes. "Ludana, you've got to stay strong until we can figure out a way to get all of you out of here. You've done a great job for a long time. You can keep it up for a little while longer, okay?"

The young petty officer nodded. Fortis turned to the team.

"Here's what we're going to do. We'll weld the hatch behind us and take the shuttle back to *Dragon's Breath*. I'll make a report to Colonel Anders, and we'll stand by in orbit while he figures out what to do. Down here, Petty Officer Vidic will carry on as if nothing has happened."

"I'd like to stay behind and help Ludana," Lou said.

"Request denied."

"But, Lucky—"

"Absolutely not. We can't risk discovery. If the collaborators or slavers get ahold of you…"

"You should go," Vidic said. "I can take care of myself."

"It's settled then." Fortis gestured to the team. "Grab your gear, and let's go." He turned to the petty officer. "Vidic, stay safe, and I promise you that we will be back for you as soon as we can."

Fortis led the team outside and waited while Bender sealed the door.

"It won't be perfect, but after a couple days I don't think anyone will be able to tell we cut the weld."

"Hey, Lucky, we've got trouble!" blurted Tweak.

"What is it?"

The electronics technician patched the comms circuit into the team common frequency, and Fortis heard Bugs' voice. The operator faded in and out through bursts of static. In the background, they could hear gunshots and shouts.

"Falling back—Tweak can you—pod. Cheese!"

The transmission abruptly cut out.

"What the hell's going on up there?" Fortis demanded.

"I don't know," Tweak replied. "I got the circuit up when we got outside and that's what I heard. Bugs shouted something about Stoat and then the shooting started."

"We gotta get up there, fast!" Cujo took off for the shuttle. "Let's go!"

They followed the pilot and scrambled inside the shuttle. Everyone dove into their seats without stripping off their ECW suits and belted in while Cujo went through the startup checklist.

"Here we go!" he shouted over the intercom. The shuttle jerked into motion as Cujo shoved the throttles forward and taxied the craft to the far end of the runway. He reversed the thrust on the port engine and the shuttle pivoted until it was pointed back down the runway. The engines revved, and the shuttle leapt forward when Cujo released the brake.

"Tweak, are you getting anything?" Fortis asked through gritted teeth.

"Negative. The circuit is dead."

The shuttle lifted off and began climbing. Suddenly, the craft banked sharply.

"Holy shit!" Cujo shouted.

"What the hell's going on?" Bender shouted.

"Something just flew past us, and crash landed over behind *Imperio*," Cujo replied.

"What was it?"

"I think it was an escape pod."

Cujo piloted the shuttle in a slow circle above the crash site while Fortis and Bender stared at the heads-up display. Stubby wings were visible on the stricken craft, but they couldn't make out further details.

"That definitely looks like an escape pod," Cujo concluded. "There's only one place it could have come from."

"Why would *Dragon's Breath* drop a pod here?"

"You heard that transmission from Bugs. Something went very wrong up there."

"What do you want me to do, Lucky?' Cujo pointed to the fuel readout. "We can't keep circling in this atmosphere forever or we won't have enough juice to get back into orbit."

"Set us down, and let's investigate the pod," Fortis ordered.

* * * * *

Chapter Twenty

As soon as Cujo got the shuttle stopped, Fortis threw open the hatch and jumped down the ramp. The team crunched their way across the frozen surface to the crashed pod where gouts of steam rose, froze, and fell in a shower of ice crystals. Fortis approached the pod and saw the front end was crushed and one wing stuck up at a crazy angle, but the craft was otherwise intact. He reached for the access lock and Lou stopped him.

"Wait. Let's find out if there's anyone in there first." She unlatched a small door next to the hatch and exposed an intercom panel. Lou pressed the call button and the response from inside the pod was immediate.

"Get us out of here!"

It was Bugs.

"We're working on it," Lou replied. "Are you okay?"

"Cheese caught one in the back, and he's lost a lot of blood."

"Do you have your ECW gear?"

"Didn't have time to grab it. All we have in here are the emergency exposure suits."

"Put them on while we figure out how to make this work."

She turned to Fortis. "How do you want to do this?"

"As soon as they're suited up, we'll pop the hatch. Tweak and Cujo, lead Bugs to the shuttle, and I'll help Bender carry Cheese.

Lou, run ahead and break out the trauma kit and get ready for Cheese."

Two minutes later, Bugs called over the intercom.

"We're ready to go. What's the plan?"

"As soon as you open the hatch and climb out, Tweak will grab your arm and lead you to the shuttle. Bender and I will grab Cheese and be right behind you. We need to move fast because those exposure suits won't protect you for long out here."

"We're ready when you are."

"Go!"

The escape pod hatch opened, and Bugs clambered out. Tweak and Cujo grabbed his arms and half-dragged him toward the shuttle. Bender stepped into the pod, scooped up Cheese in his massive arms, and followed a few steps behind Bugs. Fortis stayed close, but there was little he could do to help Bender.

Lou waited until the last second to open the shuttle hatch, and the group crowded in.

"Lay him here, on the deck," she told Bender.

"He got hit high on the left side," Bugs told her as he struggled out of his exposure suit.

Lou cut away Cheese's exposure suit, and Fortis saw a bloodstained dressing tied around his torso. Blood leaked past the makeshift bandage and spread across the shuttle deck.

"I did the best I could," Bugs explained.

Lou worked quickly to clean the gaping wound and apply a layer of elastic skin to seal it and stop the bleeding. She applied a fresh layer of gauze, and Tweak helped her wind it tight around Cheese's chest. When she was finished, she sat back and drew a deep breath.

"The bullet is still in him," she told Fortis. "I'll need more than a trauma kit to treat this wound."

Fortis frowned and turned to Bugs.

"What the hell happened up there?"

"We were in the cargo area listening for you on the circuit when Stoat rushed in and shouted something about pirates and how we were going to get the hell out of there. Cheese drew on him and said there was no fucking way we were leaving you down here. That's when his guys busted in and shot Cheese in the back.

"They had us pinned down for a few seconds, but we dropped two of them and escaped. I don't know how Cheese stayed on his feet, but he made it all the way to the escape pods. There's not much to say after that. A couple ragged-assed mercenaries ran us off." He took a uneven breath. "I didn't want to run, but Cheese was yelling and bleeding, and they had rifles against our pistols. Shit was flying everywhere, and there wasn't much else we could do except fall back." He lowered his head and a sob escaped his chest.

Bender knelt and put an enormous arm around Bugs' shoulders. "You did great, Marine. You're here, you're alive, and you saved your buddy's life. That's all anyone can ask of you."

The team sat silently as Bender comforted his distressed comrade. Fortis caught Lou's eye and nodded toward the cockpit.

When they were out of earshot, he turned to her.

"What's the prognosis?"

"Not good. He's got a large caliber round still in there. Without a scan, the best I can do is fish around and hope to find it. I'm sure he's got a bleeder or two in there as well."

"What do we need?"

Lou scoffed. "We need a ride out of here, but that just left. An operating room to get the bullet out and sew up the bleeders would be good, but there's not much chance of that. Beyond that, we can transfuse him, but it's just a matter of time."

Her eyes shined with unshed tears, and Fortis felt his own eyes burning. Just then, Cujo joined them.

"Are we going after those bastards?"

"In this? No way. From what Bugs reported, *Dragon's Breath* is already gone. Even if she was still there, Stoat's not going to let us dock, and we don't have a way to board her."

"What are we going to do? We can't stay here forever!" Cujo's voice rose.

"First you're going to calm down. Panicking is not going to make our present circumstances any better." He gestured toward the cabin. "Cheese needs a lot more help than we can give him here." He looked back at Lou. "There's an entire hospital on *Imperio*. What are the chances we can find what we need over there?"

"Vidic said the slavers stripped the ship, but maybe they left something behind."

"Let's do this. You, Bender, and Tweak head back over there. Find Vidic and see if *Imperio* has what you need. I'll stay here with Bugs and Cujo to look after Cheese."

The team agreed to the plan, and the trio prepared for their trip back to the training ship.

When they were gone, Fortis, Bugs, and Cujo settled near Cheese and waited. The silence in the shuttle was tense and uncomfortable, and Fortis couldn't shake the feeling that they were keeping a deathwatch over Cheese. The wounded operator's skin had turned a purplish shade of gray, and his chest rose and fell in shallow, irregular intervals.

Finally, Bugs couldn't take it any longer, and he jumped to his feet.

"I'm gonna kill Stoat if it's the last thing I do! I don't care if I have to chase him past the edge of known space. I'm gonna find him and I'm gonna kill him."

"I'll do the flying," Cujo added. "That backstabbing sonofabitch needs to die for this."

Cujo's vehemence toward Stoat surprised Fortis. It had become obvious as they traveled to Menard-Kev that the two men had had a relationship before Fortis contracted for *Dragon's Breath*. Cujo hadn't struck Fortis as the kind who would favor killing someone, even someone who betrayed the team like Stoat did.

"What exactly did Stoat say when he came into the cargo area?" he asked Bugs.

"He came in and said he was going to haul ass. Cheese told him we weren't going anywhere without you guys and drew on him. Then they started shouting. The next thing I know, Stoat's guys started blasting."

"Why would he abandon us?" Cujo asked.

Bugs grimaced. "Man, I don't know. That dude is totally sketchy. What the hell's been going on down here, anyway? Did you find the distress beacon?"

Fortis related what they had discovered under the massive ice mound and Vidic's story of how *Imperio* came to be on Menard-Kev. Bugs listened, open-mouthed.

"That's unbelievable," he blurted when Fortis finished." He looked at Cheese. "I wish I could tell him." His eyes grew wide. Cheese's face had turned completely white. "Oh, shit!"

Bugs jumped down beside Cheese and put his ear to the wounded man's chest.

"No, Goddammit, no!" He tipped Cheese's head up and breathed into his mouth. "Come on, Cheese. *Breathe.*"

He switched to chest compressions and looked at Fortis and Cujo.

"Don't just sit there. Help me!"

Fortis knelt down and delivered two breaths whenever Bugs paused. Cheese's chest rose and fell as Fortis breathed for him, but he didn't begin to breathe for himself.

After fifteen minutes, Bugs sat back on his heels, his chin on his chest, his hands folded in his lap.

"He's gone."

No matter how many times Fortis encountered death it always affected him, and Cheese was no different. He swallowed the lump growing in his throat and glanced at Cujo. The pilot sat, stone faced, and stared at the dead operator.

Fortis expected more tears from Bugs, but the Marine sat quietly for a long time. Finally, he leaned over Cheese and kissed the dead man on the forehead.

"I will make them pay for this, brother. I swear it."

* * * * *

Chapter Twenty-One

Lou's voice came over the circuit.

"Lucky, this is Lou. Bad news. All the medical equipment was stripped by the slavers. How's Cheese?"

Fortis swallowed and tried to speak in a normal voice. "He's gone."

"Damn it."

Bugs let out a ragged sob. Silence hung heavily over the circuit.

"Do you want to camp out in the shuttle or over here, boss?" Bender asked.

Cujo made a chopping motion across his neck. "We can't stay here. If we wear the batteries down on lights and heat, we won't have enough juice to get the engines started."

"Cujo says we can't stay here, so we'll make the move over there. Someone will have to come back for Bugs; his emergency exposure suit won't hold up."

"Roger that. Call when you're close, and I'll have someone standing by the hatch."

Fortis looked at Cujo and Bugs.

"Change of plans. Bugs, I'll give you my ECW gear and wait here while you three head over to *Imperio*. When you get over there, send my gear back here with Bender."

Bugs looked at Cheese. "Maybe I should stay here."

"No. You're going over with Cujo and Lou. I need a few minutes of peace and quiet to think through our next steps, and it's safer to be alone over here. DINLI."

"DINLI, indeed."

Bugs grumbled as he donned Fortis' gear, but he did as he was ordered. By the time he was dressed, his natural ebullience began to emerge, and he managed to joke about fouling the ECW gear.

"I'll leave you a nice warm present in the seat of your suit, Lucky."

Fortis chuckled. "That won't be necessary. A thank you will suffice. Before I forget, take a few cases of pig squares over there, too."

As the trio lined up by the hatch, Cujo leaned close to Fortis.

"Body bags are in the medical compartment."

Fortis nodded, and the trio left the shuttle. After they were gone, Fortis located a body bag in the medical compartment. After some awkward maneuvering, he got Cheese into the rubber bag and zipped it up. It was an unpleasant task, and he was relieved when he was finished. Afterward, he sat back and contemplated their situation.

The betrayal by Stoat wasn't a complete surprise. Cujo had recommended the bonus to head off the possibility, but the bonus might have caused his betrayal. Two million credits was a lot of money, even shared among the crew. Perhaps Stoat's fear of being in Maltaani space finally outweighed his greed, and he lost his nerve. Still, the unidentified signal seemed to be evidence that Stoat had something planned when they sailed. In fact, Cujo—

Fortis jerked like he'd been shocked.

Before they sailed, Cujo had claimed he didn't personally know Stoat, but during the transit it became obvious they'd known each other for some time. Fortis frowned at yet another example of Cujo's lack of candor.

What is Cujo's game?

He pushed those thoughts aside. Whatever Cujo was up to, it could wait until they were back on Terra Earth, or at least off Menard-Kev. Rescue was his number one priority. The question was, how?

One possibility was for Cujo to take the team into space on the shuttle so they could communicate with Anders on a more suitable circuit, but he didn't know whether the shuttle had comms gear with the range to reach back to Terra Earth, or even the jump gate. If not, Tweak might be able to rig something. He made a mental note to ask Vidic about the smaller ice-covered lump next to *Imperio*. If it was another craft, perhaps there was something usable on it.

The VLF transmitter was the second option. Colonel Anders had assigned someone to monitor the signal, so if Tweak could get access to it, she might be able to change the message. The data rate was slow, but a one-sentence message announcing the discovery of *Imperio* would likely be enough to set the wheels of a rescue mission in motion.

The downside to that plan was the risk of discovery by the rest of the captives on the ship. Vidic's report about the Cadre disturbed Fortis. The prospect of imminent rescue should make most of the cadets happy to see the team, but there was no way to predict how they or the collaborators would react, especially when they found out the team couldn't offer anything more than vague promises of rescue.

The slavers were a wild card. Vidic said the Cadre had a way to communicate with them, but how effective was it? Could they communicate at range, or did the slavers have to be in orbit? He made another mental note to ask Vidic how many cadets were in the Cadre and whether she knew anything about their communicator.

Fortis finally had the loose outline of a plan. The team would hide aboard *Imperio* and investigate the shuttle option. If that failed, they would gradually reveal themselves to the cadets based on Vidic's recommendations. Their first priority would be whomever was responsible for the distress signal. After that, they would talk with whatever leadership existed among the loyal cadets. If everything went to plan, the team would have a sizable group of people on their side before they exposed themselves to the Cadre.

Someone pounded on the hatch and broke his train of thought. Bender climbed aboard with Fortis' ECW gear in his arms.

"How's Bugs?" Fortis asked after they secured the hatch.

"He's okay. A little tender right now, but he's a tough kid. You know, Bugs and Cheese were privates together. They served together a long time."

"Sheesh."

Bender shook his head. "Shot in the back by a low-life traitor. That's no way for a Space Marine to die. Stoat is a dead man walking."

"I agree, but, first things first; we have to get out of here."

The two men sat in an impromptu moment of silence. Finally, Bender said, "Did you come up with a plan?"

"Yes, I did. On the count of three, I'm going to wake up in my own bed back on Terra Earth and realize this whole thing was just a very realistic nightmare."

The pair shared a laugh and then Fortis got serious. He outlined his thoughts about the comms situation, *Imperio*, and the Cadre. Bender nodded in agreement.

"I hadn't thought about the cadets. We need to be careful with them. Two years is a long time to be locked up, and there's no way to predict how they'll react."

"The first thing we're going to do is get back to *Imperio* and get some rest," Fortis said as he zipped up his ECW. "How many rations did you take over there?"

"We took four cases and left two here, so we're good for a couple months if everyone doesn't mind skipping a few meals."

"What have the cadets been eating for the past two years?"

Fortis and Bender stared at each other.

"No way."

"Not cannibalization. No chance."

The image of a thousand starving cadets slaughtering their teammates unsettled Fortis, and he was suddenly anxious to get back to *Imperio*.

"I'm all set. Let's go."

They returned to Vidic's hiding place and the team greeted them with smiles. Everyone exchanged handshakes or hugs as they enjoyed their reunion. The dangers of the mission had seemed abstract until the death of Cheese. Now they were refocused on their goal and happy to fortify the bonds they'd forged with their teammates. Even Vidic was pulled into a group hug, and she cracked a long overdue smile.

Everyone settled down, and Fortis briefed them on the plan.

"Before I begin, I need to know if the shuttle is equipped with comms gear that can reach Terra Earth."

"No," Cujo replied. "She's got point-to-point comms capability with a mothership and a short-range system for talking to the surface, but nothing for broadcasting through a jump gate."

Fortis looked at Tweak. "Do you think you can rig something up?"

"Sure, if I had some parts to work with. From what Vidic said, there's nothing here."

He turned to Vidic. "What can you tell me about the other ship next to *Imperio?*"

The young petty officer looked confused. "Other ship? What other ship?"

"There's another ship, smaller than *Imperio*, about fifty meters away. You didn't see it?"

"Nobody's been outside since we got here. The slavers took all our suits and welded the hatches shut. When we tried to tunnel out through an escape trunk in the main propulsion space, a bunch of guys drowned before they could get the hatch closed."

"Drowned? How?"

"They opened the outer hatch at the bottom of the escape trunk and water gushed in. Only one guy got out, and he had to drop the hatch at the top to stop the flooding."

"Where did the water come from?"

"We're floating on it. Under all that ice outside is hot water."

"Menard-Kev is a gnamma," Bender said.

"A what? What the hell's a gnamma?" Cujo asked.

"Ah, it's a word we use back home, mate. A gnamma is a rock hole that collects water. Out here, we use it to describe a water planet."

"Hold on a second," Fortis interjected. "Vidic, how do you know all this?"

"*I* don't. I mean, I know what the cadets say about it. Some of them studied this stuff at the Fleet Academy, you know, planets and whatnot. What *I* know is that when they opened the outer hatch, water poured in. *Imperio* has been slowly sinking ever since."

"Sinking?"

Vidic nodded. "There was a lot of damage belowdecks when we landed. Interior bulkheads cracked and hatches warped. Everything was okay until they opened the outer hatch and couldn't get it closed. That's when the water started coming in."

"How long has *Imperio* been flooding?"

"A little over four months."

"How fast the ship is flooding?"

"My job is to mark the water level in the auxiliary spaces. It's been about one centimeter a week, depending on if the hatch has been opened or not. When it's opened, it floods faster."

"That's why the air rushed out when we opened the hatch," Tweak said. "The force of the water pushed it."

"That's how I knew you had opened the hatch," Vidic said. "I felt the breeze pick up."

"Huh. Well, one centimeter a week doesn't sound too bad for a ship this size," Fortis said. "With any luck, we'll be out of here before it becomes a problem."

"Did you notice the deck is tilted? That's because the water collects on one side of the ship and makes it unstable. *Imperio* isn't equipped with a system to move the water, so they say she'll probably roll over before she sinks."

"They?"

Vidic shrugged. "I don't know…cadets who study that kind of stuff."

"I guess we better put our plan in action before we roll over."

* * * * *

Chapter Twenty-Two

Fortis asked Vidic about the VLF transmitter, but she didn't know anything about the distress call or where the transmitter was located.

"It's probably up near the operations room. I don't go up there, but I can ask around if you want."

"No, don't do that. If you're not supposed to know about it, it will be suspicious if you start asking questions. For now, we'll head over to what we think is another ship and see if we can find anything useful."

The team suited up for the trek to the other ship, then Fortis gave Cujo some bad news.

"You're going to stay here with Bugs," he told the pilot, who started to protest until Fortis cut him off with a wave of his hand. "I don't want to leave anyone here alone. I need Bender and his torch, and Lou and Tweak are our computer and electronics experts."

Bugs slapped Cujo on the shoulder. "You get to hang out with me, old timer."

Cujo rolled his eyes, and Bender laughed.

The wind had picked up, and the team had to lean forward as they trudged toward the other ice-covered lump. There was no defined walkway like there was around *Imperio*, and the team walked all the way around it, looking for an access. It was only by chance that Tweak noticed a depression in the otherwise smooth surface.

"If that's a hatch, it's been a long time since anyone went through it," Lou observed.

Bender used the torch to melt away the ice along one edge of the depression and before the water froze solid again he caught sight of a hinge.

"Definitely a hatch."

He defrosted the hinges before turning his attention to the locking mechanism. Instead of the usual lever release, there was a wheel in the center of the hatch that presumably operated a set of dogs inside. Once the wheel was free of ice, he cut the plate holding the hatch closed and stepped back.

"Here goes nothing," Tweak said, grasping the wheel. She strained with all her strength, but it wouldn't budge.

"Here, let me try." Bender handed the cutting unit to her and grabbed the wheel with his massive hands. He grunted with effort, and the wheel slowly relented.

Suddenly, the hatch flew open, and Bender fell backward. Three individuals in unfamiliar exposure suits emerged from the craft, grabbed Lou, and dragged her inside. It happened so fast that the hatch slammed shut, and the wheel engaged before anyone else could react.

"What the hell was that?"

"Lou? Lou, can you hear me? Are you okay?"

Lou didn't respond. Fortis grabbed the wheel and put everything he had into it, but it wouldn't budge. Bender joined him, but the wheel didn't move.

Bender grabbed the cutting torch. "Fuck it, I'll cut the bastard."

Sparks flew, and steam billowed as flame touched metal. Slag dripped and froze into metallic stalactites as the crack widened.

"Lucky, can you hear me?" Fortis heard Lou's voice on the circuit.

"I can hear you. Are you okay?"

"Yes, I hear you. I'm fine. Everything's fine. Please, stop cutting on the door."

"We're coming in after you, Lou."

"No, don't come in here. We're coming out."

"Look." Tweak pointed. The wheel began to turn slowly.

Bender stepped back, set the cutting unit down, and drew his pistol. Fortis and Tweak had their weapons drawn and at the low ready as the wheel stopped spinning, and the hatch cracked open. Lou stuck her head out.

"Put your guns away. There's no need for them."

Fortis and Bender traded looks.

"Honest. No tricks."

They holstered their weapons, but their hands hovered close. The hatch widened, and Lou stepped out. She gestured behind her, and one of the people in the strange exposure suits stepped out with her.

"Who the hell is this, Lou?" Bender demanded.

"Her name is Maardat. She's a Maltaani."

Fortis drew his pistol and pointed it at Maardat. Lou stepped in front of him and waved her hands. "Put it away, Lucky! She's unarmed. They're all unarmed."

"What is this, Lou?"

"Put your weapons down, and I'll explain. Please!"

"Not until that hatch is closed."

Lou bade the Maltaani to step forward and she pushed the hatch shut. Fortis holstered his pistol again.

"What are Maltaani doing here?"

"I didn't have a lot of time to talk, but it seems the slavers hijacked their ship, just like *Imperio*."

Maardat motioned to the hatch and said something to Lou.

"I think she wants us to go inside. I don't think her suit is meant for this extreme cold."

Fortis looked at Bender, who shrugged.

"We might as well go in, Lucky. Nobody's going to believe us anyway."

Maardat led the operators inside the Maltaani ship, and Fortis saw seven more Maltaani dressed in exposure suits like Maardat.

"How many are there?" he asked Lou.

Lou translated the question and nodded at the answer. "This is all they have left from a crew of thirty."

"How long have they been here?" Tweak asked.

Lou shook her head. "I learned from my interviews with Aardvark that the Maltaani don't measure time like we do. Our system is based on star observations from Terra Earth, but theirs is something much different. I don't think it's been very long though."

A Maltaani stepped forward and doffed his helmet. He had the familiar Maltaani facial features; square and prominent cheekbones and chin, and his eyes were solid black. He said something to Lou and gave a brief bow.

"His name is Jinkaas, and he is the senior crewmember on their ship. He wishes to greet our leader."

Fortis removed his helmet and held out his hand. "My name is Lucky."

Lou translated what Fortis said, and Jinkaas looked at Lou and then back to Fortis. He held out his hand, and the two leaders shook.

"Have they signaled for help?"

"I don't think so," Lou said. After a brief exchange with Jinkass, she turned back to Fortis.

"The slavers killed their officers and stripped the ship. They welded the hatch shut and haven't been back since."

Several of the Maltaani talked together and gestured toward Fortis. He didn't understand what they said, but he thought he heard his name.

"What are they saying, Lou?"

She gave a brief smile. "I think they recognize you."

"Recognize me? How?"

"Aardvark, maybe."

Bender groaned. "Is there anyone in the universe who doesn't know who you are?"

Jinkass approached Fortis and held out his hand again.

"Faartees," he said.

The two shook again, but this time they clasped forearms, and the Maltaani pulled Fortis in and hugged him with his other arm. After a brief hesitation, Fortis returned the embrace. When they parted, Jinkass said something and clapped Fortis on the shoulder.

"He said you're a great warrior," Lou explained.

Fortis grinned and clapped Jinkass on his shoulder.

"I think he's a great warrior, too."

All the residual tension between the groups evaporated, and they mingled, exchanging smiles and greetings. The Maltaani marveled at Bender's enormous size, and two of the females seemed especially impressed.

"Watch out, Bender's going to score," Tweak teased.

Fortis, Lou, Maardat, and Jinkass congregated and engaged in a rudimentary conversation about the situation on Menard-Kev. It surprised the Maltaani to learn there was another ship nearby, but Fortis was unsuccessful when he tried to explain who they were and how long they'd been imprisoned.

The differences in time measurement created difficulties in other ways, too. Fortis learned the remaining Maltaani food stocks were dwindling, but he couldn't understand Maardat and Jinkaas when they tried to explain how much food they had left.

The discussion turned to rescue.

"They don't have any comms equipment," Lou told the team. "The slavers took it all."

"What's next, boss?" Bender asked.

"We can forget about getting radio components here," Tweak said.

"Looks like we have to use the VLF transmitter." Fortis turned to Lou. "Tell Jinkass that I promise we will include them in our plans for escape. We have a plan to signal for rescue, and when they arrive I will demand the Maltaani are rescued as well."

Lou spoke in a slow and deliberate tone. The Maltaani leader seemed to understand what she was telling him. His eyes narrowed, but he nodded.

"I hope I explained it well enough," she told Fortis. "I don't have the vocabulary for this."

Jinkass and Fortis clasped forearms, and the Maltaani nodded.

"Faartees," he said.

"Jinkass," Fortis replied. He looked at Lou. "I think he understands."

The team fastened their ECW gear for the trip back to *Imperio*, waved goodbye to their new friends, and set off to rejoin Cujo and Bugs.

They found their teammates in Vidic's hiding spot, but the petty officer wasn't there.

"Somebody came over the intercom and called everyone to muster in one of the hangars," Cujo explained. "What did you find over there? Is it another ship?"

"It's another ship, all right. A Maltaani ship."

Bugs and Cujo jerked like they'd been shocked. *"What?"*

"It's a Maltaani ship, buried under the ice just like *Imperio*. What's more, there are eight live Maltaani trapped aboard."

"You didn't kill them?" Bugs asked.

"They're unarmed and no threat to us."

"But they're the enemy!" Cujo blurted.

Fortis shook his head. "They're not the enemy on Menard-Kev. The Maltaani are in the same situation we're in. Slavers hijacked their ship, crashed it here, stripped it, and welded them in. The slavers are the enemy here."

Cujo turned to Bender. "You're okay with this?"

"Yeah, and so are you." The massive operator pointed a finger at Bugs. "You, too."

"Everybody, stand down," Fortis interjected. "There's no reason to get worked up about this. The Maltaani are unarmed and no threat to us. We could have killed them all, but it wouldn't change a thing about our situation. Forget about the Maltaani."

The hatch slammed open and Vidic rushed in. The team drew their weapons and prepared to fire.

"Whoa! Whoa! Wait!" Vidic cringed and threw her hands up. "Don't shoot! It's just me."

Fortis let out a deep breath as he lowered his weapon.

"You guys, you gotta hide! The slavers are back!"

* * * * *

Chapter Twenty-Three

Everyone reacted at once.

"Holy shit!"

"The shuttle is out there!"

"They're gonna see the weld!"

"Quiet!" Lou's voice cut through the confused talk and silenced it. "You sound like a bunch of panicked schoolgirls." She looked at Vidic. "How long do we have?"

"I don't know, exactly. The Cadre announced that they arrived in orbit and would be down here soon."

Fortis, embarrassed by his reaction to the news, snapped out orders.

"Vidic, we've got to get the shuttle out of sight and fix the door, or the slavers will know someone's been here. All of you grab your gear and suit up, we've got to beat feet."

"What about me? I don't have a suit," Bugs replied.

"Then I guess you're staying here."

Bugs opened his mouth to protest, but Fortis cut him off.

"There's no time to argue. Hide here and be ready to fight like hell if they find you. We'll be back as soon as we can."

"DINLI," Bender said.

Bugs only managed a nod.

Fortis stood by the door. "Everyone ready?"

The team responded with thumbs up all around, and he led them to the exterior hatch. When they were outside, he split the team.

"Bender, Tweak, weld the hatch shut and haul ass for the shuttle. The rest of us will meet you there. If the slavers show up, we'll move the shuttle and return for you when it's safe. Escape and evade as best you can. Hide out on the Maltaani ship if you have to. Go!"

Fortis, Cujo, and Lou took off running for the shuttle. They barely had time to belt in before the pilot had the engines started and ready for takeoff.

"Where do you want to go, Lucky?" Cujo called from the cockpit.

"Can we stash this thing behind the Maltaani ship?"

"I can park it anywhere you want. Do you think they'll see it?"

"Beats me. If they don't know to look for it, maybe not. We shouldn't go too far in case Bugs needs help."

"Let's try it then."

The comms circuit crackled. "Lucky, it's Bender. We're on our way to the shuttle."

A minute later, Bender and Tweak clambered into the shuttle and flopped into their seats.

"The door is welded. I melted some ice over it, hopefully they won't notice it's been opened."

"We're going to hide this thing behind the Maltaani ship and shut it down. We'll be out of sight from the runway but close enough in case something happens."

The shuttle bumped over the uneven surface as Cujo guided it around the Maltaani ship. He parked as close as possible, and the engines wound down. Silence settled over the shuttle.

"I need to secure power to preserve the batteries," he advised Fortis.

"Roger that." Fortis looked to Bender. "Do you think we should post someone outside to watch for the slavers?"

"Good idea." The hulking operator stood up. "I'll find a good observation post and take the first watch. I'll call for relief in a couple hours. Until then, the rest of you should shut down."

After Bender was gone, Fortis did his best to get comfortable in his seat and grab some shuteye. The last time he could remember sleep was aboard *Dragon's Breath*, and the mission, while not physically taxing, had been an emotional rollercoaster. One final thought stuck in his mind as he drifted off to sleep.

The shuttle.

* * *

Fortis woke to a hand on his shoulder. He was momentarily disoriented when he discovered that he was in his ECW gear.

"Lucky, it's time to wake up," Tweak said. "The slavers are here."

"Wha-what?" Fortis groaned as he sat up.

"Lou is outside in the observation post, and she reported the arrival of a shuttle."

"Slavers?"

"Who else?"

"Ah, shit. Sorry, I'm a little groggy. How many?"

"She reported twelve went aboard *Imperio*."

"Huh. Any sign that they saw us?"

"She didn't report it."

"Okay."

Fortis' mind raced. An idea plucked at the edges of his consciousness, but he couldn't quite grasp it. Suddenly, it came to him.

The shuttle. The slaver's shuttle. That's what he'd been thinking about as he fell asleep.

"Hey, Bender, you up for a fight?"

"I could use some exercise. What do you have in mind?"

"I've been wracking my brain for a way to use our shuttle to get out of here, and the answer just landed. We grab the slaver shuttle, ride up to their ship, and hijack it."

The circuit was silent for a long second.

"It's not your worst idea ever," Bender said. "It depends on how many slavers are still up there and whether we can fool them into allowing us to dock."

"We would have to prevent their shuttle crew from warning the mothership," Tweak said. "Otherwise, we're toast."

"What about the slavers already aboard *Imperio*?" Cujo asked. "How do we stop them from calling the mothership?"

"Speed," Fortis said. "Speed and confusion. If we hit the shuttle fast, we can overwhelm the cockpit and prevent them from warning the mothership or the slavers on *Imperio*. After that, it's four on twelve, and we have the element of surprise."

"Don't you mean five on twelve?"

"We'll need you to stay in their cockpit after we grab the shuttle. Especially if we can keep their pilot alive. It would be good for the mothership to hear a familiar voice."

"Why not hit them while they're on *Imperio*? Bugs would definitely improve our odds."

"Because I forgot to ask Vidic how many cadets are in the Cadre. If the Cadre came in on their side, we might end up in a fight with a hundred guys, or they might disperse and then we'll never find them."

"How do we stop the Cadre from warning the mothership? They have a communicator, remember?"

Fortis thought for a second. "That might not be a bad thing. Let's say they warn the mothership and the mothership leaves. We'll still have both shuttles, and we'll have the comms gear from their shuttle. Tweak and Lou ought to be able to put something together from that, right?"

Lou nodded, and Tweak shrugged.

Bender stood up. "Enough bullshitting. Let's roll."

Even in the perpetual near darkness that hovered over Menard-Kev, Fortis felt dangerously exposed as the team moved across the icy ground toward the slaver shuttle. He expected shouts of discovery and incoming fire with every step, and he was surprised when they reached the ramp without an alarm being raised.

"Bender and Cujo, go forward and secure the cockpit. Me, Tweak, and Lou will secure the cabin and cover your back. If at all possible, we want the pilot alive. Ready?"

Lou grasped the hatch handle, and Bender and Cujo crouched, ready to charge aboard.

"Go!"

Lou opened the hatch, and the team flowed onto the shuttle. Fortis, Tweak, and Lou discovered the shuttle cabin was deserted. They found a false bulkhead that divided the cabin into two spaces. The forward space had rows of seats. The rear space was empty except for some eyebolts welded to the deck.

"Great place to chain down prisoners," Lou said.

Fortis heard Bender grunt and Cujo shout.

"Stand by," he told his team before he went forward to the cockpit. He found Bender and Cujo engaged in a wrestling match with a nude man and a scantily clad woman. Bender had the man pinned to one of the seats with a front headlock while Cujo struggled to control his opponent. Fortis grabbed an ankle and wrist and Cujo was able to subdue her.

"Don't kill him," Fortis reminded Bender. The brawny soldier released his grip on the man, and he flopped to the deck, unconscious.

"Which one of you is the pilot?" Fortis demanded from the woman.

The woman sneered and lashed out at him with a kick aimed at his groin. He deflected the attack with his knee and struck her with openhanded slap that sent her sprawling.

"What the hell, Lucky?" Cujo protested as he bent down to help her up. She connected with an unexpected groin kick at Cujo. The pilot clutched his crotch and groaned as he sank to his knees.

Bender laughed at Cujo as Fortis grabbed the woman by the hair and yanked her into a seat.

"I asked you a question. Which one of you is the pilot?"

The woman glared but said nothing. Fortis raised his hand again.

"Leave her alone," croaked the nude man on the deck. He wriggled into a seated position and rubbed his throat. "We're both pilots."

"How many of you went to *Imperio*?"

Fortis knew the answer was twelve, but he wanted to test the pilot.

"Don't tell them anything!" the woman spat. Fortis slapped her again.

"If you don't answer my questions, I will hurt her. If you lie to me, I will hurt her. Do you understand?"

"Yes, yes. I understand. Just stop hitting her."

"How many of you went to *Imperio*?"

"Twelve."

"What kind of weapons?"

"Pistols and cattle prods."

"How many prisoners are they going to bring out?"

"Eight. Eight slaves."

Fortis raised a fist as if to strike the man. "They're not slaves, they're prisoners. What kind of exposure suits for the prisoners?"

The man shrugged. "Man, I don't know. Regular exposure suits, I guess. They dress them, chain them together, and hustle them out here."

"How many of you are on your mothership?"

The man looked over at the woman, who glared at Fortis with hate in her eyes.

"Don't look at her, look at me. How many of you are on your mothership?"

She lashed out again, this time at the man crouched on the deck next to her. Fortis grabbed her by the face and shoved her toward Bender.

"Subdue this bitch, would you? If she moves, snap her fucking neck."

Bender wrapped an enormous arm around her neck and squeezed, and the woman went limp.

"There's no need for that," the man protested. "Don't hurt her."

"Last chance, lover boy, and then my friend here will give your love story a tragic ending. How many of you are on your mothership?"

"Fourteen. No, fifteen. Yeah, fifteen."

Fortis nodded to Bender, who twitched his arm and made the woman flinch.

"Fifteen. You're sure?"

"Yes, I'm sure. Fifteen. Now please, stop hurting her."

Fortis nodded again, and Bender allowed the woman to slump to the deck.

"Who are you guys?" asked the naked man. "You're not from *Imperio*."

Fortis ignored the question.

"Cujo, go find Lou and Tweak. See if there's anything back there to tie up these two."

The pilot gave Bender and Fortis a suspicious look before he left the cockpit.

Fortis motioned for the man to get up and sit in the flight engineer's seat. He picked up a flight suit discarded in a corner and threw it at him.

"Here; get dressed."

Allowing the man to dress was a calculated move. The flight suit might give the slaver some emotional armor and reduce his feelings of vulnerability, which could make him uncooperative. If that happened, Fortis would have Tweak and Lou strip it from him. Conversely, the pilot might be grateful for the favor and willingly provide the team the information they needed.

The woman groaned and sat up. She saw her partner dressed in the flight suit and scowled.

"I had to tell them," he told her.

Cujo returned to the cockpit with a handful of cargo straps in one hand and shackles in the other.

"We can tie them up with these. I couldn't find keys for the shackles."

Fortis looked at the man. "Where are the keys?"

"Nust has them. On *Imperio*."

"Who's Nust?"

"Enus Nust. He's the overseer. He's in charge of handling the slaves—er...prisoners. We're just shuttle pilots, man."

"Do you have comms with Nust or your mothership?"

The man hesitated. Fortis grabbed a handful of the woman's hair, and she cried out in surprise and pain.

"Yes. Yes, okay, we have comms."

"Both?"

"No. Just the mothership. *Alharib*."

"That's the name? *Alharib*?"

"Yeah."

Fortis motioned to Bender and Cujo. "Take her all the way back, tie her up and gag her."

The woman struggled as Bender hoisted her up and carried her out of the cockpit, but she was no match for the massive Space Marine. Fortis slid into the seat next to the pilot.

"What's your name?"

"Tench. Philip Tench."

"Okay, Philip Tench. Here's what's going to happen: your friends are going to come back with a group of prisoners. We're going to kill them and grab the prisoners, and you're going to take us up to your mothership. When we get there we're going to hijack it and fly it home."

Tench's eyes widened. "You're nuts. There's only five of you. Nust is a stone-cold killer."

Fortis gave him an icy smile. "We're no strangers to killing."

* * * * *

Chapter Twenty-Four

Bender returned to the cockpit and escorted Tench aft to the cabin. Fortis saw the woman hogtied across a row of seats in the back and chuckled. They bound Tench's hands and feet and left Cujo, Tweak, and Lou to watch over the prisoners while they returned to the cockpit to talk.

"There are twelve slavers armed with pistols and cattle prods on *Imperio*. They're here to get eight prisoners, so they should be headed back out soon."

"How do you want to hit them?"

"They have to hustle the prisoners out to the shuttle, so they'll leave at least one guy behind to weld the door. I'd like to hit them on the ice, but eleven targets mixed in with eight friendlies in the near-dark is a lot to ask of four shooters."

"Hit them at the hatch?"

"Yeah, I think so. We'll turn off the interior lights and start blasting when the hatch opens. Kill everyone without chains and then hunt down the welder."

"What about the prisoners?"

"For now, we get them aboard and sit them down. Cujo can keep an eye on them until we get back. After that, we'll get Bugs and go grab the slaver mothership."

"You make it sound so easy. Now I know why you're an officer."

Fortis chuckled and stood up, but Bender stopped him with a hand on his arm.

"You were pretty rough with that woman. I thought I was the heavy."

"You are. I was acting, mostly. We could have beaten Tench to a pulp and gotten a bunch of bullshit answers before he died. A couple slaps to his woman, and he couldn't talk fast enough. I'm supposed to be a mercenary leader."

"Okay. Slavers or no slavers, I'm making sure you remember we're the good guys."

Fortis nodded. "I got no pleasure from smacking her around. You can do it from now on."

"DINLI, right?"

"Yeah, DINLI."

* * *

They went back to the cabin, and Fortis pointed Tench. "Will Nust call you when he comes back from *Imperio?*"

Tench shook his head. "I don't know. This is my first time here. I doubt it. He orders everyone around and doesn't worry about stuff like that."

Fortis glanced at the newly gagged woman.

"She wouldn't know. It's her first time, too."

"Yeah, I noticed," Fortis said dryly. When Tench didn't respond, he stuck a finger in the pilot's face. "If anything goes wrong, the last thing you'll see before you die is her brains all over you. You understand?"

Tench nodded as he turned a sickly shade of gray.

Fortis turned to the team. "Let's get ready. It shouldn't be long now. When the hatch opens hit the ramp and start shooting. They have us three-to-one so we can't give them time to react. After we clear the ramp, Bender and Tweak will go kill the welder while Lou and I herd the prisoners aboard the shuttle."

The shuttle hatch was designed to open inward and then slid sideways on tracks. Fortis crouched in front on one side of the hatch with Lou pressed against his back. Bender and Tweak assumed the same posture on the other side. The minutes dragged by as they waited for the slavers to return.

Finally, the hatch lock disengaged with a clunk, and the hatch popped open.

Fortis emerged, his pistol at the ready. The first three he encountered on the ramp were slavers and he dispatched them with single shots to the head. He advanced down the side of the ramp to avoid the mass of shackled prisoners lined up in the middle. Fortis spotted another slaver, but before he could engage the slaver tumbled backward with two holes in his visor. Lou slammed Fortis on the shoulder, and they pressed forward.

Fortis heard Bender and Tweak attacking the other side, but he was too focused searching for targets on his own side to gauge their progress. Two more slavers emerged from the gloom, and Fortis double-tapped them center mass. Lou stepped around him and took the lead when he dropped to one knee to reload. She blasted another slaver at the bottom of the ramp. The prisoners had ducked when they heard the shooting start but were starting to mill around trying to escape down the ramp. Several of them fouled Fortis' line of fire at a slaver who turned and ran into the darkness.

"I'll get him," Lou called, and she took off after the fleeing slaver. Before Fortis could stop her, she disappeared into the gloom.

"Lou, stop!" he ordered over the circuit. "There's nowhere for him to run."

A salvo of shots from Bender and Tweak sent Fortis sprawling. A slaver who tried to hide among the prisoners fell next to him with a bloody hole where his visor used to be.

"We got seven. Number eight is on the run," he announced.

"Three on this side. That's eleven, plus the welder. We're clear," Bender replied.

Suddenly, they heard Lou scream. Her cry was cut short.

"Lou! Lou, what's your status?"

There was no response.

"Stay here," Fortis ordered as he took off in the direction Lou had disappeared. "I'll get her."

He advanced at a fast walk through the gloom. He caught sight of a shape on the ice. As he got closer, he recognized Lou. The slaver was nowhere in sight.

"Lou?"

The operator was unresponsive, so Fortis heaved her over his shoulder and started back toward the shuttle. That's when he noticed her pistol was gone.

"I've got her," he announced to the team. "She's unconscious and her pistol is gone. We're heading back now."

Fortis returned to the shuttle's ramp. It was clear of prisoners and slaver bodies. He pounded on the hatch, and Tweak opened it, pistol in hand.

"What happened to her?" Bender asked as Fortis lowered Lou to the deck.

"I don't know. She took off after one of the slavers, and, by the time I caught up with her, she was like this."

Lou's helmet and ECW gear appeared undamaged. When Tweak slid her helmet off, they saw a trickle of blood under her nostrils.

"I don't see any bullet holes. It looks like she got clobbered," she said.

"What's that?" Bender was pointing to a burn mark on Lou's leg.

"Tench said the slavers used cattle prods," Fortis said.

"Bastards."

"Hey, I need some help back here," Cujo called out.

* * *

"I got this," Tweak said. "Go help the old timer."

The Fleet Academy cadets who had been herded into the rear compartment must have sensed something was very different about their new captors. They rattled their shackles and pressed toward the pilot. When Fortis and Bender arrived in the space, they had to push the cadets back.

Fortis pulled off his helmet. "You're safe now. Sit back down and relax. You'll all be unlocked as soon as we find the keys."

He grabbed Tench and dragged him out of the space.

"You told me Nust has the keys to the shackles. How do we identify him?"

"He's a big guy with brown hair and a bushy mustache. He wears an earring and has a diamond tooth, too."

Fortis shoved the slaver back onto the deck. Lou had regained consciousness and was talking to Tweak.

"I was following him and somehow he got behind me and zapped me with a cattle prod." She touched the scorch mark on her leg. I went down and he kicked me in the head. Then I woke up here."

"He got your pistol," Fortis said. "Do you remember how many rounds you had left?"

Lou shook her head and winced. "I don't know. I think I shot two of them." She patted her equipment belt. "My spare mags are here."

"Okay, so at worst he has six shots," said Tweak.

"There's six of us," noted Bender.

"He can't stay out there forever, but we still have to deal with the welder," Fortis said. "Bender, come with me and we'll check the bodies on the ramp. Tweak, police up the weapons outside and then stay here and look after Lou and Cujo. We'll tap three times, wait a second, and tap twice. Shoot anyone else who bangs on the hatch."

Fortis and Bender ducked outside and scanned their surroundings. Bender maintained a watchful eye as Fortis went from body to body and removed helmets. It was clear that none of the dead slavers was Nust.

"He's running around out there somewhere," Bender said.

"Tweak, this is Lucky. None of these dead guys is Nust. We're going over to *Imperio* to see if we can find him over there."

When the two men returned to the training ship they saw the weld was cut open.

"He's inside."

* * * * *

Chapter Twenty-Five

Fortis and Bender crouched next to the hatch and prepared to board *Imperio*.

"Hey, Lucky, did you happen to notice whether the slavers had any low light or IR on their helmets?"

Fortis mentally kicked himself for overlooking this key detail. "No, I didn't."

"Neither did I. Don't worry about it." The hulking operator grasped the handle. "Go left and stay low. I'll go right."

"Roger that."

Bender opened the hatch, and Fortis jumped through, immediately sidestepping to the left with his pistol at the ready. The wave of hot, humid air from inside the ship fogged up his visor for a brief second. Fortis heard the hatch close behind him but remained focused on the threat axes.

"Clear." Bender's voice was steady and calm.

"Clear," Fortis replied. "Take point and move out for Vidic's hideout. Let's go find Bugs."

Bender moved with the slow smoothness that was a trademark of skilled operators as he led the way. Fortis felt clumsy by comparison, and he struggled to keep up without making any noise.

"Where the hell have you guys been?" Bugs demanded when they were safely inside Vidic's hiding spot. "Did you have any trouble?"

Fortis recounted their assault on the slaver shuttle and the attack on Lou. "The head guy Nust got away. We're pretty sure he's somewhere here on *Imperio* with the welder."

"Fuck him. Let's leave him here."

"We can't. He's got the keys to the shackles they used on the prisoners."

"All right then, let's go get the bastard." Bugs jumped up. "All this sitting around is making me crazy."

"Hold on a second. Where's Vidic?"

"I don't know. She left after you did, and she hasn't been back."

"I'm sorry to tell you this but we can't have you moving around in the dark," Fortis told Bugs. "We don't know if the slavers have night vision and it's too dark on the ship to move without lights."

"Aw, c'mon, Lucky. You can't leave me here again." He turned to Bender. "Please!"

Bender shrugged. "We could set him up in an ambush position by the hatch as a backstop in case the prick gets past us. If anybody but us opens the hatch he could blast them."

"All right, let's do that. Nust is a big guy with brown hair, a bushy mustache, and an earring. Try not to kill anyone but him."

Fortis and Bender left Bugs concealed near the hatch and headed deeper into the bowels of the massive ship. After thirty minutes they paused in a cargo handling area to reassess their plan.

"I think we're wasting our time, Lucky. There are a million places he could be hiding. It would take days to search this place. Even you're not that lucky."

They heard a loud bang in the darkness ahead. A man cursed, and a second man shushed him.

Bender shook his head. "You gotta be shitting me."

Fortis led the way as they crept down a passageway toward the sound.

"What the fuck are we doing, Nust?" a pained voice demanded. "I damn near broke my neck."

"Keep your voice down! Those mercenaries will hear you if you keep bitching."

The conversation faded to a murmur. Fortis and Bender heard them whispering but couldn't make out what they were saying.

"How do you want to handle this?" Bender whispered even though both operators wore their helmets.

Fortis whispered back, "Slip close enough to figure out which one is Nust and then hit them. I don't care what happens to the welder but we have to get those keys."

"Dead or alive?"

"It doesn't matter to me. There's no telling who might hear us, so we should keep the noise to a minimum."

"Okay. Follow me."

They slipped through the darkness until they saw a dim light approaching. They ducked into a side passage and waited as the light grew brighter. Bender jumped out and clobbered the man with the light while Fortis butt stroked his companion behind his ear. Both slavers went down without a fight.

Bender and Fortis dragged their captives into a nearby space for interrogation. Fortis saw Nust was the slaver he had knocked out. He searched the unconscious man's exposure suit and discovered a set of keys and Lou's pistol.

"You want to leave them here?" Bender asked.

"Yes, but I want to talk to them first. Tench told me there are fifteen more of these pricks on their mothership, but I don't trust him. Let's see what Nust and his pal have to say."

"Sounds good." Bender grabbed Nust by the front of his suit and sat him up. He slapped the insensible slaver across the face with the tips of his fingers. "Wakey, wakey, princess."

Nust grunted, and his body twitched as he woke up. He struggled against Bender's grip until he opened his eyes and saw the massive Space Marine hunched over him.

"Who—"

Bender slapped him with the palm of his meaty hand. "We're asking the questions here."

"What—"

Another slap, harder this time. "Are you deaf?"

Nust opened his mouth to protest but stopped, and Fortis almost laughed at the hurt expression on his face. Nust was no different from any other bully who turned cur when he collided with someone bigger and stronger.

"Better." Bender looked at Fortis. "You want to take over?"

Fortis looked Nust in the eye. "How many of you are there on *Alharib?*"

Nust's eyes widened, but he didn't respond. Fortis nodded, and Bender hit the slaver in the ear with an open hand that knocked him flat. Bender yanked Nust upright.

"How many of you are there on your mothership?"

Nust hesitated and his eyes flicked between Fortis and Bender. Fortis nodded again, but the slaver cringed and began to sputter before Bender could hit him again.

"Hey c'mon, you don't have to do that," Nust whined.

"How many?" Fortis demanded.

"Ah, shit. There's...uh...twenty-four if you count the crew. Yeah, twenty-four."

Fortis and Bender exchanged glances as if to say, *Tench lied.*

Nust sensed their unease. "Look, I don't know who you're working for, but I can pay you double what they're paying you. Maybe more."

Bender raised his hand to silence the slaver.

"Let him talk," Fortis said.

"Yeah, yeah, that's right. We've got connections. *Corporate* connections. They pay top credits. I saw you on the ramp. The way you moved tells me you're more than just run of the mill mercenaries. I know I could get you a fat deal. They'll pay big money for experienced guys like you."

"Who do you work for?" Fortis asked.

"Aw, hey, I can't really say, you know. I'm just a middleman. I get an order for slaves, and I fill it."

"Who orders them? Where do you take them?"

"Everywhere, man. I've delivered to asteroid mines, protein wells, even pleasure ships." Nust gave Fortis an exaggerated wink. "This ship is packed with young girls that have been here a while. They need cleaned up to be saleable, but they bring big prices."

Fortis could barely conceal his anger. "Don't they resist or report you after you sell them?"

Nust scoffed. "That's what the scrambler is for." He motioned toward the ceiling with his thumb. "We have a machine on *Alharib* that fries their brains. A couple zaps and they become docile and forget everything. After that—" he shrugged, "—you can do whatever you want with them. Hit them. Rape them. Kill them, if that's your thing. It's an expensive kink, but I'm nobody's judge."

Bender lunged at the slaver and dragged him to his knees by his head.

"Hey! Whoa!" Nust protested. He struggled but was no match for the strength-enhanced Space Marine.

Bender squeezed the slaver's head under his arm with all his strength and gave one hard jerk as he twisted away. There was a mushy *pop* and the slaver went limp. Fortis stared at Bender in shock.

"We're the good guys, remember?"

"That piece of shit deserved a lot worse," Bender said by way of explanation as he let the dead man fall to the deck.

"It would have been good to find out what he meant by 'corporate connections,'" Fortis said coldly. "What the fuck?"

Bender squeezed his eyes shut for a moment. "My best mate's daughter is a cadet at Fleet Academy. My goddaughter, Phaedra."

Fortis' anger turned to incredulity as Bender's words sank in. "She's *here*?"

Bender managed a nod.

"You've known this whole time? Why didn't you say something? We have to find her!"

Bender shook his massive head. "No, sir, we do not. We need to stick to the plan and get all these kids out of here as soon as possible. If we start playing favorites it will create havoc among the cadets. What if she's not here?"

"I'm sorry to say it but you're right." Fortis put a hand on the bigger man's shoulder. "If there was some other way…"

"DINLI."

Fortis sighed. "DINLI."

The other slaver had regained consciousness and witnessed the attack on Nust. He made a noise in his throat, and they turned their attention on him.

"What do you want to do with this one?" Bender asked.

"I'm just a grease monkey," the man protested. "I work on the engines. That's it. I only came down here because nobody else knows how to use the portable welder. Look!"

He held out his trembling hands, and Fortis saw thick grease under his fingernails.

"What's your name?"

"F-F-Faraday. I'm a machinist." He looked at Nust and gulped. "I never liked that prick anyway."

"How do you want it? Pistol? Knife?"

"There's no need for that. I'll tell you whatever you want to know. Just let me go."

"Go where? You're on a crashed spaceship with a couple thousand Fleet Academy cadets who would tear you to pieces if they found you."

"Okay then, take me with you, and I'll tell you anything you want to know."

Fortis thought for a second and then nodded. "Take the exposure suit off Nust while I talk with my partner."

Fortis and Bender retreated to the other side of the space while Faraday wrestled with the dead slaver."

"You really want to take him with us?" Bender asked.

"He seems like he's on the up and up. He might come in handy now that we know Tench can't be trusted. It would be good to know the layout of the mothership since six of us have to fight through twenty-four of them to capture it."

"That's a good point. I've been thinking about how to hijack their ship, and I had an idea. It's going to sound crazy, but this whole trip has been a circus, so why stop now?"

*****

Chapter Twenty-Six

"You're out of your fucking minds," Bugs exclaimed after Bender explained his idea.

"Bugs, our attack on the shuttle ramp worked because we had the element of surprise. Six of us against twenty-four slavers spread out around their mothership is a disaster in the making. We can't seize and hold the bridge and the engine room with only six people. Our chances go way up if we get the eight Maltaani to join us. In exchange, we give them a ride home."

"What about the cadets we rescued? Why not use them?"

"Those cadets have been locked up in the dark for two years. Half of them barely made it up the ramp into the shuttle. I'd rather gamble on a bunch of Maltaani than some sick kids who will fall out before the action starts."

"I'm all for thinking out of the box, but that's just nuts. You know we're are war with them, right?"

Fortis snorted. "Better than most."

Bender shut down the debate. "We're going over to the shuttle with Faraday, and we're going to present the idea to the team. Unless someone has a better objection than 'the Maltaani are the enemy,' we're going to give it a try. Besides, the Maltaani might tell us to go to hell, in which case we go with Plan B."

"What's Plan B?"

Bender shrugged and tipped his chin at Fortis. "I have no idea, mate. Ask the idea guy."

* * *

Fortis keyed his mic as the group approached the shuttle ramp. "Tweak, it's Lucky. Open up. We're at the hatch with Bugs and a prisoner."

"Roger that. What's the password?"

"What?"

"The password. How are we supposed to know it's you?"

"Geez. Okay. Tap tap tap. Tap tap. Satisfied?"

The hatch swung open and the knot of men scrambled inside.

Tweak looked Faraday up and down. "Who's this guy?"

"Faraday. He's an engineer on the slaver mothership," Fortis said as he pulled off his helmet. "He's going to draw a diagram of the ship for us."

"Anything you want." Faraday gasped when Bender yanked off his helmet. "Anything at all."

Lou sat up from where she was reclining in one of the shuttle seats. "Where's Nust?"

Fortis shook his head. "He didn't make it."

She stared at Fortis for a long second before she shook her head. "Pity. I would have liked a little payback."

"Where's Vidic?" Tweak asked.

"She disappeared from her hiding place after you guys left and never came back. I don't know where she went," Bugs said.

"What's been happening here?" Fortis asked Tweak.

"Cujo has Tench and his girlfriend under guard in the back. The cadets settled down after we gave them some food and water. Lou is concussed but her leg is fine. Just another day at the office."

Fortis produced the shackle keys and handed them to Bender. "Put Faraday in the back row and unlock the cadets. They can watch the prisoners while we discuss our next move."

Bender put Faraday's helmet back on so the engineer couldn't listen in on their plans. The team gathered forward by the cockpit door, and Fortis looked from face to face.

"Our plan to hijack the mothership has hit a pretty big snag. The shuttle pilot Tench told me there are fifteen additional slavers up there. Six of us versus fifteen of them were terrible odds, but doable. Nust told us there are twenty-four. Too many for six of us to take on."

Cujo scoffed. "What if they're both lying and there are forty of them?"

"Then we go down fighting and take as many of those sonsofbitches with us as we can. What we can't do is sit down here forever." Fortis gestured to the massive operator. "Bender came up with an idea that I think has a lot of merit."

Bender stepped forward. "When we visited the Maltaani ship, they had a lot more fight in them than the cadets. I propose we enlist them in the attack on the slaver in exchange for a ride home."

Tweak gasped, and Cujo laughed aloud. "You're out of your fucking minds," the gray-haired pilot said. Bugs elbowed Bender as if to say, "See, I told you so."

"No, we're not," Fortis replied. "It makes perfect sense. Six of us aren't enough to capture *Alharib* by ourselves. Fourteen versus twenty-four sounds a lot better to me."

Cujo looked around at the rest of the team. "Are you guys listening to this? This is madness."

"It's not madness. It's our best chance to get out of here. The odds of another ship coming out this way are almost nil. Colonel Anders will be hard pressed to get authorization to launch an effort to rescue the rescue team. Combover and the rest of the bean counters would probably just write us off. Does anyone want to end up like the cadets?"

The team shook their heads.

"Lou and I will head over to the Maltaani ship to make the offer. Whether they agree or not, we'll take off for *Alharib* as soon as we return and conduct the assault." He pointed at Cujo. "That includes you."

Bender motioned aft where the cadets watched over the prisoners. "Lucky, what do you want to do with Tench? 'If you lie to me, I'll hurt her.' Remember that?"

Fortis nodded. "Yeah. C'mon."

The pair of operators went back to where the prisoners waited. Fortis yanked the woman up to her knees and pulled the gag out of her mouth.

"You fucking pig!" she croaked.

Fortis drew back and delivered a stinging open-handed slap to the side of her head that sent her sprawling.

"Hey what the fuck was that for, asshole?" demanded Tench.

Fortis shoved his fist under Tench's nose. "You lied to me, so I hurt her. I'll ask you one more time. How many slavers are on *Alharib*?"

Tench looked at Faraday, who shrugged. He hung his head and answered in a defeated voice. "Twenty-four."

Fortis leaned over the groaning woman and cocked his fist. "Are you sure?"

"Yeah. Twenty-four."

Fortis turned and abruptly left the space with Bender close behind.

"Damn it, mate, you're a scary bloke when you want to be."

"DINLI."

"Indeed."

* * *

"Here goes nothing."

Fortis pounded on the hatch of the Maltaani ship. He and Lou waited nervously but there was no response. He pounded again. The wheel spun, and the hatch opened a crack.

"Faartees," Fortis called. "Friend."

The hatch opened wide, and the Maltaani beckoned for Fortis and Lou to enter. After the hatch closed the operators removed their helmets.

"Faartees," said Jinkaas as he stepped forward. They clasped forearms like they had before.

"Jinkaas," replied Fortis. The Maltaani leader seemed pleased that the human remembered his name.

The Maltaani stared at Fortis expectantly.

"Here we go, Lou." He cleared his throat and smiled. "Jinkaas, our groups are in the same situation." He paused so Lou could translate and waited for Jinkass to nod his comprehension. "We have no ship and no way to call for help. There is no hope of escape without a ship.

"There is a ship in orbit above this planet. It belongs to the vile slavers who have imprisoned us here. We have captured their shuttle, but we are too few in number to capture their ship."

Jinkass turned and talked to Marrdat and the other Maltaani gathered behind them.

"What are they saying, Lou?"

"He's talking so fast that I'm only getting bits and pieces. I think he's explaining my translation."

Jinkass turned back to Fortis and waited.

"I propose to join forces with you to seize the slave ship. After we capture it, I promise we will safely deliver you and your comrades into the arms of your people before we depart for home."

Jinkaas' eyes widened as Lou spoke. When she was finished, he turned back to his companions and conversed in rapid-fire Maltaani.

"Are you getting any of this?" Fortis asked from the side of his mouth.

Lou shook her head. "No. I heard your name a couple times but the rest of it is too fast."

The Maltaani discussion grew louder. An argument sprang up between Jinkaas and a dark-haired female Maltaani. She periodically glared at Fortis, and he knew she was arguing against his proposal.

"Apparently she served on Balfan-48," Lou said. "She told him you weren't trustworthy."

"This was a mistake. We need to get the hell out of here."

The argument ended abruptly and Jinkaas turned to face Fortis. He spoke in a slow and measured tone that allowed Lou to translate as he went.

"Jinkass says it would be a great honor to join forces with a warrior such as yourself," she said. "He regrets that he has to turn down your request."

"Why? Are they going to sit here and hope someone comes looking for them? It hasn't worked for the cadets on *Imperio*."

Jinkaas didn't wait for Lou to translate Fortis' response before he began to speak. Lou nodded and turned back to Fortis.

"He is embarrassed to report that they cannot join our effort because they don't have suitable weapons."

Fortis locked eyes with Jinkass for a long moment before he unholstered his pistol and held it out, butt-first. A murmur ran through the Maltaani as Jinkaas accepted the proffered weapon.

"Tell Jinkaas that we have plenty of weapons."

"Do you think that was a good idea?" Lou asked as the Maltaani gathered around Jinkaas and admired his new pistol.

"Calculated risk, Lou. Look at it from their perspective. We're human and so are the slavers. There have been hostilities between our races, and we're supposed to be at war. Then we show up and ask them to join us in an attack on our own. That female was right when she said I wasn't trustworthy. Maybe that will change her mind."

Jinkaas turned back to Fortis with a broad smile on his face. "Faartees," he said as he nodded.

"Jinkaas friend," Fortis replied.

Lou spent several minutes explaining their intentions to the Maaltani. They would accompany the operators back to the slaver shuttle and prepare for takeoff. They would brief the actual assault on *Alharib* on the ride up using Faraday's input to guide them. She made sure Jinkaas understood that everyone would be armed with either a captured slaver pistol or cattle prod, and they would have to pick up weapons as they progressed through the slave ship.

Lou turned to Fortis when she was satisfied that Jinkaas understood everything she'd told him.

"It's your show, boss."

He walked to the hatch and motioned for the Maltaani to follow him.

"Let's get the hell out of here."

* * * * *

Chapter Twenty-Seven

"Bender, this is Lucky. We're headed your way with eight Maltaani. Make sure everyone stays cool when we come aboard. The Maltaani are not the enemy right now."

"Got it. Tweak is standing by the hatch."

Fortis looked back when he got to the hatch. The Maltaani had stopped to look at the bodies of the slavers scattered around the ramp.

"If that doesn't convince them that we're on the same side, nothing will," Lou said.

The Maltaani followed Fortis up the ramp, and he pounded on the hatch. Tweak secured the hatch once they were all aboard and joined the rest of the team, who watched their visitors with interest.

Fortis pulled off his helmet and the Maltaani followed suit.

"This is Jinkaas. He's their leader. This female is Maardat. Maybe Lou can help out with the rest of their names." He nodded to Jinkaas and pointed to each member of the team. "This is Bender, Cujo, Tweak, and Bugs. You've met Lou, and I am Faartees."

Jinkaas smiled and patted Fortis on the shoulder. "Faartees friend."

"Why does that Maltaani have a human pistol?" Bugs asked.

"Because I gave it to him as a gesture of good will. The slavers stole their weapons when they captured the Maltaani ship."

"So, you gave him yours?"

"Yeah, Bugs, I did. They first refused to join us because they don't have any weapons. I told them we had plenty of weapons and gave him my pistol. It was either that or we assault *Alharib* by ourselves."

Bugs scowled but didn't respond.

"I had Faraday draw a diagram of *Alharib* while you were gone," Bender said. "It's pretty basic but it gets the point across. The captain's name is Mansoor. Black hair, black beard, dragon tattoos on his neck."

"Make sure everyone knows who we're looking for."

"I also sent Bugs and Tweak over to bring Cheese over here. We can't leave without him."

"Good idea. Let's get the Maltaani into their seats and we can take a look at this diagram." Fortis looked at Jinkaas and motioned to the row of seats. "Please. Friend."

Jinkaas and the other Maltaani sat.

Fortis pointed to the pilot. "Cujo, you said you could fly anything. Time to prove it."

"You got it, boss. Maybe I should take Tench with me in case *Alharib* hails us."

"Do it. Tweak, give him a hand."

Tench couldn't conceal his amazement when Cujo and Tweak led him through the cabin.

"Those are Maltaani!"

Tweak shoved him forward. "Keep moving, or I'll let them deal with you."

Fortis positioned himself in the front of the cabin where everyone could see him. Bender stood next to him, and Lou sat in the row with the Maltaani to translate.

"This is our plan to capture *Alharib*. It's barebones and subject to change at a moment's notice. Sound off if you see any problems or have any questions. Bender?"

Lou finished translating, and Bender pointed to a drawing on the forward bulkhead.

"This is the basic layout of the target ship. The shuttle will dock here. As soon as the docking doors are closed and the hangar is pressurized, we will launch our assault.

"The engine room is just aft of the shuttle bay. Me, Lou, and six Maltaani will move through the main passageway and take control there. We'll take Faraday with us just in case. I don't expect a lot of armed resistance so we should get there quickly. We'll have two pistols and six cattle prods.

"Lucky, er, Faartees, will head forward to the bridge with Bugs, Tweak, Cujo, and two Maltaani. You have to go up two decks and a hundred meters forward so the slavers will have more time to put up a fight. Everyone on that team will be armed with pistols. Once we have control of both spaces the remaining crew will be given a chance to surrender or be airlocked."

"The Fleet Academy cadets will remain aboard the shuttle and guard Tench and the other pilot."

Fortis watched Jinkaas out of the corner of his eye while Bender briefed the assault plan. The Maltaani leader nodded at the mention of his forces and grunted in apparent satisfaction when Lou explained that they would be involved in the capture of both the engine room and the bridge.

Bender looked at Fortis. "That's all I have. Do you have anything to add?"

Fortis smiled and gestured toward Jinkaas. "I'm pleased to have Jinkaas and his Maltaani warriors with us to capture the slave ship," he started. "All of us have suffered at the hands of the slavers, and it's time everyone was returned to their rightful homes." He became serious. "Our priority is to capture the engine room and the bridge. Any resistance must be crushed with overwhelming force. Remember who these animals are and what they've done."

"Take no prisoners," Bender snarled.

Fortis looked at Lou. "Would Jinkaas like to say a few words?"

The Maltaani leader beamed as he stood up.

"This is a good plan," Lou translated. "We are pleased to join our new friends in battle, and we look forward to victory."

Jinkaas extended his arm and clasped Fortis' forearm. The two leaders stared into each other's eyes for a long second, and Fortis got the same weird sensation he had when he traded looks with Fuck You Too on Balfan-48.

The shuttle engines wound up, and Cujo's voice came over the intercom.

"Buckle up folks. Lucky, please come to the cockpit."

Fortis went forward to the cockpit. "What's up?"

"Tench said he needs to contact *Alharib* and let her know we're taking off."

Fortis looked at Tench and the slaver shuttle pilot shrugged.

"They're going to be suspicious if we just show up."

"Okay. Give him the mic." He grabbed a handful of Tench's flight suit. "No tricks. One wrong word or one false move, and I'll let the Maltaani and the Fleet Academy cadets have you. Understand?"

The blood drained from Tench's face, and he nodded.

"*Alharib*, this is the shuttle. We're taking off at this time."

There was no response.

"*Alharib*, this is the shuttle. Do you read me?'

"Yeah, shuttle, we read you. What took so long?"

Tench looked at Fortis.

"Make something up."

"We, uh, had some difficulty picking the best slaves," Tench reported. "We've got it all sorted out now, and we're on our way."

"Okay. We'll have the barn doors open for you."

"Roger that." Tench took off the headset and let out a deep breath. "They don't suspect a thing."

Fortis looked at Tweak in the flight engineer's seat. "Make sure it stays that way."

He returned to the cabin and slid into a seat next to Bender.

"Everything okay?"

"We're good. Tench wanted to call *Alharib* and let them know we were coming. Not us, I mean the shuttle." He craned his neck to look back toward the compartment where the cadets were sitting. "Have you talked to the cadets and let them know what's going on?"

Bender nodded. "I told them that we needed them to watch over the prisoners while we captured the slave ship. They're good to go."

"Do they know who we are?"

"No. At least I don't think so. I told them we were mercenaries hired to destroy the slavers. I don't know if they bought it or not."

"Any word on Phaedra?"

"I can't bring myself to ask. It's better that I focus on the task at hand. There will be time for questions later."

Fortis felt cold anger rising in his chest when he saw Bender's distress. "Let's kill these pricks, and we'll get them all home."

The pitch of the shuttle engines became a shriek, and they were pressed back into their seats as the spacecraft accelerated down the runway.

"Airborne," Cujo reported over the intercom.

The shuttle climbed at a steep angle and began to rumble and shake. Fortis looked at the Maltaani. Jinkaas was wide-eyed. He smiled and winked in a universal gesture of reassurance. The Maltaani returned the smile.

"We're clear of the atmosphere," Cujo announced. "We should dock with *Alharib* in eighteen minutes."

Fortis unbuckled his harness and stood. "Let's get the teams organized and issue weapons," he told Bender. "Make sure the Maltaani in your team know who the friendly humans are."

Fortis was surprised when Jinkaas and Maardat joined his team. For some reason he figured the Maltaani leader would go with Lou and the engine room team. He stripped off his ECW gear and piled it on his seat. He wouldn't need it on *Alharib,* and he was more comfortable moving around without it. Jinkaas watched him for a second and then removed his own exposure suit. The rest of the Maltaani followed suit, and Fortis saw they all wore a similar uniform.

"What's their uniform from?" he asked Lou. She translated his question and Jinkaas' response.

"They're members of the Maltaani space survey corps," she said. "At least I think that's what he said. Their ship had just returned from a mission through the Maduro Jump Gate when the slavers captured them."

"We're on final approach," Cujo reported. "The hangar doors are open, and their retrieval boom is extended."

The shuttle pilot had a bullseye to aim at as he approached the mothership. The boom would mate with a fitting on the top of the shuttle and lift the smaller craft into the hangar. The retrieval system eliminated the need for the pilot to guide the shuttle into the hangar and was low-tech enough that it could be operated by hydraulics alone in case of power failure.

Fortis heard a loud *thunk,* and the shuttle jerked as the boom locked in.

"Mating complete. Commencing shutdown."

The engine noise dwindled away, and a tense silence settled over the shuttle. The seconds crawled by as they waited to hear that the hangar doors were secured.

"Doors are closed, pressurization is in progress."

Fortis breathed a sigh of relief and caught Jinkaas smiling at him. The Maltaani winked, and Fortis almost laughed aloud. Tweak reappeared with Tench in front of her.

"Tie him up back there," Bender ordered.

"I should go with you," Tench said. "You might need me on the bridge."

Fortis shook his head. "No chance. I'll send for you if I need you. In the meantime, you can stay back there with the Fleet Academy cadets you kidnapped."

"I'm just a pilot!" Tench protested as Tweak shoved him down the aisle. "Just a pilot!"

The assault teams lined up in stacks by the shuttle hatch. Fortis and the bridge team had the farthest to go so they would exit first, with Bender and the engine room team right behind them. Fortis flashed a thumb's up to the members of his team. After a brief pause Jinkaas and Maardat returned the gesture.

"Hangar pressurization complete." Cujo's voice boomed through the overhead speakers.

Fortis unlatched the interlock and slid the hatch open.

"Go! Go! Go!"

* * * * *

Chapter Twenty-Eight

Fortis charged through the hatch and jumped down to the hangar deck. An *Alharib* crewman standing next to shuttle stared in astonishment as the rest of the team poured out behind him. Jinkass was right behind Fortis and delivered a vicious blow that knocked the man out cold.

The team raced up a ladder, out of the hangar and past the retrieval boom control station. Fortis saw a man inside the station fumble with a communicator handset, and he aimed and fired. The shot punched a hole through the glass and tore the top of the slaver's head off in a spray of blood and brains.

Fortis threw open the hatch and entered the main passageway running down the center of *Alharib*. He almost collided with two crewmembers jogging toward the hangar.

"Did you hear shoot—"

Fortis shot them both without breaking stride and ran for the hatch Faraday said went up one deck to the bridge. He reached the hatch and turned to look for the rest of his team as a slaver burst into the passageway, a pulse rifle at the ready. Jinkass and Maardat fired simultaneously, and the man somersaulted backward from the impact of the slugs.

"Grab that rifle," Fortis ordered Bugs as he opened the hatch. A burst of energy bolts from above sprayed the hatch and narrowly missed him as he slammed the hatch closed.

"We've got to go the other way." He pointed to a cross passageway. "Bugs, take point and move fast. Everyone else stay alert. They know we're here."

Bugs sped through the passage with Tweak and Cujo close behind. Maardat and Jinkaas trailed them by several paces, and Fortis brought up the rear. When Bugs reached the end of the passageway, he signaled for the team to halt. He peeked around the corner and held up two fingers. Tweak patted him on the shoulder and they stepped around the corner and opened fire. Tweak looked back and waved her hand.

"Let's go!"

The coppery smell of blood mixed with ozone tickled Fortis' nostrils as he stepped over the dead slavers. One of them had taken a pulse rifle blast to the face and the back of his head was a gaping crater. The other had taken a ballistic round to the throat that nearly tore his head off.

Bugs paused at a door marked "Bridge" and waved Fortis forward. Jinkaas and Maardat crowded forward and motioned for the others to follow them. Bugs and Fortis exchanged glances and stepped aside.

Maardat tried the doorknob and shook her head.

Locked.

Bug placed the barrel of the pulse rifle inches from the knob. Everyone stepped back, and he blasted the door open. Jinkaas and Mardaat led the team through the shattered door into the bridge.

A wild melee ensued. Several slavers had taken cover behind the various consoles and equipment throughout the bridge and opened fire as soon as the team appeared in the door. Jinkaas bellowed in pain and went down immediately. Maardat grabbed an arm and tried to pull him to safety. An energy bolt struck her between the shoulders, and she went down on top of him.

Cujo and Tweak moved left while Fortis and Bugs moved right. A head popped up from behind an upended desk and Bugs vaporized it. Blue-white ricochets of energy showered the operators as the slavers fired wildly in both directions. Fortis fired at a shadowy figure moving across the front of the space, and he heard a scream when his target went down.

"We gotta secure the other door," he shouted to Bugs.

"I got it. Cover me!"

Bugs jumped up and crossed the room in several big strides. Fortis unloaded his pistol at the consoles where he'd seen movement, and Bugs added a salvo from the pulse rifle. Sparks flew and acrid smoke from damaged electronics filled the air.

On the other side of the bridge, Tweak and Cujo killed two slavers before a third pinned them down with sustained pulse rifle fire. Bugs took aim at the spot where the shooter disappeared and fired when he reappeared. The slaver went down with a massive hole in his chest.

"Cease fire!" Fortis shouted.

"Clear!" Bugs answered after he advanced through the wreckage and inspected the fallen slavers.

"Clear here," Cujo called.

"All clear," Fortis announced. "Cujo, secure the main door and watch for counterattacks. Tweak, take the back." He saw Jinkaas kneeling next to Maardat, who was lying facedown on the floor. "Bugs, see what you can do for them."

Fortis keyed his communicator. "Bender, this is Lucky. The bridge is secure."

"Roger that. We're in the engine room. There are a couple of the crew playing hide and seek around the machinery, but the Maltaani are chasing them down."

"Any casualties?"

"Bumps and bruises. Lou got scratched by a ricochet but she's okay. You?"

"Jinkaas and Maardat are wounded. Slaver body count is nine."

"We've got four prisoners plus two or three still hiding. Say fifteen total between us?"

Fortis nodded. "Affirmative. Have you seen the captain, Mansoor?"

"Negative. I haven't seen anyone by that description."

"Okay. I'll get on the address system and tell the rest of the slavers to surrender. If they don't, we'll have to hunt them down."

"Tell them to report to the passageway between the engine room and the hangar. I've got the extra bodies for crowd control. Warn them we will shoot at the first sign of a weapon."

"Will do. Lucky out."

Fortis searched until he found an internal communications panel on the ship control console. He pressed the button for "General Announcing" and keyed the mic.

"Attention *Alharib*. My name is Lucky, and I'm the leader of the assault team that just seized control of the ship. We have killed or captured most of the crew. If you surrender you will be fairly treated. Continue to resist, and we will hunt you down.

"You have ten minutes to muster in the main passageway outside the engine room. If we see any signs of a weapon we will shoot to kill. This is a one-time offer. In eleven minutes, we will hunt you down and kill you. That is all."

Fortis set the mic down and went to the door where Cujo stood lookout.

"See anything?"

Cujo shook his head. "Nothing. I heard a hatch slam down that way, but nobody came through. How much longer—"

A klaxon blared from the ship control console.

"What the hell is that?"

"Stay here!" Cujo leaped to his feet and ran to the console. He scanned the blinking lights and stabbed a button, silencing the alarm.

"Someone has overridden the interlocks on the hangar doors. They're trying to launch the shuttle!"

"Shit!" Fortis cast around and found a pulse rifle on the deck. "Let's go, Bugs. The rest of you stay here and hold this space."

Jinkaas tried to stand but Bugs pushed him down before he grabbed his own rifle and joined Fortis at the door. A quick glance revealed the passageway was empty and they ran toward the hangar.

"Bender, someone's trying to launch the shuttle," Fortis called over his communicator.

"Yeah, they have us pinned down in here," came the reply. "Two Maltaani are down, and Lou caught another fragment in the arm."

"Sit tight and stay low. Bugs and I are on the way."

They hurdled the bodies from their previous passage and paused at the cross passageway.

"You want to go that way or back the way we came?" Bugs asked.

"Go that way," Fortis replied. "I don't want to end up pinned down next to Bender."

Bugs led the way, and they soon arrived at the ladder to the hangar passageway.

"Hold up," Fortis ordered. He keyed his communicator. "Cujo, this is Lucky. What's going on in the hangar?"

"Someone has taken local launch control in the hangar, but they aren't making much progress. The outer hatches are still closed, and the space is pressurized. They activated the safety interlocks to secure the inner hatches but one of them is stuck so they can't launch. The boom status panel up here is all shot up, so I don't know if they've engaged with the shuttle or not."

"Is there any way we can get through a hatch secured by the interlocks?"

"Maybe. The interlocks were designed for safety not security. There should be an emergency access panel next to the hatch. Look for it and follow the directions."

"Okay, thanks."

Fortis patted Bugs on the shoulder. "Let's go."

Bugs descended the ladder two steps at a time and crouched at the bottom until Fortis joined him. He cracked open the hatch and peeked out. After a long second, he held up four fingers and signaled Fortis to lean in close.

"Four guys with two pulse rifles covering the engine room door," he whispered. "I'll start left, you start right."

Bugs opened the hatch wide and stepped out. Fortis was right behind him. One of the slavers turned and saw them just as they opened fire. Fortis concentrated his shots on the two slavers to the right and they went down in an eruption of energy sparks. One of Bug's targets got off a shot and Fortis heard the energy bolt crackle as it whizzed past his head.

"Bender, it's Lucky. Your door is clear."

The engine room door cracked open, and Bender looked out. Bugs waved, and the door opened wide.

"Any trouble?" Fortis asked.

"Nah, mate. The Maltaani caught up with the last of those bastards down in the bilges and settled them right down." He chuckled. "They're pretty enthusiastic with those cattle prods."

Fortis flashed back to the Maltaani butchery of captured Space Marines during the Battle of Balfan-48. He blinked away the memory and grimaced. "They can get pretty enthusiastic. How's Lou?'

"I'm right here, Lucky." Lou stepped into the passageway and Fortis saw a bloodstained bandage wrapped around her midriff.

"That's a hell of a scratch."

She shook her head. "A piece of shrapnel bounced along my ribcage. Hurts like hell but it's all for show."

Fortis pointed down the passageway to the hangar hatch. "Let's find out what the hell's going on in there."

He found the emergency access panel exactly as Cujo described. He found a black and gold striped lever with the warning "For Emergency Access Only" in big red letters above it.

"You ready?" Fortis asked Bender and Bugs.

Both operators nodded, and Fortis turned the lever.

* * * * *

Chapter Twenty-Nine

An alarm screamed from somewhere in the maze of pipes running across the top of the hangar and an amber light flashed over the door. The three men moved into the space quickly with Bender in the lead. He blasted two slavers standing in the retrieval boom control station while Bugs sent a stream of energy bolts at two more on the far side of the hangar. His shots were wild, and the pair returned fire before they ducked behind the shuttle.

"Oh."

Bugs dropped his rifle and fell backward. Blood spurted from a gaping hole in his abdomen, and he clutched at his stomach.

"Bugs is hit! Cover me!" Bender grabbed the fallen man under the arms and dragged him behind a stack of toolboxes.

Fortis poured suppressive fire where he'd seen the slavers take cover and then ducked behind a set of heavy lockers. "How is he?"

Bender held up a blood-soaked hand. "Not good."

"Shit." Fortis chanced a look over the locker but there was no one in sight. He looked up at the shuttle and saw the hatch was ajar. "They're in the shuttle."

Mansoor stepped onto the platform outside the shuttle. He held a Fleet Academy cadet in front of him, an arm around her neck and a pistol pointed at her head.

"That's him," Bender said in a low voice. "That's Mansoor."

"Hey!" the slave ship captain shouted from behind his human shield. "Back off or I'll kill her."

"Do you have a shot?" Fortis whispered to Bender.

"Negative. You?"

"Yeah, kind of. It's pretty close though."

"Did you hear me?" Mansoor shouted.

"I heard you," Fortis replied.

"Back off, or I'll kill her," Mansoor repeated.

"I heard you the first time."

There was a long pause. "What didn't you understand? Get the fuck out of here, or I'll waste this bitch."

"I don't care about a slave. You're going to die today," Fortis yelled.

Mansoor shook the cadet, and she cried out. "Leave now, or I'll kill her."

Fortis saw another cadet emerge from the shuttle behind Mansoor, cattle prod in hand. He stood up to stall for time.

"Let her go, and I'll let you live."

Mansoor laughed. "No way—arggh!"

The slaver convulsed when the cattle prod touched his neck. His hand spasmed and he fired two shots, but his captive had already twisted out of his grip. The shots ricocheted harmlessly across the hangar, and the slave ship captain fell to his hands and knees.

The two slavers Fortis and Bender had chased behind the shuttle emerged from hiding and fired at Fortis. One of the shooters had squeezed around the shuttle to catch the two operators in a crossfire, but the ambush was hastily conceived and poorly executed.

The Space Marines reacted immediately.

Bender and Fortis fired at the slaver closest to the shuttle. One energy bolt struck him in the shoulder and spun him around. A second bolt hit him in the neck and took off his head. Before the headless body hit the deck, the operators redirected their fire at their second slaver. Near-misses cracked overhead as Bender blasted him. He hit the man with three center-mass shots, and the man disintegrated in a flash of blue-white energy and gray-red viscera.

Mansoor struggled to get to his feet. The Fleet Academy cadet gave him another shot with the cattle prod. His body jerked as she screamed and jabbed him repeatedly.

"Wait! Don't kill him!" Fortis shouted as he raced for the ladder.

The cadet looked at him and gave the slaver a final jolt.

Fortis kicked Mansoor's pistol off the platform. The slaver groaned and rolled over, his hands held in front of his face. The two cadets huddled together by the hatch, and Fortis gave them his biggest smile.

"Good work," he told them. They smiled back and retreated into the shuttle.

Bender joined Fortis as he stood over Mansoor.

"Get up you piece of shit." The hulking operator grabbed Mansoor by the front of his coveralls and yanked him to his feet. "We've got some questions for you." He shoved the slaver inside the shuttle.

Fortis keyed his communicator. "All stations, this is Lucky. We've got Mansoor, and the hangar is secure. Cujo, get on the intercom and repeat my instructions about surrendering. The hunt begins in one minute. Lou, keep an eye on the passageway in case anyone takes us up on the offer."

Cujo and Lou acknowledged his order, and he followed Bender into the shuttle.

Bender had restrained Mansoor in one of the seats, and the slaver glared at Fortis.

"I don't know who you are but you're going to pay dearly for this," the slaver spat.

Fortis nodded, and Bender delivered a massive slap to the side of Mansoor's head. The meaty *thunk* made Fortis wince. He leaned down until he was nose-to-nose with their captive.

"You're going to die today. How you die is up to you."

Fortis let his words sink in for a moment, but Mansoor's expression didn't change. He nodded again, and Bender lashed out. Mansoor's face turned bright red, and blood trickled from his nose. His chin lolled around on his chest, and Fortis yanked his head back by the hair.

"I'm going to ask you some questions. Your manner of death depends on how you answer. If you tell me the truth, your death will be quick. If you lie to me, I will turn you over to the cadets and my Maltaani friends. Do you understand?"

Mansoor didn't respond. Fortis backhanded him with the tips of his fingers. The stinging slap got the slaver's attention.

"Do you understand?"

"Yeah."

"First question. Who do you work for?"

Mansoor shook his head. "I don't work for anybody."

"C'mon now, we both know that's not true. Somebody pays you to kidnap people and scramble their brains."

Mansoor looked up sharply when Fortis said "scramble." Fortis nodded.

"Yeah, that's right. I know all about how your operation works. We spent some quality time with Nust after we caught up with him. He had some very interesting things to say."

It was a bluff. Nust had mentioned corporate connections, but Bender had killed him before Fortis could get more information. He continued, "The way I see it, if someone is paying you to supply them with slaves, they'll pay me. So, who is it?"

Mansoor looked away.

Fortis tipped his chin toward the aft compartment where the cadets were watching over Tench and his girlfriend.

"Go check on the cadets," he told Bender.

When the larger man was gone, Fortis leaned in close and spoke in a level tone.

"I meant it when I said you were going to die today. Why do you want to suffer on the way out? You don't think I can find out who you've been doing business with?"

Mansoor remained silent.

Fortis sighed. "My big friend is going to come back in here in about five minutes. He's going to lose his temper when he hears you won't talk to me." He shrugged. "Nust tried to be a tough guy and that made him mad. Bender gouged his eyes out with his thumbs, and we turned him loose on *Imperio*. I guess we'll find out how tough he was when we come back for another load of slaves."

Mansoor squeezed his eyes shut and shook his head. He looked up at Fortis.

"Painless?"

"You won't feel a thing. I promise."

Mansoor hung his head. "Okay. There's a guy named Leishman. Theo Leishman. He's the one who arranges our deliveries."

"I'd very much like to meet this Leishman. How do I contact him?"

"You don't. He'll contact you."

Fortis poked Mansoor in the forehead with his forefinger. "Remember what I said about lying?"

Mansoor twisted away. "I'm not lying, man. I only met Leishman one time in this place on SOMO."

"I don't believe you."

"It's the truth. Me and my crew are salvage pirates. We ambush ships at the jump gates and grab them when their crews are disoriented and easy pickings. We strip them bare, disable the engines, and set them adrift."

"You murder the crews."

"No. We set them adrift."

"On a disabled ship in the middle of deep space. You murder them."

"They have a fighting chance."

Fortis fought back the anger rising in his chest. "How did you get into slave trading?"

"A ship came through the Maduro Jump Gate, and we grabbed it. A huge ship. Biggest one yet. The score of a lifetime."

"*Imperio.*"

Mansoor nodded. "*Imperio.* We didn't know what she was until after Nust and the boarding team seized the bridge and killed a bunch of the crew. After that there was no going back."

"Nust led the boarding team. Not you."

"I stayed here on the bridge. Nust is a maniac. Totally unpredictable and capable of extreme violence without warning. I don't mind admitting that I'm a little scared of him."

"Then what happened?"

"Nust and his guys handled the crew while the rest of us stripped the ship of as much stuff as we could carry. That's when Tench came up with the idea of putting *Imperio* in orbit around a remote planet on the far edge of space until we could come back and finish the job."

"It was Tench's idea?"

"It's hard to believe he and Paloma are qualified to fly everything up to and including ore trains. They make a helluva bridge team."

Ore trains were kilometers-long ore cars linked together and pulled through space by massive high-powered engines. They were the most efficient way to move large amounts of raw material to processing plants. Driving the engines required a great deal of skill.

"Who's Paloma?"

"She's our other pilot. If you met Tench, you met Paloma. They're always together."

"Yeah, I met her. Didn't catch her name. Continue."

"I ordered the salvage crew to leave the engines intact, and we took *Imperio* to Menard-Kev. Somebody fucked up and stripped the orbital thruster controls and the ship had a kinetic deorbit."

"It crashed."

"Yeah, but it was a controlled crash. I mean, it didn't just fall out of the sky."

"You still haven't explained why you turned to slavery."

"We sold the first load of salvage on SOMO, and somebody talked. That's when Leishman appeared. He said he heard we had a couple thousand prisoners and asked if I'd be willing to sell some. I never considered slaving, but he offered so much money that it was impossible to say no. My crew would have mutinied if they found out I turned down that much cash. Leishman gave me the scrambler and we were in business."

"You've been selling slaves to Leishman for two years?"

"Not just Leishman. Sometimes he calls with order from other clients."

"Like who?"

Mansoor chuckled. "C'mon man. This isn't the kind of business where people use their real names, you know? They don't ask me, and I don't ask them. Everybody's anonymous."

"What about the Maltaani ship next to *Imperio*? You're dealing with the Maltaani?"

"No. That was a mistake. We hadn't grabbed a ship for a long time, and the boys were getting bored. We staked out the Maduro Jump Gate and snagged the first thing that came through. It was just like *Imperio*. We didn't know what we had until it was too late. Leishman got all excited when he heard we had a bunch of Maltaani salvage. He bought the entire load, sight unseen. We couldn't sell the Maltaani as slaves, though; they draw too much attention."

"So, you left them there to die."

"They're Maltaani. Fuck 'em."

Bender emerged from the back of the shuttle.

"The Maltaani might not make good slaves but they're damn fine soldiers," Fortis told Mansoor. He looked at Bender. "Throw this bastard in the back with Tench and his girlfriend."

"Wait!" Mansoor struggled as Bender hoisted him over a massive shoulder. "You can't do this. You promised!"

"I lied."

* * * * *

Chapter Thirty

Faraday helped with the ship-wide search for surviving slavers and identified the bodies of his dead comrades. When Fortis was satisfied that all the slavers were accounted for, he called everyone to the engine room passageway. It gladdened him to see Jinkaas, and he greeted the Maltaani leader with a sad smile as they clasped forearms.

"I'm sorry so many Maltaani warriors fell today," he told Jinkaas. Lou translated the reply.

"We do not mourn those who fall in battle. They wait for us in paradise."

They were brave words, but Fortis sensed Jinkaas struggled to contain his emotions at the death of Maardat. Fortis fought to remain stoic when he thought about Bugs, but the idea that Bugs was in a paradise with Cheese was strangely comforting.

Fortis took a moment to survey the team. Lou's wound was painful but not life-threatening. Jinkaas took an energy bolt in the leg that gave him a pronounced limp. Bender was hit by metal splinters across the shoulder during the assault, but he didn't notice until Lou pointed out the blood. Fortis smashed two fingers somewhere along the way, but his fingers didn't start throbbing until his adrenaline rush faded.

Lou and Tweak went to work repairing damaged consoles on the bridge to make *Alharih* spaceworthy while two of the Maltaani tended to the Fleet Academy cadets. Mansoor had beaten several of the cadets when he boarded the shuttle. The assault was devastating in their already weakened state.

The cadets marveled at the Maltaani. They had been imprisoned when the two races made first contact, so they were unaware of the hostilities that had ensued. Fortis was pleased to see the cadets and the Maltaani interacting through a system of hand signs and rudimentary words.

They had nine prisoners bound and gagged in the slave compartment on the shuttle. Faraday was given free run of the ship with an armed Maltaani escort, and he worked with Lou and Tweak to restore engine control to the bridge.

Fortis had no medical or technical skills to contribute so he sat in a seat on the shuttle and tried to stay out of the way. Jinkaas tried to sit next to Fortis, but his wound forced him to stretch out on the deck. Bender sank into the seat beside him.

"Four KIA and some walking wounded," Bender said. "It could have been a lot worse."

Fortis nodded his agreement. "Now we have to figure out how to get Jinkaas and his people home without getting attacked."

Fortis had a solution by the time Lou and Tweak reported that their repairs were complete.

"We'll put Jinkaas on the circuit and let him dial up whatever frequency he needs. We can arrange to meet a Maltaani ship at the Maduro Jump Gate to transfer him and his people."

"What about the rest of the cadets?" Bender asked.

"That's a little more complicated. Do you think our mission is still a secret?"

"I guess so. Nobody but Vidic knows who we are. The slavers think we're mercenaries and the cadets don't know what to think."

"Isn't Fourth Division on deployment aboard *Colossus* right now?"

"They were when we left. I have no idea where they are now."

"What if Fourth Division captured a slave ship named *Alharih* and in the course of their investigation they discover *Imperio*?"

"You want Fourth Division to get the credit for this?"

"I don't care who gets the credit. These kids need to get back home. We can't do it ourselves."

"What about us? Getting captured for slavery by Fourth Division might raise a few eyebrows at headquarters."

"We need Anders to arrange a ship to meet us just before *Alharih* is captured. If the assault team does some playacting, they can convince the prisoners and cadets that we've all been killed, and we slip away with our identities protected."

Bender scoffed. "Are your plans ever simple, mate?"

"What? It's not that complicated. We drop off the Maltaani and then link up with another ship and Fourth Division. We put on a show, and we're free. Piece of cake."

"And the whole thing falls apart if the Maltaani decide to resume hostilities or the ship that Anders hasn't arranged for yet is late or gets lost."

"Anything could happen, but we have to have a plan. You need to relax. This is what I do."

* * *

Fortis asked Lou to come to the shuttle and translate while he explained his plan for Jinkaas and his comrades.

"We will proceed to the jump gate where you were captured by the slavers," he told the Maltaani leader. "We will wait there for one of your ships and transfer your people so you can go home."

Jinkaas smiled at the news. "Faartees friend."

"Jinkaas friend. I have a small request though."

"Anything you wish."

"There are almost two thousand humans still imprisoned aboard their ship. I have to arrange their rescue. Given the uncertain nature of relations between our people, I think it would be wise to arrange safe passage for a human fleet to rescue them."

Jinkaas frowned. "I cannot grant this request. The admiral who commands the sector must do so."

"I understand. How do I contact the admiral?"

"The admiral will be on the ship that meets us. You can make your request then."

"Thank you."

* * *

"So now you're a diplomat?" Cujo exclaimed when Fortis briefed the team.

"No. I'm a Space Marine trying to get fifteen hundred kids back to Terra Earth without sparking a massive fight with the Maltaani. What do you think would happen if the Maltaani detected a fleet of human ships operating on this side of the Maduro Jump Gate?"

"You're setting them up for ambush if the Maltaani know they're coming."

"Do you have a better idea?"

Cujo scowled but said nothing.

"Tweak, you're in charge of getting Jinkaas whatever comms he needs to contact his people. Cujo, break orbit and get us pointed toward the Maduro Jump Gate. Be ready to run for it if the Maltaani refuse to meet us."

Tweak caught up with Fortis in the passageway after the meeting.

"Hey, Lucky, I don't know if this means anything but I think you should know. Me and Lou finished fixing the comms panels on the bridge and left to go below. I went back to get a tool I forgot and walked in on Cujo typing on the teletype circuit."

"Who was he typing to?"

"I don't know. He deleted the message and got real squirrely when I asked him what he was doing. He mumbled something about a loop back test, but we'd already tested the circuits."

"Huh. What do you think he was doing?"

"Beats me. Cujo is a weird dude so there's no telling what he was up to. I just thought you ought to know."

"Thanks, Tweak. Let's keep this between us, okay?"

"Sure thing. I'm going to go get Jinkaas set up with a circuit."

"Thank you."

Fortis continued down to the shuttle.

What is Cujo up to?

* * *

Fortis waited nervously with the team in the passageway while Jinkaas communicated with his people. Fortis ordered the bridge cleared because the Maltaani leader insisted on privacy while he dialed up the frequency and made the call.

"We shouldn't have left him alone in there," Cujo complained. "What if he's changing our flight plan?"

"Would you relax?" Bender said. "You're beginning to make me nervous."

"You should be nervous. Haven't you heard what they did to prisoners on Balfan-48?"

"If they were going to try something they would have done it by now, mate. There are more of them than there are of us, and they've been armed this whole time. I'm pretty sure we're safe."

Jinkaas opened the bridge door and smiled at Fortis.

"The admiral has agreed to meet us and will talk with you about your request."

"Excellent."

* * *

The atmosphere on *Alharib* grew tense as they approached the rendezvous with the Maltaani at the Maduro Jump Gate. Fortis tried to project a confident air, but Cujo's doubts gnawed at him. The Maltaani *were* the enemy. They might refuse safe passage to Fourth Division and capture *Imperio* for themselves. They might grant safe passage but then ambush the fleet. They might take the opportunity to exact revenge against the Space Marine who led the fighting on Balfan-48.

Anything was possible, and not knowing was aggravating. Fortis finally forced himself to dispel all those thoughts when Bender quietly pointed out that his nervousness was becoming noticeable.

Fortis spent several hours talking with Jinkaas through Lou. He learned that Jinkaas was from a large family and had graduated from their version of Fleet Academy. The Maltaani was reluctant to share other personal details and answered several of Fortis' question with a shrug as if to say "I don't understand."

Cujo called Fortis from the bridge when they were three hours from the Maduro Jump Gate.

"Someone is calling on the hailing circuit, but I think they're speaking Maltaani," the pilot told Fortis.

"We're on our way."

The two leaders and Lou went to the bridge. After several minutes of rapid-fire conversation on the circuit Jinkass turned to Fortis.

"They want us to proceed to the gate and be prepared to transfer passengers via their shuttle," Lou interpreted. "Including you."

Fortis had anticipated traveling to the Maltaani ship, and he nodded. "It will be my honor."

And maybe my death.

* * *

Faraday showed Fortis an airlock they could use to transfer passengers from *Alharih* to the Maltaani shuttle and explained how it worked.

"We don't need a collar or anything. Once we're in a hover their shuttle can approach, and we crack the hatch. Passengers jump from ship to shuttle. You'll be safe as long as you don't miss."

"That's easy for you to say," Fortis replied dryly.

Faraday laughed. "You'll see. We transfer slaves like this all the time, Lucky. It's no big deal if one misses—"

A sharp look from Fortis cut the words off in Faraday's throat. For a moment the slaver had forgotten he was a prisoner himself.

"Eh, yeah. It works well."

Cujo brought *Alharib* to a stop near the jump gate beacon. Jinkaas called the Maltaani ship and explained how their shuttle should approach. He joined Fortis and the team as they gathered near the airlock to don their exposure suits.

"Faartees friend," the Maltaani leader said. He held out the pistol Fortis had given him back on Menard-Kev. "Friend."

Fortis accepted the weapon and clasped forearms with Jinkaas. "Jinkaas friend."

They wrapped Maardat and the other two Maltaani casualties into exposure suits and tethered them to the other Maltaani for the jump to the shuttle. It was a grim task that left everyone in a somber mood, but a round of handshakes and hugs between the two races soon lifted everyone's spirits.

"The shuttle is alongside," Cujo announced over the intercom. "Ten meters."

"Be careful," Bender told Fortis and Lou before he stepped out of the airlock.

A green light flashed once the interior hatch was closed and locked. Fortis heard a *whoosh* as the pressure equalized between the airlock and the vacuum of space outside. Lou twisted the handle on the exterior hatch, and it slid open.

The ten meters between vessels looked like a hundred kilometers to Fortis when he leaned out. There was nothing around the two ships except the gaping blackness of deep space and he felt a twinge of vertigo.

"'You'll be safe as long as you don't miss,'" Lou quoted Faraday. The operators exchanged looks and laughed.

A hatch opened on the Maltaani shuttle and Fortis saw several figures inside beckoning them to make the jump. The first to go were the Maltaani, who towed the bodies of their comrades. The rest of the Maltaani followed until only Jinkaas, Fortis, and Lou remained.

"Faartees friend," Jinkaas said before he launched himself across the gap.

Lou gestured to the hatch. "Lead the way, boss."

Fortis took a deep breath and stepped through the hatch. He pushed off and glided to the Maltaani shuttle. Lou followed close behind. When they were safely aboard the shuttle the hatch slammed shut, and the craft headed for the Maltaani ship.

* * * * *

Chapter Thirty-One

The twenty-minute ride to the Maltaani ship was nerve wracking for Fortis and Lou. Even the presence of Jinkaas couldn't mitigate the hostile vibes Fortis got from some of the Maltaani crew.

"I feel like an unwelcome party guest," Lou told him. "Or a puppy that just peed on a new carpet."

Fortis snorted. "I wonder if any of these guys were at the Battle of Balfan-48?"

"Oh my God, Lucky. Don't even talk like that."

The shuttle docked, and Jinkaas led them into an enormous hangar area crowded with Maltaani crewman in various uniforms. Fortis felt the weight of a thousand stares and forced himself to maintain a friendly smile. He and Lou instinctively held hands as Jinkaas waved them forward.

"Faartees friend," the Maltaani repeated as they approached a knot of Maltaani dressed in uniforms adorned in gold braid and stars who Fortis assumed were the admiral and his staff. Jinkaas turned and briefly addressed the admiral before he bowed and stepped aside.

"Follow my lead," Fortis muttered to Lou as he gave a slight bow. The admiral acknowledged him with a tilt of his head but said nothing.

"Admiral, thank you for agreeing to meet with me." Fortis kept his voice steady and spoke at a pace that Lou could interpret without rushing. "My name is Abner Fortis, and I'm here with a request."

A low buzz rose from the crowd at the mention of his name. Sharp glances from the officers gathered around the admiral cut off conversation.

"I am Admiral Vaarden." The admiral looked at Lou, and she nodded. "Thank you for rescuing my people. How may I repay your kindness?"

"There are many humans still on the planet where we discovered Jinkaas and his people. The slavers held them there against their will and their situation is desperate. My ship is not capable of rescuing them. There is a fleet operating within a few days of the Maduro Jump Gate and I am here to request safe passage for that fleet to affect the rescue of our imprisoned people."

"You have the authority to make such a request?"

"I am the captain of *Alharib* and I am the senior military officer present. It is our custom that I have broad authority to take whatever actions are necessary to protect human life."

Vaarden turned and engaged in a whispered conversation with several of the officers gathered around him. Lou squeezed Fortis' hand.

"That was good," she said out of the corner of her mouth.

The admiral addressed Fortis. "What assurance do I have that the human fleet will not use this mission as cover for a preemptive strike against my forces?"

"Sir, I can't offer you anything but my word of honor. The human fleet will be on a mission of mercy and will remain there no longer than necessary to complete that mission."

Admiral Vaarden stared at Fortis for a long moment before he nodded. "I will grant your fleet safe passage to rescue your people."

Relief washed over Fortis as the admiral approached and extended his hand. The two men clasped forearms and Vaarden embraced Fortis as Jinkaas had.

"Faartees friend."

"Vaarden friend."

Jinkaas stepped forward and handed a small package to Vaarden and the admiral passed it to Fortis.

"It is our custom to exchange gifts on such occasions."

Lou winced. "Sorry, I didn't know."

Fortis' face burned with embarrassment. "Admiral, I deeply regret that I have no gift to offer you."

Vaarden shook his head and gestured to Jinkaas. "You have given me the greatest gift of all. My son."

Jinkaas laughed at Fortis' shocked expression and gestured at the package.

"Please open your gift."

Fortis unwrapped the package with trembling hands. Inside was a small dagger with a jeweled handle and sheath. The craftsmanship was stunning.

Fortis was speechless.

"In our culture, the dagger is a symbol of a great warrior," Jinkaas explained.

"This is too much," Fortis protested.

Jinkass put his hands on Fortis' shoulders, and they locked eyes. Fortis felt the same unnerving sense of familiarity he'd had before.

"Faartees friend."

A sense of comradeship rushed over Fortis. "Jinkaas friend."

Lou was exuberant during the shuttle ride back to *Alharib*.

"You did it! That was fantastic."

"The plan is working out so far. Now comes the hard part. Selling it to Colonel Anders."

* * *

The jump back through the Maduro Jump Gate went smoothly, and everyone breathed a sigh of relief when they were through. Fortis instructed Cujo to put *Alharib* in orbit around the beacon until he finished his report to Anders and received further instructions.

Bender and Lou found Fortis hard at work on his report.

"What are you going to tell him?" Lou asked.

"The more difficult question is *how* am I going to tell him," Fortis replied. "We left all our encrypted comms gear on *Dragon's Breath* so I have to be vague and specific at the same time."

Bender smiled. "As if you could be anything but, mate."

"I hope he can read between the lines. And who knows? He might order us to return directly to Terra Earth."

"That would be too easy." Bender elbowed Lou. "I have a thousand credits that say we take the path of greatest resistance."

After several hours or writing and rewriting, Fortis decided on a simple message that hopefully conveyed the urgent nature of their discovery and Fortis' follow-on plan.

From: Team Leader X5D1
To: ISMC ISR Chief

1. *Transmission source confirmed. Unable to send detailed results due to unforeseen circumstances.*

2. *Request ISR chief authorize X5D1 to contact nearest military commander for urgent secure communications.*

3. *X5D1 aboard Alharih in orbit near Maduro Jump Gate awaiting further orders.*

/Team Leader X5D1/

"Do you think he'll understand?" Fortis asked when he showed the message to Lou and Bender.

"It looks good to me," Lou said.

Bender nodded in agreement. "Those cadets can't wait much longer. If he doesn't get it, I say send the whole bloody story unencrypted and let the world know."

"He'll get it." Fortis hit the Send button. "He has to."

They received Anders' terse reply nineteen hours later.

From: ISMC ISR Chief
To: Team Leader X5D1

1. *Remain in current orbit. Will advise.*

/ISMC ISR Chief/

* * *

Alharih loitered in the vicinity of the jump gate for three days. The waiting was interminable, but it gave Fortis a chance to talk with Bender about Cujo.

"What do you know about Cujo?" he asked Bender when they were alone.

"I dunno. I've done a couple missions with him with no issues. I don't know him all that well. Now that I think about it, nobody does. Why?"

Fortis sighed. "There's something about him that doesn't seem right. Ever since SOMO, I have this weird vibe that's he's got his own agenda. He told me he'd never met Stoat before, but you saw how they were on the trip out here. Did they seem like strangers? What about his reaction when we found out Stoat marooned us on Menard-Kev? He was furious."

"So was everyone else."

"Yeah, but his anger was different. It felt personal. And then there's the time Tweak found him typing on the bridge teletype circuit after she and Lou got it working. He deleted the message before she could see it and then made up a story about testing the circuit after they had already done so."

"I'll talk to him if you want."

"No. Don't do that. Now that I've put all this into words it sounds pretty thin."

"Intel work can make you crazy. The paranoia can reach a fever pitch if you let it."

"It's probably nothing. Still, keep an eye on him. If he's up to something I don't want to be the only person to see it."

"Will do."

Fortis also spent several hours reconstructing the mission to date. He talked with each of the team members to get their input and verify his own recollections. He passed the document around the team for a final scrub. When he was finished, Fortis had a comprehensive seven-page record of their operations.

On the morning of the fourth day, Colonel Anders contacted them.

From: ISMC ISR Chief
To: Team Leader X5D1

1. Rendezvous with Cosmic Falcon *in eighteen hours for further instructions.*

/ISMC ISR Chief/

"Finally!" Cujo exclaimed when he heard the news. "Maybe now we can get things moving."

"What's the rush? You got a hot date with Charlotte?" Bender smiled but the look on Cujo's face was anything but amused.

"What's wrong with you? Do you like sitting out here in the middle of nowhere?"

Bender shrugged. "At least it's not raining."

"Does anybody recognize the name *Cosmic Falcon*?" Fortis asked the team. Nobody answered. "It's critical that we keep this rendezvous a secret within this team. If the prisoners or cadets find out about this, it might blow our cover story. Hopefully someone on *Cosmic Falcon* will have answers for us."

* * * * *

Chapter Thirty-Two

"*Alharih*, this is *Cosmic Falcon*. Do you read me?" Cujo scrambled for the mic to answer the hail. "This is *Alharih*. Go ahead."

"Stand by to receive a shuttle in fifteen minutes to transport Lucky to *Cosmic Falcon*."

"This is *Alharih*. Roger." The pilot turned to Fortis, who had been dozing in one of the bridge chairs. "Suit up, Lucky."

When Fortis arrived aboard *Cosmic Falcon*, a crewman bade him to strip off his ECW and then led him to an elaborately furnished passenger cabin. It surprised Fortis to see Colonel Anders waiting for him.

"I can tell you didn't expect to see me," Anders said with a smile.

"Nice digs."

Anders waved Fortis into the seat next to his. "*Cosmic Falcon* is the new flagship of the ISR Division. She used to be a deep space cruiser, but the previous owners decided it wasn't luxurious enough for them to live aboard. I was off on other business when I got your message. Now, tell me your story."

Fortis unfolded his report and offered it to Anders. "It's all right here, sir."

The colonel started to read but paused after the first page. "How did Cujo locate Stoat and *Dragon's Breath*?"

"He talked with someone he knew at the bar where his ex-wife works."

"A fat guy with a ridiculous handlebar mustache and bad teeth?"

Fortis shook his head. "I didn't get a good look at him. He was fat, but I couldn't see his face."

"Huh." Anders resumed reading. He stopped after the second page. "In here you say Stoat recognized you. Then you report Tweak detected those data transmissions. Do you think they're related?"

"I don't know, sir. It's possible. It's also possible that someone was tracking Stoat for a reason unrelated to our mission. Maybe one of his crew was working for a rival or an unhappy client. We weren't in a position to investigate. Tweak strangled their comms, and I thought that was sufficient."

"I concur."

Fortis couldn't control his expression when the colonel got to the part where the team encountered Vidic and learned they had discovered *Imperio*. Anders' eyebrows shot up, and his jaw dropped. His hands fell into his lap, and he stared at Fortis.

"You found *Imperio*?"

It was Fortis' turn to laugh at the colonel's surprise. "Yes, sir."

"And they're alive?"

Fortis' face fell. "Not all of them, sir. Read on."

Ander's expression darkened into an angry scowl as he digested Vidic's story. "Fucking slavers." His scowl deepened, and his neck turned red-purple. "Cadet traitors. This is disgraceful." He read a little further. "Cheese is dead?"

"Yes sir. Cheese and Bugs."

"Stoat killed them both?"

"No, sir. Bugs was killed in the assault on *Alharib*."

Anders slumped back into his seat. "Ah, fuck. They were good operators."

"Top notch."

"Dammit!" The colonel fixed Fortis in a steady gaze. "Remember the name Stoat."

"I won't forget."

Anders turned his attention back to the report. He stopped and looked up. "*Imperio* is floating?"

"She's reportedly floating on an ice-covered thermal vent or hot spring. Vidic said the ship is flooding about a centimeter a week because bulkheads and hatches were damaged during their crashlanding."

"We need to get them out of there before it sinks." After another page, Anders looked up in shock. "You've got to be shitting me. Maltaani?"

Fortis laughed again and nodded. "Yes, sir. Maltaani."

Anders read the next page, rubbed his eyes, and read it again. "You armed the Maltaani and teamed up with them to capture *Alharib*?"

"I had no choice, Colonel. Six of us weren't going to be enough."

"And you still have them with you aboard *Alharib*?"

"Keep reading."

A minute later, Anders dropped the report onto his lap and began massaging his temples with his fingers. He took deep a breath and released it as though he was trying to control himself. He finally looked up and fixed Fortis with a piercing glare.

"Please tell me that you made this up. Please tell me that you, an ISMC first lieutenant who reports to me, did not negotiate a truce with the Maltaani."

"It's not a truce, sir. It's a temporary accommodation to allow a human fleet to rescue the cadets without starting a shooting match with the Maltaani."

"You don't have the authority to make that call, Lieutenant. Hell, even *I* don't have the authority to make that call. You're way out of line on this one."

"Colonel, if I overstepped my bounds to rescue those kids, then I'll gladly face the consequences." Fortis struggled to keep his voice level. "Do you think there's an admiral or general in the Fleet who would have traveled to the Maltaani flagship and made that request?"

"No. The stakes are too high, and the risks are too great."

"Exactly. They would have launched an invasion through the jump gate with guns blazing, and a lot of people would have died unnecessarily. Instead, a dumbass first lieutenant risked his life to find a way for Fleet to rescue those cadets and look like heroes without firing a shot."

"You understand there are no guarantees that Fleet Command will agree to this? They might decide to do exactly what you said: invade with guns blazing."

"Maybe. Maybe Fleet Command doesn't have to get involved. There's a way to do this involving only local commanders but it will require some finesse."

"Oh? This ought to be good. Let's hear it."

Fortis detailed the plan he described to Bender. "You arrange for *Colossus* and Fourth Division to capture *Alharib* here, near the Maduro Jump Gate. During their interrogation of the slavers, they'll get information about *Imperio* and proceed to Menard-Kev. They'll rescue the cadets and cover themselves in glory while our cover remains intact. The only people who know the entire story are us, the Fleet admiral aboard *Colossus*, and the commanding general of Fourth Division. We'll need the boarding party that captures *Alharib* to do some playacting, but they won't know anything about the agreement with the Maltaani."

"What about our team?"

"Just before they grab *Alharib*, we'll transfer to *Cosmic Falcon* and ride back to Terra Earth with you."

Anders stroked his chin thoughtfully. "You've got this whole thing figured out, don't you?"

"Yes, sir, I do. Our first priority has to be the fifteen hundred cadets on *Imperio*. If we can maintain our mission secrecy without impeding their rescue, we should. Otherwise, call *Colossus* right now and tell them what we found. Either way, Admiral Vaarden has promised our ships safe passage."

"I'm going to need some time to digest this," Anders said as he stood up. "But I will give it due consideration and let you know what I decide. Right now, I need to get word to our assets on SOMO to find Theo Leishman. If we go ahead with your plan, he'll disappear as soon as news of *Alharib* gets out."

"Makes sense to me, sir." The two men shook hands.

"Anything else?"

"No, sir. We'll be standing by on *Alharib* when you make your decision."

"Very good."

* * * *

Fortis gathered the team on the bridge when he returned. "I briefed Colonel Anders on the progress of our mission."

"Was he surprised?" Lou asked.

Fortis chuckled. "Surprised is an understatement. Astounded would be a better word to describe his reaction."

Cujo raised his hand. "Are we heading home then?"

"Not yet. The colonel is considering options to rescue the cadets. He said he'll get back to me as soon as possible."

Cujo swore under his breath and shook his head. "We should have left when we had the chance. There's nothing left for us to do here. Let Fourth Division handle it."

"What's your hurry, mate?" Bender said. "The mission isn't over until Anders and Lucky tell us it's over."

Bender's restraint impressed Fortis. If there was a member of the team with a legitimate reason to speed up events, it was Bender. Somehow the giant Australian managed to keep his composure despite the knowledge that his goddaughter might be among the cadets on *Imperio*.

Seven hours later, Fortis was summoned back to *Cosmic Falcon*.

* * * * *

Chapter Thirty-Three

Fortis found Anders in the same cabin. There was a camera and holographic display set up on the table in front of him. The colonel pointed to a chair positioned out of camera view.

"We're getting set up for a teleconference with *Colossus*. The signal travels on a beam of light, so it's as close to real time as we can get. Sit there. There's no reason for anyone to see your face."

"Who are we meeting with, sir?"

"Admiral Downing and General Tsin-Hu. Fleet commander and the commanding general of Fourth Division."

Fortis blinked in surprise.

"I had to reach out to Admiral Kinshaw to vouch for me so they would agree to the meeting."

Admiral Kinshaw had commanded the Fleet during the Battle of Balfan-48, and he was critical to providing support to Fortis and the Space Marines on the surface. After the battle, he coordinated with Anders and Fortis to protect the reputation of Ninth Division and the commanding general.

"Is Liz coming?" Fortis quipped.

Liz Sherer was the Terra News Network reporter who had embedded with Fortis and Third Platoon during the Battle of Balfan-48. Her post-battle reporting had been critical in shaping the news to portray the battle as a hard-fought victory and not a strategic foul up.

Anders gave him a sharp look. "Don't even joke about that, Lucky. If a *rumor* of this meeting gets out, we're going to prison. There won't be a court-martial. Just prison."

"Are you ready, Colonel?" came a disembodied voice from the holograph speaker. A shimmering holograph of a female Fleet officer flickered to life.

"I'm standing by," Anders replied. "I have both visual and audio feeds."

"The admiral and general will be with you shortly." She vanished.

"What do you want me to say?" Fortis whispered.

"Don't say anything unless I prompt you," Anders answered.

A plain-faced Fleet admiral and a stern looking ISMC general appeared.

"Admiral, General, thank you for taking the time to meet with me," Anders began. "I'm Colonel Nils Anders, chief of—"

"We know who you are, Colonel," the general snapped. "Burle Kinshaw told us all about you. What he didn't tell us was why we should talk to you."

Anders was momentarily nonplussed by the general's question, but he quickly composed himself. "Last week, ISR operators followed a distress signal beyond the Maduro Jump Gate to a frozen planet in The Menard system. When they deployed to the surface, they discovered the Fleet Academy Training Vessel *Imperio*."

Both officers leaned forward. "What?" exclaimed the admiral. "*Imperio?*"

"Yes sir. *Imperio.*"

"How did she get there?" asked Admiral Downing. "She wasn't operating anywhere close to The Menard."

"She was hijacked by slavers and crash landed on Menard-Kev. The slavers have been using her as a sort of prison to hold the cadets captive ever since. They've been returning periodically to take some of the cadets away to sell into slavery."

"Oh my God."

Anders continued. "When my team left, there were almost fifteen hundred cadets still alive aboard *Imperio* awaiting rescue."

"Why the hell didn't your people rescue them?" asked the incredulous general.

"General, their ship wasn't large enough to carry fifteen hundred passengers. Nor was it equipped to feed and care for them."

"He should have brought out as many as the ship could carry."

"How could the officer commanding the mission choose which cadets to bring out first? The sickest? The healthiest? The sons and daughters of important politicians? How does he explain that to the cadets left behind?"

"You would do well to guard your tone, Colonel," the admiral warned him.

"My apologies, but it was an impossible situation. The cadets were unaware that they've been discovered so he decided it was best to leave them in situ and go for help."

"And you support that decision?"

"One hundred percent, General. It was a gut-wrenching call but the correct one."

"Why are you bringing this to our attention?" asked the admiral.

"*Colossus* and Fourth Division are best positioned to affect the timely rescue of the cadets."

Downing and Tsin-Hu stared through the camera. "We've received no such orders from Fleet Command," the general said.

"I understand that sir, but the cadets are in pretty rough shape after two years imprisoned in *Imperio*. If we wait for Fleet Command to act a lot of them won't survive."

"I don't think you do understand, Colonel," Tsin-Hu snarled. "Menard-Kev is deep in contested space. The risk to *Colossus* and Fourth Division is too great if we jump through the gate without proper authority."

"I have excellent intelligence that the Maltaani forces will not confront a human fleet engaged in rescuing those cadets."

"Oh really? And how did you come up with *that* nugget of information?"

Anders remained silent.

"That's what I thought. Guesswork and supposition." The general pointed a holographic finger in Anders' face. "Let me tell you something. We're not going to risk the lives of everyone on *Colossus* and her escorts based solely on your 'excellent intelligence.' The last time we followed excellent intelligence Ninth Division was destroyed. Submit your report to Fleet Command. If they deem it credible, they'll issue orders and then we will act." He turned to someone off-camera. "How the hell do I turn this thing off?"

Fortis had heard enough. "Wait a goddamn minute!" He grabbed the holograph camera and stuck his face in it. "We're not done here."

"Who the fuck are you?" Tsin-Hu demanded.

Anders tried to take the camera from Fortis. "Lieutenant Fortis, this meeting is over."

"It's *not* over!" Fortis fended off Anders' hands. "It's not over until *Colossus* is on her way through the jump gate to rescue those kids."

"You're Lieutenant Fortis?" Downing's surprise was evident in his voice.

"Yes, sir. Lieutenant Abner Fortis. I command the ISR team that discovered *Imperio*. If you don't act immediately, a lot of innocent kids are going to die."

"Lieutenant! This meeting is over! Stand down!" Anders made another attempt to grab the camera.

The general was standing now. "Hold it there! I don't care whose ass you kissed to get here, Fortis. There had better be a damned good reason for your insolence."

"Abner, please." Anders had given up trying to take the camera. "Stop this now."

"It's too late, Colonel." Fortis stared into the lens. "As we speak, there are fifteen hundred Fleet Academy cadets imprisoned Menard-Kev. They are dying. You have the power to rescue them."

"But the Maltaani—"

Fortis cut the admiral off. "*I* am the source of the excellent intelligence that says the Maltaani will not engage you while you rescue those kids."

"And how would you know what the Maltaani will or will not do?" Downing demanded.

"Because I went to the Maltaani flagship and requested safe passage for our fleet. Admiral Vaarden, who commands their fleet, granted my request. *That's* how I know it's safe to jump and travel to Menard-Kev."

Downing gasped and Tsin-Hu made a choking noise.

"You made a deal with the Maltaani?" the general croaked.

"Yes, sir, I did."

"On whose authority?"

"Mine. Exigencies of the situation demanded it. I saw an opportunity, and I seized it."

"And you trust this Maltaani admiral…what's his name?"

"Vaarden. Admiral Vaarden. I trust him because he owes me a favor."

Downing squeezed his eyes shut and pinched the bridge of his nose. "How exactly does a Maltaani admiral owe you a favor?"

"I rescued his son from the same slavers who kidnapped the Fleet Academy cadets."

Tsin-Hu slapped his forehead. "You did *what?*"

"Admiral, General, *please*. Our mission was a complex operation and frankly it doesn't matter how we got to this point. What matters right now is that I have a plan for *Colossus* and Fourth Division to rescue those cadets and paved the way so you can do it without interference from the Maltaani."

Downing and Tsin-Hu exchanged glances. "Can you believe the balls on this guy?" the general asked in disbelief.

Anders took the camera from Fortis' hands and set it back on the table. "Admiral. General. I realize how incredible all of this sounds. Insane, even. But Lieutenant Fortis is an experienced officer who has earned my complete trust. If he says the Maltaani have agreed not to interfere with a rescue mission, then I believe him. I urge you to do the same. At least listen to his plan with open minds."

Tsin-Hu scowled but Downing nodded. "Okay, Colonel. We'll listen to your plan. If it's as crazy as the rest of this story, we'll wait for guidance from Fleet Command."

Relief washed over Fortis, and he almost shouted in triumph. Instead, he cleared his throat. "The plan is straightforward. My team captured the slave ship *Alharib* along with the captain and several crewmembers. We also rescued a dozen Fleet Academy cadets from them. All of them are under the belief that my team are mercenaries who have gotten into the slavery business. If *Colossus* and Fourth Division assault *Alharib* and capture it from us, you would discover the cadets and learn of *Imperio* from the slavers. You can then jump through the gate and rescue the remainder of the cadets.

"Nobody outside of this call has to know the true identity of my team or the agreement with Admiral Vaarden. *Colossus* and Fourth Division will get the credit for the rescue."

The senior officers sat in silence while they considered Fortis' plan. Downing opened and closed his mouth several times as if to speak but changed his mind. Tsin-Hu's customary scowl softened. The general finally spoke.

"I've heard worse plans." He looked at the admiral. "I don't see a downside except that we have to trust the Maltaani."

Downing nodded slowly. "I agree. Colonel, it looks like you've got a workable plan. I'll order *Colossus* to the Maduro Jump Gate at best speed. We're twenty-two hours out."

Admiral, General, there are two important details your assault force need to know. First, there's a petty officer named Vidic imprisoned on Imperio. She gave us critical assistance and knows who we are. Second, a number of cadets were recruited by the slavers and turned into trustees or jailers. They assist the slavers accounting for the prisoners during round-up."

"That's outrageous!" Downing blurted.

"Yes sir, it is. Your assault team will need to identify and separate them from the rest of the cadets, and I believe Vidic will be very useful in that regard."

* * * * *

Chapter Thirty-Four

Fortis returned to *Alharih* to prepare for the Space Marines to "capture" her. He gathered the team on the bridge where they could speak in private.

"*Alharih* and *Cosmic Eagle* will loiter here and wait for *Colossus*. The slavers will remain locked up on the shuttle, and the cadets will stay in the passenger compartment. Just before the ISMC boarding party arrives from *Colossus* we'll put on a show for the cadets and slavers. We have to convince them that we plan to resist the boarding and then transfer to *Cosmic Eagle*. The boarding party will use plenty of flash bangs and smoke grenades for their part of the show and report all mercenaries KIA. After they get everyone else off *Alharih*, they'll jump through the gate and head for Menard-Kev. We'll ride home with Anders.

"Remember not to breathe a word of this to anyone outside this room. It only succeeds if the cadets and slavers believe what they hear." He looked at Tweak and Lou. "Go through the ship's logs and erase any traces of our rendezvous with the Maltaani."

"What about Faraday?"

"Tie him up and put him with the rest of the slavers. I'll mention his name to Anders, but he's going to be tried along with all the others."

"What's the timeline?" Cujo asked. "How long until *Colossus* arrives?"

Fortis started to answer but at the last second decided to keep that information to himself. "I don't know. They only said that they would make best speed and we should be ready to evacuate *Alharib* at a moment's notice."

When the meeting broke up, Tweak caught Fortis and Bender in the passageway. She beckoned them to follow her into a vacant space and closed the door.

"Cujo is definitely up to something. I saw him use the teletype today while you were on *Cosmic Eagle*. I don't know who he was talking to, but he was on there for a while before I interrupted him."

"You think he's talking to Charlotte?"

"On the teletype? No way. It doesn't have the power to reach all the way back to SOMO."

"Can you disable the teletype without being obvious?"

"Sure. I can trip the breaker for the antenna. He'll be able to type all he wants but his transmissions won't go through."

"Will he be aware of it?'

"Yeah, I think so. He'll see a transmission failure indicator on the screen."

"Trip the breaker and let's see how he reacts."

Tweak left in search of the correct electrical distribution panel and Bender held Fortis back.

"What is it with you and Cujo, mate?"

Fortis sighed. "I don't know. He's performed well on this mission but there's something about him that makes me distrust him. This teletype business is suspicious."

"Well, we're on the home stretch. When we get back tell Anders you won't accept any more missions if Cujo's on the team."

Fortis chuckled. "We have a choice of missions?"

"Yeah. DINLI."

"Indeed. By the way, we have about twenty hours until *Colossus* is in range."

"I thought you didn't know?"

"I don't know why, but I didn't want to share that information with the group. The paranoia of this intel business will make you crazy."

Bender nodded and clapped Fortis on the shoulder. "Only if you let it. Take it easy, Lucky. Things are looking up. Your plan is coming together, and we're less than a day away from *Colossus* and Fourth Division."

"Yeah, I know. I just hate that nagging feeling that I missed something."

"She'll be right, mate. From where I'm sitting you've hit all the high points. The details will work themselves out." Bender cleared his throat. "What do you want to do with Cheese and Bugs? We can't leave them here for the assault team to find."

"What do you think?"

"We can take them with us across to *Cosmic Eagle*, but we already decided we weren't bringing bodies back on this one. Friendlies or not, the sky marshals will put us in quarantine and our cover will be blown. It becomes a choice between burying them here or over there."

"Shit." Fortis pinched the bridge of his nose between thumb and forefinger. "They deserve better than an airlock."

"No argument here, but we really don't have any choice, do we?"

"DINLI."

"Indeed."

Two hours later, the team assembled at the airlock with the body bags containing Cheese and Bugs. After a moment of silence, Fortis cleared his throat.

"Jinkaas told me that the Maltaani don't mourn the death of a warrior because they believe the warrior waits for them in paradise. I like to believe that Cheese and Bugs are together in paradise waiting for the rest of us."

"Cheese and Bugs were good operators and good Space Marines," Bender said. "They died like warriors, with a song in their hearts and a smile on their faces. We will never forget them."

Bender was dressed in his ECW gear, and the team helped him move the bodies into the airlock and secured the hatch behind him. They heard the hiss of air as the pressure equalized. Fortis imagined Bender opening the exterior hatch and gently floating the bodies of his friends into space. There was another hiss as the airlock was pressurized again and Bender stepped back through the interior hatch.

"Cujo, go up to the bridge and tell *Cosmic Eagle* we're moving away from this spot."

* * *

Eighteen hours later Cujo summoned Fortis to the bridge. "*Colossus* just hailed us. Are they supposed to be here already?"

"I guess they made best speed. Are you ready to start the show?"

"I sure am. Is everyone else?"

"They're all standing by. Give me ten minutes and then do your thing."

Fortis went to the shuttle to check on the cadets. They were in good spirits and looked healthier after several days of the improved diet aboard *Alharib*. He was sorely tempted to tell them they were about to be rescued. Instead, he went back and opened the door to check on the slave compartment. Mansoor, Tench, and the rest of the slavers were bound and gagged. After a quick glance he closed the door. There was no reason to gloat.

They'll get what they deserve.

He lingered in the passenger compartment until he heard Cujo's voice on the general intercom circuit.

"Lucky, come to the bridge! The UNT Fleet has found us!"

Fortis cursed and ran from the shuttle, slamming the hatch shut behind him. "Everyone standby to repel boarders!" he shouted as he scrambled up the ladder out of the hangar. Once he was in the passageway, he turned and headed for the airlock. The rest of the team was already there and dressed out for the jump to the shuttle from *Cosmic Eagle*.

"Hurry up! The shuttle is waiting," Cujo urged.

The transfer to the shuttle was easy. Fortis caught sight of *Colossus* before he jumped, and the sheer size of the vessel amazed him. He had deployed on *Atlas*, her sister ship, but there were no viewports on the shuttles or dropships, and he'd never seen the vessel from the outside. He smiled when he saw another shuttle approaching.

Right on time.

* * *

Cosmic Eagle remained in the vicinity of the action until they received a message from *Colossus* reporting the boarding was complete. The ISR Branch vessel steered a course to stay clear of the flagship and her escorts and began the long trip home.

Colonel Anders called the team together in the same cabin where he'd met Fortis and held the holograph conference with *Colossus*.

"You have performed magnificently," Anders told them. "Your discovery of *Imperio* and the capture of the slaver vessel *Alharib* were remarkable feats for which you deserve high praise and recognition. Unfortunately, this is the intel business so you'll have to settle for a 'Well done' from your commanding officer."

"How about a pay raise?" Cujo quipped.

"Let me think about it." Anders put a forefinger to his chin and feigned thought. "No."

The team laughed at Anders' response and the colonel grew somber.

"We have some unfinished business." He gestured behind Lou. "Lou, please get the glasses from the cupboard behind you and pass them out." Anders pulled a flask from his uniform smock. "I didn't know why I packed this before we left. Now I do.

"This was a tough mission and we lost two friends and teammates. Cheese and Bugs were top-notch operators, and they'll be sorely missed." He poured a shot for each team member. "Lucky told me you held a funeral on *Alharib* but there was one thing missing. It's our tradition to remember fallen Space Marines with a toast." He raised his glass. "To the dead and the living."

Anders tipped a tiny splash from the flask and then took a healthy slug. Fortis and Bender tossed back their drinks. The other operators bravely followed their lead. The raw alcohol made them sputter and choke and the Space Marines got a good chuckle from their discomfort.

The trio of Space Marines shouted in unison.

"DINLI!"

* * * * *

Chapter Thirty-Five

Colonel Anders used the downtime during their transit home to debrief the team on the mission. He met with the team members individually and as a group. When he was finished Anders called Fortis to his cabin to review the results.

"This was an extraordinary mission. I am amazed every time I read your report," Anders said. "The sad part is that we'll never be able to tell anyone about it and the team will never get the credit you deserve."

Fortis shrugged. "I think the team would agree that it doesn't matter who gets the credit as long as the cadets are brought home safely."

Anders gestured to Fortis' report. "My question for you now is this: what didn't you include in here?"

"Sir?"

"I've been in the intel field long enough to recognize a recitation of facts overlaid on a timeline. We deal in a lot more than that. I want your impressions, your feelings, and your instincts. For example, you interacted with the Maltaani in ways that humans have not up until now. We have a lot of questions about them, and you might have some of the answers."

Fortis thought for a long moment. "I don't believe the Maltaani are the savage race we've led ourselves to believe. They fought aggressively on Balfan-48 and their treatment of prisoners was barbaric, but I don't think that's all Maltaani. There are humans capable of the same degree of brutality and they don't define the entire human race."

"Their technology is comparable to our own in many ways," Anders said. "Is it possible for a civilization to have advanced technology and brutal cultural norms?"

"My experience with Jinkaas and Admiral Vaarden tells me they have behavioral norms approximating our own. They knew who I was, but I felt little hostility on the Maltaani flagship. How many engagements have there been with the Maltaani since the Battle of Balfan-48?"

"Three that I know of. All of them were single ship encounters with no real damage or resolution. There are also many who blame the Maltaani for the attack on *Repose* and the disappearance of *Nelson*."

Repose was the flagship of a religious sect called the Science Church. The sect sent out a group of pilgrims from Terra Earth to find another planet to colonize. When the pilgrims stopped reporting, Fleet Frigate *Nelson* was dispatched to look for them. *Nelson* had the first known encounter with a Maltaani craft while searching for *Repose*. *Nelson* discovered *Repose* floating in space with her engines disabled and the ship deserted. Shortly after that, *Nelson* herself disappeared. Suspicion immediately landed on the Maltaani.

"Colonel, from what I've learned about how slavers operate, I think it's safe to assume *Repose* fell victim to slavers. *Nelson* isn't the first vessel to simply vanish out here."

"False correlation between those disasters and the Maltaani, you mean?"

"Yes, sir. I'm beginning to wonder if the Battle of Balfan-48 wasn't the result of a series of misunderstandings that went kinetic. The Maltaani landed there without considering we would consider that move a threat to Terra Earth. Maybe they thought it would serve as a warning. Or it may have been a deliberate provocation. We responded by dropping Ninth Division on the planet. They threatened us, we threatened them, and the fight was on. We proved that we can slaughter each other in large numbers, and neither side has made a serious move since."

Anders nodded thoughtfully. "It's worth more study when we get another chance to interact with them."

"If we ever stop shooting at each other."

"True. Anything else?"

"This is a weird one. After we captured the Maltaani soldier on Balfan-48 I went to see him up close. I stared into his eyes and felt a strange connection with him. I didn't think much of it at the time, but I got the same feeling from Jinkaas. It reminded me of a zoology elective I took at university. A primate researcher talked about the common ancestry he felt with the apes he studied." Fortis shook his head. "I can't describe the feeling except to say that I somehow recognize them on a fundamental level. When I look at the Maltaani I feel a primal connection. It's like I'm looking at me. Lou told me about a theory that they're actually distant relatives of humans."

"Hmm. That's interesting."

"Something else to look into."

"What about the team? Any comments or complaints?"

"They all performed their duties in exemplary manner. Except…"

"Except whom?"

"I don't know if this is worth going into. I don't want to cause trouble, but I had some difficulties with Cujo."

"Really? How so?"

Fortis told the colonel about Cujo's behavior on SOMO and later on *Dragon's Breath*. He included Tweak's observations of Cujo on the *Alharib* teletype.

"Who was he talking to?"

"I don't know. Who's out here within teletype range?"

"It could be anybody. Did he react to the failure of the antenna?"

"Tweak didn't say anything, sir. *Colossus* arrived soon afterward so maybe he didn't have a chance to get back on the circuit."

"Huh. Have you questioned him about any of this?"

"No. I was more interested in convincing *Colossus* and Fourth Division to rescue the Fleet Academy cadets on Menard-Kev than worrying about Cujo. He really hasn't done anything wrong to question him about. If he's up to anything nefarious he'll have a story ready anyway."

Anders nodded. "Cujo is a holdover from my predecessor. Before this mission I only used him twice to transport personnel and supplies. In this business it's not uncommon for independent contractors like Cujo to pad expense reports or encounter cost overruns after they lowball contract bids. He's probably working some kind of grift."

"I think we're okay. We're almost home and he's not flying anymore on this mission. You might consider vetting him again before you send him out."

"I'll do that. Anything else?"

"Bender's goddaughter is one of the Fleet Academy cadets on *Imperio*. Her name is Phaedra."

"Holy shit. Did you find her?"

"No. Bender didn't want to look. He said it would be a distraction from the mission. I think he's a little afraid of what we might have found. Those kids have been there a long time and the slavers sold a lot of them off."

"I had no idea. That man is a rock."

"He's probably going to need some time off when *Colossus* and Fourth Division return to Terra Earth with the cadets."

"That won't be a problem."

They lapsed into silence for a long moment before Fortis spoke again.

"Colonel, that's about all I have right now. I'll let you know if anything else comes to me."

"Very good." Anders stood and the men shook hands. "You and your team performed brilliantly, Abner. Beyond the humanitarian miracle of discovering *Imperio*, I think you might have saved the ISR Branch."

"Saved it from who?"

"Before the United Nations of Terra was formed and our militaries merged, some countries had what they called special operations forces. Those forces underwent specialized training and had generous budgets, and they operated outside the control of the regular military. Those forces were disbanded when the ISMC was formed. Over time we've discovered that the ISMC is not the proper tool for every job and the ISR Branch was created."

"We didn't do anything that a platoon of Space Marines couldn't do."

"That's where you're wrong. We have some very skilled Marines, but the ISMC doesn't have pilots capable of flying everything from a civilian shuttle to a multi-engine spacecraft like Cujo can. Nor do we have computer technicians on par with Tweak and Lou. We simply don't have the need or budget to recruit, train, and retain them.

"It's more cost effective to marry up some of our warriors with outside technical specialists for a specific mission like we did here. Unfortunately, some generals see the existence of the ISR Branch as a threat and there are some on the Council that agree. Your mission is officially a secret, but it won't stay that way forever. Allowing *Colossus* and Fourth Division to take credit for the discovery of *Imperio* was an unintentionally brilliant move and should go a long way to bolstering our reputation and tamping down some of our critics. I would also venture a guess that your ISMC career prospects will improve as well." He smiled and put a hand on Fortis' shoulder. "Who knows, a one-legged company commander might not be such a bad thing."

* * * * *

Chapter Thirty-Six

Cosmic Eagle's previous owners spared no expense when they refitted the craft, and the team availed themselves of the luxurious accommodations as they traveled to Terra Earth. The most popular indulgence was the three-dimensional food printer. The printer combined bulk raw materials like water, fat, protein, and carbohydrates with vitamins and minerals, added the appropriate spices, and produced restaurant quality meals. Instead of the prepackaged dried or frozen meals the team was accustomed to, they feasted on fresh cuts of meat, vegetables, and decadent desserts.

"Oh God, I'm going to gain ten pounds if we don't get home soon," Tweak declared as she pushed her plate away. Tweak was the last person on the team who needed to concern herself with gaining weight, and everyone laughed.

"Too bad we can't get back to the daily dozen when we get home," Bender replied. "The workout room on this tub reminds me of a health spa."

"Am I the only person who won't miss the daily torture routine?" Cujo quipped.

Bender's remark subdued the group's cheerfulness, and nobody laughed at Cujo. It wasn't the threat of a rigorous workout but the realization that the team would disband when they returned to Terra Earth. Tweak, Lou, and Cujo would return to their civilian lives while Fortis and Bender would go into standby as they waited for another mission.

"I hope we get the chance to work together again," Fortis said. "It's been an honor and a pleasure to lead X5D1."

Lou sniffed and then giggled with embarrassment. "I think—"

An urgent voice came over the general intercom circuit and cut her off. It made the hairs on Fortis' neck stand up. "Colonel Anders report to ship control. Colonel Anders report to ship control immediately."

"What's going on?" Tweak asked in a panicked voice.

"No idea," Fortis replied. "Everyone stand fast until we get more information."

After a few minutes Fortis couldn't wait any longer. "Bender, take charge here. I'm going to see what's up."

Fortis climbed the ladder to the ship control space and stopped just inside the door. Anders was seated at one of the consoles with a circuit headset on, staring intently at the display in front of him. One of *Cosmic Eagle*'s crew stepped to Fortis' side.

"What's going on?" Fortis muttered.

"We were hailed by a ship claiming to be UNT Fleet Frigate *LJM de Bourbon*. They ordered us to heave-to for a safety inspection. I refused because I've never heard of such a thing in open space. They threatened to fire on us, and that's when Colonel Anders got involved."

"I demand to know the name of your commanding officer," Anders' voice boomed over the circuit.

"Did you get a look at them?"

"Only for a second, and that was at long range. *Cosmic Eagle* doesn't have the visual surveillance capabilities that most Fleet vessels have; we only have docking cameras. I happened to catch a glimpse when they first hailed us. Now they've taken a position two kilometers astern."

"*Cosmic Eagle* this is Fleet Frigate *LJM de Bourbon*. Heave-to and stand by for safety inspection. Comply immediately or we will be forced to fire on you."

Fortis almost laughed aloud at the absurd accent he heard over the speaker. It would have been comical if the speaker wasn't threatening to engage them.

"What's really weird is that we're only broadcasting a generic identification signal and our destination. We haven't even registered the name *Cosmic Eagle* yet, but somehow they know it," the crewman added.

Fortis agreed. "That is weird."

Cujo.

Anders took off the headset and looked around. "Can anyone back there tell me what the hell's going on here?"

"Maybe they're pirates, Colonel," said the crewman standing next to Fortis.

"Pirates taking prizes within two days of Terra Earth?" The colonel shook his head. "I don't think so. They would have to be the dumbest pirates in the universe."

"It could be mistaken identity. They don't know this is not the property of an ultra-wealthy person anymore," Fortis said.

"They're calling us *Cosmic Eagle*. That's a new name."

"Is this guy's accent for real? It sounds like he's parodying a French accent."

"If he is, the joke's on him. Fleet Frigate *John Young* is about an hour away. When they arrive we'll find out who these clowns are. I'm certain they're not Fleet."

"*Cosmic Eagle* this is *LJM de Bourbon*. Comply or we will fire on you."

Anders keyed his mic. "What is the name of your commanding officer?"

Fortis returned to the mess decks to update the team. "Someone impersonating a Fleet vessel is tailing us and demanding we stop for a safety inspection."

Tweak and Lou exchanged nervous looks while Cujo smothered a laugh and shook his head.

"Pirates?" Bender blurted.

"Not here. We're too close to Terra Earth. We don't know who they are, but Anders isn't stopping."

He returned to the ship control space where Anders continued the verbal jousting with their hopeful assailant. The absurdity continued for another thirty minutes. *Cosmic Eagle* maintained her course and speed while the unknown vessel demanded they stop. Anders continued to respond to their demands with demands of his own. Fortis realized there was something vaguely familiar about the voice on the circuit, so he recorded parts of the conversation on his communicator to listen to later.

"*Cosmic Eagle* this is *John Young*. I have you on my sensors. Who's your friend?"

Fortis smiled when he heard the friendly voice over the encrypted Fleet circuit.

Anders switched channels. "This is *Cosmic Eagle*. We don't know who they are. They claim to be the *LJM de Bourbon* but that's obviously false."

"Roger that. When we got underway yesterday *LJM de Bourbon* was pulling in. Maintain your course and speed; we're going to maneuver around behind her to get a good look."

"This is *Cosmic Eagle*, wilco."

Two minutes later, *John Young* came back up on the net. "*Cosmic Eagle*, *John Young*. Looks like your friend has changed his mind. I guess they saw us because they turned away and accelerated. Did they exhibit hostile intent?"

"Negative, *John Young*. They only demanded that we heave-to."

"Then I can't shoot them, and I don't have on-station time to chase. Sorry."

"This is *Cosmic Eagle*, you've done enough. We appreciate the assist."

"Our pleasure. By the way, have you heard the news? *Colossus* discovered *Imperio*."

Anders turned and flashed a big smile at Fortis. "No kidding? That's incredible!"

"They found it crash landed on a frozen planet in the middle of nowhere. It's a miracle that some of the cadets survived."

"Amazing."

"Yes, sir, it is. Anyway, we're out of here. Have a safe journey home. *John Young*, out."

Anders took off his headset and joined Fortis by the door. "Pretty awesome news, isn't it?"

Twenty minutes later, Fortis beckoned Bender into his stateroom. "I need you to listen to something." He played the recording of the radio conversation. "Does that voice sound familiar to you?"

Bender's face screwed up as he thought about it. "Play it again."

Fortis played the recording again, and Bender nodded. "It sounds like Stoat except for that ridiculous accent, mate."

"That's what I thought."

"We need to go get that bastard."

"Let's not get ahead of ourselves. 'Sounds like' doesn't mean it's him."

"Ask Cujo. He'll know."

Fortis shook his head. "I think that's a bad idea, and I'll tell you why. The watch stander in the control space told me they haven't registered the name *Cosmic Eagle* yet. We've been broadcasting a generic identification signal this entire trip. How would this guy know who we are unless someone on this ship told him?"

"You think it was Cujo?"

"I don't know who else it could be. I don't want to get carried away with suspicion but it's possible. It doesn't make sense to me why he would do it though. Let me get Tweak and Lou up here and see what they say."

The two women agreed with Bender. "That sounds like Stoat," Tweak said.

Lou was more certain. "There's no doubt in my mind. That is definitely Stoat."

"You're sure?"

"Lucky, I'm a trained linguist. I'd bet your next paycheck on it."

Fortis looked at Bender. "There you have it. It's Stoat."

"Are you going to tell the colonel?"

"I have to. We have unfinished business with him, and Anders has the contacts to help us find him."

Later, Anders expressed skepticism at Fortis' analysis of the identification issue and the team's conclusion about the recording. "I respect Lou's skill as a linguist, but I'm not convinced that's Stoat. How much time did she spend in conversation with him?"

"I don't know, sir. Not a lot. None of us did, except Cujo."

"I'll query my sources and see what they've come up with on Stoat. The identification issue might be nothing. The control station watch stander responded to the hail before I got up there; he might have inadvertently responded with our name without realizing it." He let out a deep sigh. "I can't imagine what Cujo would be up to by disclosing our identity and location. It simply doesn't make sense to me."

"Nor to me. The pieces fit but there's no motive to bind them together."

Anders clapped Fortis on the shoulder. "Welcome to the intel world."

* * * * *

Chapter Thirty-Seven

The remainder of the voyage to the TEJG was tense. Fortis split his time between his stateroom and the ship's workout room. He tried to avoid staring at Cujo when the team met for meals, and he was grateful that the pilot wasn't a gym rat.

The ship's workout room was well-equipped with machines to maintain muscle tone, but they didn't offer enough challenge to the strength-enhanced Space Marine. Fortis pounded out many kilometers on the treadmill while his mind chewed over the details of their mission. His exercise sessions left him physically exhausted but gave him no clear answers to his questions about Stoat or his suspicions of Cujo.

Colonel Anders called the team together for a final meeting as *Cosmic Eagle* approached TEJG orbit. He handed each team member an envelope with their name on it.

"Here are your contract payouts and tickets for the shuttle down to Terra Earth," he told the civilians. "For you two—" he looked at Fortis and Bender, "—you get shuttle tickets and leave papers. I'll see you back at the ISR building in two weeks. The ladies leave in an hour and then the three of you are on the next shuttle.

"I don't have anything to add to what's already been said. You all performed magnificently and a lot of Fleet Academy cadets owe their lives to you. Just remember that you were never there, etcetera, etcetera. The shuttle is standing by to take you to the jump gate."

After a round of handshakes with the colonel, Fortis led the team to the shuttle for the brief flight to the jump gate. They lingered at the arrival area long enough for another round of hugs and handshakes. Fortis got a thick feeling in his throat, and he had to blink away the sudden unexpected pressure in his eyes.

Lou and Tweak headed for the Terra Earth shuttle gate, and Cujo turned toward the SOMO gate.

"I'd love to hang around, but Charlotte's waiting, boys." The pilot smiled as he saluted them with his envelope. "I've got a paycheck burning a hole in my pocket."

Bender chuckled and shook his head as they watched him disappear into the crowd. "Well, mate, I could use a drink while we wait. Join me for a beer?"

"Sounds good to me. Let me check what time our shuttle departs." Fortis unsealed his envelope and pulled out his ticket. "We have three hours. Hey, what's this?" He pulled out a folded sheet of paper and read it aloud. "Barnaby Rausch, AKA Stoat, has contracted with the Galactic Resource Conglomerate to transport personnel and supplies between Terra Earth and the Eros Cluster aboard his vessel *Anusha*."

"Sounds like our friend is trying to make himself scarce around here," Bender said. "Let's take a look at the departure schedule."

The two men examined the departure screen but didn't see *Anusha*.

"Wait here, I'll ask an agent."

Bender waded through the crowd to the service counter while Fortis examined the rest of the schedule. There was a flight to Eros-69 in five hours, and he chuckled.

Looks like I might get my chance to go to the Eros Cluster after all.

"*Anusha* departed three days ago. They couldn't give me a schedule. She's a tramp not a liner so she sails when she gets a load. Her declared destination from here was Ilyich-Zeta, which is on the way to the Eros Cluster. Maybe that was her pretending to be the frigate?"

Fortis shrugged. "Could be." He pointed to the departure screen. "I don't want to chase her from station to station. We have two weeks. Let's go wait for her on Eros-69."

Bender threw his head back and laughed. "That's the best idea I've heard in months."

* * *

Bender wanted to book two seats and sleeping pods on a transport to save money, but Fortis insisted on their own cabin. "I'd rather not spend the entire trip worried someone might recognize me," he told Bender as he paid for the upgrade. "That war bond tour is turning out to be a mistake."

By the time they boarded, the craft was fully booked. Many of their fellow passengers had begun their vacations early in the bars on the TEJG, and loud voices and drunken laughter filled the passenger cabin.

Bender and Fortis retreated to their private accommodations. "I'm glad you insisted on the private cabin," Bender said as he closed the door against the noise. "It's a madhouse out there."

The two men spent their time watching holographic movies, sleeping, and talking. They exchanged life stories, and Bender got a kick out of Fortis' reasons for joining the ISMC.

"Student loans. Bah, what a wanker. I reckon you've regretted that decision at least once."

Fortis gave a wry smile. "Yeah, maybe once. What about you? What made you join?"

Bender shook his head. "A woman. Can you believe that? I loved her, and she broke my heart, so I ran away to the Space Marines." The two men laughed at their foolishness.

"We're both wankers," Fortis sputtered, and they laughed even harder.

Fortis recounted the story of Idoia Guerra's attempt on his life in the hotel workout room.

"You *are* a lucky bastard, aren't you?"

"I guess. I still have no idea why she tried to kill me."

Bender told Fortis about some of his exploits as a young Space Marine, both on and off duty. The highlight came when he lifted his shirt and exposed a thick scar that ran across his ribs. "Bloody Fleet bastard got me with a knife after I won all his money at cards." He flexed his hand and Fortis saw three parallel scars across his knuckles. "It cost me a month in the brig and a few stitches, but he got what he deserved. What about you? Do you have any interesting scars?"

"My leg, but that's not very interesting. I do have these." He dug out the necklace made from the Maltaani dog fangs and offered it to Bender. "Some of the guys had it made from the fangs of a Maltaani dog that damn near ripped my arm off on Balfan-48."

Bender examined the necklace with a smile on his face. "That's beautiful work, mate. And you say these came from a Maltaani dog?"

"Yeah, a big bastard, too. Grabbed my arm and wouldn't let go. Gunny Ystremski blew it to pieces. Saved my life."

Bender handed the necklace back. "One helluva story. I bet you get a lot of free drinks when you tell that one in a bar full of Space Marines."

"Actually, I haven't had the chance to tell anyone but you. After I was released from the hospital I went straight to the war bond tour, so I haven't spent a lot of time in bars since the battle."

"Well then, let me be the first to toast your fangs." Bender picked up a handset by the cabin door. "We need a bottle of rum and a case of beer," he told whoever answered it. He winked at Fortis. "And a couple sandwiches. Just in case."

* * *

When the transport docked at the shuttle station orbiting around Eros-69, Bender led the way into the terminal area. "We need to find out how they get cargo to the surface. If Stoat is here, that's where we'll find him."

They discovered that the shuttle station handled only passengers bound to and departing from Eros-69. "There's a cargo station in orbit on the other side of the planet," a station crewmember told them. Then she winked. "We can't have the drunks mixing with the junk."

"Let's head down to the surface," Fortis said. "We'll find out where they land the cargo and see what we can learn about *Anusha*."

The carnival-like atmosphere of Eros-69 hit them the second they stepped off the shuttle. They had to run a gauntlet of people passing out handbills for everything there was to do on the planet. On one side of the terminal, a three-piece band belted out old-time dance tunes. Men with large tanks strapped to their backs circulated through the crowd and dispensed anonymous punch drinks into giant plastic cups for newly arrived passengers.

Bender bulled through the crowd with Fortis close on his heels until they were outside. They walked past the queue for free luxury hotel ground transportation and found a taxi stand.

"Take us to the cargo terminal," Fortis told the driver.

"Are you sure? That's in another dome and there's a fee to use the tunnel."

"Yes, I'm sure."

"There's also a taxi premium. There aren't any return fares from the cargo terminal."

"When we get there, I'll pay you half and you can wait with your meter running. When we've finished our business, you can bring us back."

"How long will you be there?"

"No more than thirty minutes, but I'll pay you for the hour."

"Shoot, I might take the rest of the day off." The taxi shot into traffic. "Hang on, gents. We'll be there in no time."

The taxi stopped in front of the cargo terminal and Fortis passed a wad of credits to the driver. "Remember, you get the rest if you're here when we get back."

"You sure drove a hard bargain with him," Bender said as they climbed the steps into the cargo terminal. "Why didn't you just buy the taxi?"

"I'm not in the mood to do a bunch of haggling. Besides, if he's telling the truth, we might not have gotten a ride back any time soon."

They located the cargo master's office and Fortis spun a tale of critical inbound cargo aboard *Anusha* and repeated inquiries to the ship going unanswered.

"*Anusha* is scheduled to dock in thirty-six hours. She'll be at the cargo station for two days and then she's bound for Eros-28."

"What do you want to do for the next thirty-six hours?" Bender asked when they were back in the taxi.

"If it's girls you want, I can hook you gentlemen up with the finest Eros-69 has to offer," the driver said.

"We're okay, thanks."

"Boys?"

"No. Really, we're okay." Fortis looked at Bender. "I heard they built a beach under the dome. I've never been to a beach."

"The beach it is."

As they got out of the taxi, the driver pushed his business card on them. "Keep this, just in case. That number is good any time. Anything you want, I can get it."

Bender tucked the card into his pocket as the taxi accelerated into traffic. "Crazy bastard."

Fortis was disappointed by the beach. The dome was painted to look like a distant horizon over the ocean, but the clouds never moved. The waves were obviously man-made, and they splashed onto the sand with unnatural regularity. The whole thing was a desultory effort at creating an effect for people who'd been in space too long.

Bender was anxious to cram in as much of the Eros-69 experience into thirty-six hours as they could. He'd been there several times and had his favorite places to go, but after twelve hours Fortis had to call it quits.

"This place is so fake," he told Bender as they sat at a sidewalk bar and watched the crowds. "Everyone is determined to look like they're having the time of their lives whether they are or not."

"Except you, mate. You seem determined not to have fun."

"It's not that I don't want to have fun, I just don't want to force it. I don't know, it's hard to explain."

Bender, on the other hand, displayed a remarkable knack for attracting female attention, and he was constantly being approached by women alone and in groups. Whether it was his size, his booming laugh, or his brilliant smile, Fortis had to hand it to the massive Australian: he was a chick magnet. The lieutenant tried to fulfill the role of wingman, but Bender proved more than capable of handling the attention from more than one woman at a time.

Eventually Fortis waved goodbye to Bender and threaded his way through the mass of humanity back to their hotel.

* * * * *

Chapter Thirty-Eight

"**H**ow do you think we should handle this?" Bender asked Fortis over breakfast thirty hours later. They had just learned *Anusha* was due soon at the orbiting cargo station, and she was still commanded by Captain B. Rausch. "Get him on the ship?"

"I think we'll stick out if we go up to the cargo station. It's one thing to concoct a story to get some information, but we'd have to arrange transportation up and down. Too many people will remember us."

"We could wait for him at the cargo terminal, but there aren't a lot of people over there, either. What if he stays on the ship?"

"How about we lure him over here?"

Bender's eyebrows went up. "Sure, that might work. Send a message to the master of *Anusha* requesting a meeting to discuss a private transaction. 'Will only discuss details in person,' that sort of thing. He's shady enough. It probably wouldn't be the first time he did business that way."

"We'll need a high-roller hotel suite in case he checks out the invitation, but we need to catch him on the street, away from security cameras. I've still got a bunch of credits left over."

Bender laughed. "You didn't give Anders the rest of the money back?"

"As far as I'm concerned, we're still on the mission. Who do you think paid for the cabin on the transport?"

Fortis waited until they were finished eating to broach the next topic. "What are we going to do with him?"

"Kill him," Bender answered without hesitation. "He and his crew killed Cheese, and he left us to die on Menard-Kev. If that doesn't deserve a death sentence, I don't know what does."

Fortis nodded. "Yeah, I agree. If our mission wasn't secret, I'd try and argue that maybe we should put him on trial. Unfortunately for Stoat, that's not an option."

"You could try and argue for a trial, but you'd lose. Cheese was too good an operator to die at the hands of a backstabbing bastard and not be avenged."

The men lapsed into silence for a several minutes before Bender spoke again.

"There's a big hole in the plan. If he takes a taxi, it will drop him off at the front door of the hotel."

"Do you still have that taxi card? Maybe we could include transportation for the esteemed captain, except that he drops Stoat off in some back alley of our choosing."

"I have the card. It might work, but it means involving the taxi driver. A guy like that wouldn't have a problem getting involved in a setup, but when Stoat turns up dead, he might get cold feet. What if we go in the opposite direction? Instead of a posh hotel, let's get a room in the cheapest by-the-hour fleabag we can find, the kind of place where shady deals are made, and people mind their own business."

Fortis scratched his chin. "Yeah. If we set the meeting for midmorning, all the nighttime hustlers will be sleeping." He nodded. "I like it."

"Our exposure is the guy at the hotel desk who gets paid to remember nothing. There's only one problem."

"What's that?"

"How do we kill Stoat? It's going to be pretty obvious what happened if they find him with a broken neck."

"Drug overdose. There's China Mike here. How hard can it be to find? Just another spacefarer who succumbed to the excesses of Eros-69."

They divided up the tasks and got started. Bender left in search of China Mike while Fortis looked for a suitable meeting place. He found one and paid three days ahead to give him and Bender time to get off Eros-69 once the deed was done. Once in the room, he sat down and composed a note to Stoat on motel stationary.

Dear Captain Rausch,

My associates and I desire a meeting with you while your vessel is docked at Eros-69 to discuss a mutually beneficial business proposal. We will be at the Dark Star Motel for the next 24 hours, room 237. We look forward to meeting with you and negotiating a satisfactory arrangement.

Sincerely,

Eldon Kinch

Fortis reread the note a couple times and decided it was vague enough to suggest potentially illicit activity without being blatant about it.

It sounds like something out of a cheap gangster film.

He put it in an envelope and addressed it to Captain Rausch, care of *Anusha*, and sent it to the cargo terminal via messenger.

Bender arrived at the room with an armload of take-out and a shopping bag hanging from one elbow.

"I got the gear," he said opening the bag and revealed a syringe and a packet of white powder. "The guy I bought it from said it's good stuff." He pulled out a handful of plastic zip ties. "I found these, too. Thought they might come in handy."

Fortis eyed the paraphernalia. "Did the dealer tell you how to mix up the China Mike?"

"No, but I don't think it matters. When the time comes, we'll mix it one-for-one. That ought to do it."

The two men chewed their way through the food and then Fortis checked the time.

"*Anusha* will be dockside in an hour. I'm guessing another hour for Stoat to get the message and get over here, so we've got two hours to kill before we—well, you know…"

Bender chuckled. "Yeah, I know." He kicked off his shoes and stretched out on one of the beds. "I'm gonna take a quick nap."

Fortis wrinkled his nose at the idea of getting on the beds. "I wonder when the last time those coverlets were cleaned?" He settled into one of the armchairs, put his chin on his chest, and closed his eyes.

* * *

"Lucky, it's time." Bender shook Fortis' shoulder. "He could be here any minute."

Fortis stood and stretched. While he'd been

napping, the Australian operator had cleaned up the food trash and laid out a syringe filled with milky white liquid.

"I'll take the first watch," Bender told him. He placed a chair next to the window and cracked the shades enough so he could see the motel entrance. "Dim the lights, would you?"

"How are we going to do this? When we open the door, he's going to recognize us and run."

"That's why we won't give him a chance to run. When he knocks, I'll go to the door and wait for him to knock again. When he does, I'll yank the door open and drag him inside. Be ready to throw a coverlet over him and we'll pin him to the floor and zip tie him. No worries."

Fortis knew the smaller man would be no match for the two Space Marines, but he also knew that when anything could go wrong it usually did. He played Bender's scenario over in his head and decided to make some changes to the room. He shoved the beds together against the far wall and moved the table away from its place next to the door. The arrangement cleared the area in front of the door and lessened the possibility of getting tangled up in the furniture. He settled back into his chair to wait and was soon in the restful state of alertness that had served him well so far during his ISMC service.

Forty minutes later, Bender sat up and stared out the window. Fortis sat up as well and watched his partner.

"This is it." Bender moved to the door and quietly unlocked it while Fortis grabbed a coverlet and prepared to pounce. There was a furtive knock and Bender put his hand on the doorknob. Another knock, and he threw it open wide and seized Stoat, who was in mid-knock.

"Hey! What—"

Fortis dove on top of Stoat and threw the coverlet over the captain's head. Bender kicked the door shut and joined the fray, and Stoat was restrained in seconds. They pulled the coverlet off and Stoat blinked.

"What the hell? This—oh shit, it's you," Stoat said when he recognized Fortis. He looked at Bender, and the color drained from his face. "And you brought your big friend."

Bender slapped Stoat. "Shut up. Don't speak unless you're spoken to."

They left Stoat on the floor and dragged their chairs close enough that they could put their feet on his body.

"You killed my mate and left us to die." Bender punctuated his statement with a foot to the face.

"We had to leave. Pirates were on the way."

"Not pirates, slavers."

"Whoever they were, I didn't want to mess with them."

"You chased my men onto the escape pod and then ran for it." Fortis prodded him in the ribs. "You abandoned us. You're a fucking coward."

"What was I supposed to do? They told me to get the hell out of there, so I did."

"The slavers told you to go and you were going to leave without warning us?"

"No, not the—" Stoat caught himself.

Bender and Fortis exchanged puzzled glances.

"'Not the' who? The slavers?"

Stoat looked away.

Bender slapped him on the head. "You're supposed to speak when spoken to. I'm speaking to you. Who are you talking about?'"

Stoat shook his head but remained tightlipped. Bender yanked him up by the front of his tunic and aimed a massive fist at Stoat's face.

"Who are 'they'?"

When Stoat didn't answer, the operator crushed his nose with a powerful punch. The captain moaned as blood poured down his face. Bender shoved him back onto the floor and leaned over him.

"We've got this room for the next three days. I can do this for three days; can you?"

Fortis put up a hand to restrain the massive Australian. "Take it easy, Bender. We're never going to get any answers that way." He grabbed Stoat by the shoulder and hauled him up until he was sitting. "Your nose is a mess, but it's nothing a good doctor can't fix." He gestured to the bathroom. "Bender, can I talk to you for a second?"

They retreated into the bathroom and closed the door. "What's up, boss? You're not going soft on me, are you?"

"No, not at all. We can finish him right now if you want, but I'm curious to know who he's talking about. Now he has a chance to think about what you said while his nose bleeds. It might make him more talkative."

"Okay. You take the lead, and I'll look menacing."

The two men returned to their seats and Fortis patted their captive on the shoulder. "You understand why we're pissed, don't you?" Stoat nodded. "My friend here wants to pound on you. To be honest, so do I. Still, I'm a fair guy, and I want you to tell me the story of our mission. Who knows, maybe you'll convince us to let you go."

Stoat's eyes flicked between Fortis and Bender. "Where do you want me to start?"

"Start at the beginning. How did you find out about us?"

"Cujo came to see me on SOMO. He said there was a team that needed a ride and asked if I had a ship."

"Did you know Cujo before that?"

"Sure. I know all the pilots that fly out of SOMO."

"Okay, then what?"

"He brought you to *Dragon's Breath,* and we made our deal."

"Any strings attached? Anyone else interested in us?"

Stoat hesitated and Bender shifted in his seat. "Yeah."

"Come on, Stoat. Don't make me ask."

"Cujo was mixed up with these guys who wanted to keep tabs on the ship."

"Cujo?"

Stoat nodded. "He knows them from before. They put a transponder on the ship to track our position."

"Who are these guys? How does Cujo know them?"

"He used to fly for them. They're in the Knighthood."

"Cujo used to fly for the Kuiper Knights?"

Stoat nodded. "I thought it was kind of weird that he was with you, all things considered."

"What things?"

"You know. The bounty." Stoat looked from Fortis to Bender. "You know about the bounty, right?"

"No, I don't. How about you, Bender? You know anything about a bounty?" The hulking operator shook his head. "Tell us about the bounty."

"Fifty million credits."

"Fifty million credits for what?"

"For you. The Knighthood has put a fifty million credit bounty on your head. Dead or alive."

Bender sat back and gave a low whistle. Fortis' head swam, and he had to brace himself so he didn't tumble out of his chair.

* * * * *

Chapter Thirty-Nine

It took Fortis a minute to clear his head. The enormity of Stoat's revelation about the bounty was shocking, and Cujo's role in a scheme to collect it temporarily overwhelmed him.

Bender sat in his chair and punched a massive fist into his other palm. "I never liked that sonofabitch." *Smack.* "I'm gonna kill him." *Smack.*

Finally, Fortis found his voice. "Okay, Stoat, let's start all over again. Cujo came to see you on SOMO."

"Yeah. I had just finished refitting *Dragon's Breath*, so I needed the work. He said there was a team looking for a ride and there was an opportunity to pick up a load of extra money from a bounty. His plan was to take your team down to the surface, and my crew would take care of whoever you left behind. Then the trailing ship would shuttle over a bunch of guys to ambush you when you returned."

"Remember how upset he got when he found out we were leaving Bugs with Cheese?" Fortis asked Bender. Bender nodded. "Continue, Stoat."

"I was waiting for the Knights to show up before we took out your guys. Instead, the Knights called and said the slavers were on their way and told us to get out of there. What the else could I do? Your guys wouldn't go with us without a fight, right? We sprang the trap and everything went to shit almost before it started. Two of my guys were dead, two more were wounded, and your guys jumped to the surface in an escape pod. I did the only thing I could do, I ran."

Stoat's matter-of-fact confession about killing Cheese and abandoning the team infuriated Fortis, but he saw the logic behind those decisions.

"You left your partner Cujo behind, too."

"Hey, look, he knew the risks of getting involved in something like that. I didn't leave him behind as some kind of double-cross, it just happened"

"It was him or you, and you chose you."

"When you put it like that, sure."

Fortis looked at Bender. "What do you think?"

"Dunno. It fits. It doesn't really change things here."

"Hey, Stoat, do you speak French?"

Stoat looked surprised but said, "Yeah. Heh. That was Cujo's idea. I knew it wouldn't work, but he insisted."

"Let's waste him," Bender said.

"Ah, hey, c'mon guys. I told you the truth about bounty and Cujo," Stoat begged. "Doesn't that count for anything?"

Bender hit him in the temple with a vicious rabbit punch and the captain fell over, unconscious. "No."

The operators returned the furniture to the way it was. The blood on the carpet from Stoat's nose disappeared under one of the beds, and they didn't try to scrub it up or disguise it. Fortis cut the zip ties from Stoat's wrists and dumped him on one of the beds. He positioned the body to make it look like the captain was sitting on the edge and fell backward.

Meanwhile, Bender grabbed the syringe filled with China Mike. He instructed Fortis on how to tie the surgical tubing to make a vein in Stoat's elbow stand out.

"Last chance," Bender said.

Fortis nodded. "Do it."

Stoat convulsed and bloody foam poured from his mouth and nose when the drug entered his bloodstream. He was dead in seconds.

Bender checked for a pulse and shook his head. "He's gone."

Fortis was curiously unmoved by Stoat's death. One minute he was pleading for his life, and, in the next, he was gone. Fortis was no stranger to death, but this was the first time he'd encountered it and not felt anything. He thought about Cheese and the desperation the team had felt when they discovered they'd been abandoned.

It was a better death than Stoat deserved.

Bender stripped a pillow and tore the case into strips. They wiped down every surface in the room, starting in the bathroom and working toward the door.

"Even if they found one of our fingerprints in here, it proves nothing," Bender said as they worked. "Still, it's better not to give them a reason to ask questions."

"This room is going to be cleaner than it's been in years," Fortis said. "Oh, shit."

"What?"

Fortis pointed to a discarded condom on the carpet in the corner. "I moved the trashcan to wipe around it and found that."

"You didn't touch it, did you?"

"Fuck—" Fortis stopped when he saw the familiar mirth in Bender's eyes. "No, I didn't touch it, dickhead. I left it right where your mom dropped it."

They shared a laugh while they continued with their grim task. Fortis got the willies when he wiped down the dresser and got a glimpse of Stoat in the mirror. In his mind's eye he saw the captain sit up, and he had to turn around and check, just to be sure.

When they were finished, Fortis and Bender surveyed the room. It looked like what they imagined an accidental overdose would look like.

"Let's get out of here."

"One more thing." Bender bent over Stoat's body and lifted the dead man's shirt. "I'm not leaving this," he said as he stripped off the money belt he found around Stoat's waist.

"Do you think that was a good idea?" Fortis asked after they stepped out into the afternoon sunshine and pulled the door shut.

"He won't be needing it anymore, and if we don't take it whoever finds him will. At least we know the money will be well spent." He unzipped the money belt and pulled out a sheaf of bills. "Sheesh, look at this. There's got to be a million credits here."

"I paid him a million and a half up front and another half million when we got to Menard-Kev," Fortis said. "I guess he didn't have time to spend his cut."

"C'mon, we need to find you a disguise."

"A disguise?"

"You're the most famous Space Marine in the Corps and there are fifty million reasons why someone might want to take a shot at you."

Suddenly, the run-down neighborhood surrounding the Dark Star Motel took on a menacing look despite the bright sunshine. The skin on the back of Fortis' neck tingled as he scanned the area for threats.

"Thanks for reminding me. I'd completely forgotten."

"Yeah, well, I don't want to be around when someone tries to collect." Bender laughed at the look Fortis gave him. "Don't worry, mate. I've got your six. Still, there's no reason to make it any easier."

Fortis' disguise consisted of a floppy hat, a garish Eros-69 tourist shirt that read "I got 69'd on Eros-69!" and a tall plastic cup filled with the ubiquitous "punch" peddled by venders all over the party district.

"Here, splash some of this on your shirt and try to look drunk," Bender told him. "We're just a couple of asshole tourists on an early bender."

They finally made it back to their hotel, and Fortis breathed a sigh of relief when he closed and locked the door behind them. He took a quick look in the bathroom and closets to ensure they were alone before he allowed himself to relax.

"Stay here. I'll get us seats on the next craft headed for TEJG, and some food, too." Bender paused at the door. "Are you okay?"

"Yeah, I'm fine. I don't like sneaking around."

"I'm afraid you're going to have to until we get you back to Terra Earth."

"I wonder how many more Idoia Guerra's there are out there."

Bender stared at Fortis. "Nothing's going to happen to you on my watch, Lucky. Count on it."

Fortis looked at the door for a long time after the Australian left. *I hope you're right.*

* * *

The next transport to TEJG didn't leave until the following evening, so Fortis and Bender hunkered down in their hotel room.

"Mate, if you don't stop peeking out the window every five minutes, I'm going to throw open the drapes and put up a sign announcing that you're here," Bender said. "You're driving me crazy."

Fortis chuckled and sat down on the edge of his bed. "I'm sorry. I'd be okay if Stoat hadn't told us about the bounty."

"Speaking of Stoat, you understand that what we did here during our vacation can't be part of your written mission report to Anders, right?"

"Why not? He's the one who gave us the tip."

"Did he?"

"Yeah, of course. It was in the envelope with our tickets, remember?"

"He gave us an envelope with our tickets. Are you certain *he* put that note in there?"

Fortis thought for a second. "No."

"Do you think someone with an axe to grind against you, or Anders, or the ISMC, might be interested in a report that detailed the assassination of a civilian by ISR Space Marine operators?"

Fortis didn't know how to respond.

"I like you, Lucky, so I'm going to give you some friendly advice: this is the intel world. It's a pit full of vipers that will bite you to death if they can gain advantage by doing so do, and those are the people on the inside. On the outside are politicians, reporters, and a bunch of other people who want to see us destroyed for any number of reasons." He pointed a thick forefinger at Fortis. "You can't trust anyone. *Anyone*. Not even me."

"Why can't I trust you?"

"What we just did to Stoat is murder. A smart defense attorney could probably make the case about extenuating circumstances and blah blah blah, but we murdered him. In terms of shared secrets, that's about as bad as they get."

"Why would you tell anyone? You'd get in trouble too."

"What if I get in trouble in the future and try to deal my way out of it?"

Fortis' felt the blood drain from his face.

"Not that I would do that to a fellow Space Marine, but I could, especially if it was documented in a written report. Now do you understand?"

Fortis nodded slowly. "Yeah, I think so. Don't trust anyone. Especially you." He flopped back on his bed and rubbed his eyes with his palms. "All I wanted to do was pay off my student loans."

The pair broke into laughter and Bender threw a pillow at Fortis.

"Bloody wanker."

* * * * *

Chapter Forty

The trip to the passenger terminal was anticlimactic. Fortis donned his drunken tourist costume and they made it to the shuttle without incident. Once they were in their private cabin aboard the transport, he tore off the Eros-69 shirt and threw it in the trash.

"You don't like your shirt?" Bender taunted him.

"That thing stinks like stale liquor," Fortis told Bender. "I was going to keep it, but not now."

"We still need it, at least until we get down to Terra Earth. Rinse it out and hang it up."

The rest of their journey was unremarkable. The transport passenger cabin was far more subdued than their outbound trip, and when they arrived at TEJG, there was no rush to disembark. Fortis and Bender waited to join the last trickle of passengers headed for the Terra Earth shuttle gate. After a quick trip down to Kinshasa, they caught the next tram to the ISMC headquarters base.

"Safe and sound," Bender announced as they entered the ISR team building. "Maybe."

Fortis slugged his companion on the shoulder. "Thanks, dickhead. C'mon, let's go see the colonel."

"Nah, you go ahead. I've got to get the latest on *Imperio*."

Fortis had completely forgotten about Bender's goddaughter.

"Good luck," he said as they shook hands.

"Thanks, mate. And good luck to you, too."

Fortis rapped three times of Anders' office door, waited a beat, and entered.

"Ah, Abner, welcome home." Colonel Anders stood and greeted Fortis. He stared at Fortis' shirt. He gave a knowing smile and asked, "How was your leave?"

"Relaxing. Eros-69 was everything we could have asked for."

"Sit down and tell me all about it."

When they were seated, Fortis recounted their trip to Eros-69. He was careful not to give too many details about Stoat's fate.

"We met an old spacefaring friend there. Sadly, he was on his final journey, but we settled up an old debt and had an interesting conversation before he left."

"Really? Do tell."

"The assassin Idoia Guerra tried to kill me to collect a bounty that's on my head. The Kuiper Knights have put up a fifty million credit bounty on me."

"Fifty million credits? How did he know that?"

"Because Cujo put him up to it."

"I don't understand."

"Our pilot Cujo was part of a plot to kill me and collect the bounty. Cujo has piloted for the Kuiper Knights in the past. He and Stoat planned to ambush us when we returned from the surface of Menard-Kev with the help from an unidentified Kuiper Knight craft. Mansoor and the slavers showed up and disrupted their plan."

Anders sat back and made a steeple with his fingers in front of his face. He closed his eyes for a long moment before he sat up and put his hands flat on the desk.

"Stoat told you all this?"

"Yes, sir."

"And you believe him?"

"The pieces fit, Colonel. Take the transmissions that Tweak discovered. How could Stoat have known that we discovered them? Only Tweak, Bender, and I knew about them. What about Cujo's reaction when he found out Bugs and Cheese were staying on *Dragon's Breath*? Then there were his suspicious teletype transmissions on *Alharih*. I think he was signaling the Kuiper Knights." Fortis stood and began to pace. "Sir, I know this sounds crazy, and if it was just a story Stoat told us before we...well, before we said goodbye, I'd be more a lot more skeptical. But it's not. His story correlates to a lot of details that he couldn't have known. Oh, and when I asked him if he spoke French, he knew exactly what I was talking about. *LJM de Bourbon*."

"What do you want me to do with this information? I can have my sources locate Cujo for you."

Fortis sat down with a big sigh. "I don't know, Colonel. I know there's some bias in my thinking, and I don't have any solid evidence. We know that Stoat abandoned us, and he deserved to be punished. We don't *know* what Cujo did. Maybe Stoat's story is a remarkable coincidence. What do you think, sir?"

"I think Cujo deserves closer scrutiny. If he has ties with the Kuiper Knighthood, we need to know about them. If we find any evidence that he was part of a conspiracy to collect the bounty, then we'll act. The most important thing we need to deal with right now is the bounty. We've got to convince the Kuiper Knights to rescind it, because I can't have one of my top people unable to operate."

"How?"

"I don't know. Until we come up with a solution, I'm ordering you to remain inside this building. If La Química could find you, others can too."

"That sucks, sir."

Anders spread his hands open on the desk. "It's not too late to transfer to Logistics or Personnel."

"Screw that. I'm staying here."

"DINLI, Fortis."

"Yes, sir. DINLI."

* * * * *

About P.A. Piatt

P.A. Piatt was born and raised in western Pennsylvania. After his first attempt at college, he joined the Navy to see the world. He started writing as a hobby when he retired in 2005 and published his first novel in 2018.

His published works include the Abner Fortis, International Space Marine Corps mil-sf series, the Walter Bailey Misadventures urban fantasy trilogy, and other full-length novels in both science fiction and horror.

All of his novels and various published short stories can be found on Amazon. Visit his website at www.papiattauthor.com.

* * * * *

For More Information:

Meet the authors of CKP on the Factory Floor:

https://www.facebook.com/groups/461794864654198

* * * * *

Get the free Four Horsemen prelude story "Shattered Crucible"

and discover other titles by Theogony Books at:

http://chriskennedypublishing.com/

* * * * *

Did you like this book?
Please write a review!

* * * * *

The following is an
Excerpt from Book One of the Lunar Free State:

The Moon and Beyond

John E. Siers

Available from Theogony Books

eBook and Paperback

Excerpt from "The Moon and Beyond:"

"So, what have we got?" The chief had no patience for interagency squabbles.

The FBI man turned to him with a scowl. "We've got some abandoned buildings, a lot of abandoned stuff—none of which has anything to do with spaceships—and about a hundred and sixty scientists, maintenance people, and dependents left behind, all of whom claim they knew nothing at all about what was really going on until today. Oh, yeah, and we have some stripped computer hardware with all memory and processor sections removed. I mean physically taken out, not a chip left, nothing for the techies to work with. And not a scrap of paper around that will give us any more information...at least, not that we've found so far. My people are still looking."

"What about that underground complex on the other side of the hill?"

"That place is wiped out. It looks like somebody set off a *nuke* in there. The concrete walls are partly fused! The floor is still too hot to walk on. Our people say they aren't sure how you could even *do* something like that. They're working on it, but I doubt they're going to find anything."

"What about our man inside, the guy who set up the computer tap?"

"Not a trace, chief," one of the NSA men said. "Either he managed to keep his cover and stayed with them, or they're holding him prisoner, or else..." The agent shrugged.

"You think they terminated him?" The chief lifted an eyebrow. "A bunch of rocket scientists?"

"Wouldn't put it past them. Look at what Homeland Security ran into. Those motion-sensing chain guns are *nasty*, and the area between the inner and outer perimeter fence is mined! Of course, they posted warning signs, even marked the fire zones for the guns. Nobody would have gotten hurt if the troops had taken the signs seriously."

The Homeland Security colonel favored the NSA man with an icy look. "That's bullshit. How did we know they weren't bluffing? You'd feel pretty stupid if we'd played it safe and then found out there were no defenses, just a bunch of signs!"

"Forget it!" snarled the chief. "Their whole purpose was to delay us, and it worked. What about the Air Force?"

"It might as well have been a UFO sighting as far as they're concerned. Two of their F-25s went after that spaceship, or whatever it was we saw leaving. The damned thing went straight up, over eighty thousand meters per minute, they say. That's nearly Mach Two, in a *vertical climb*. No aircraft in *anybody's* arsenal can sustain a climb like that. Thirty seconds after they picked it up, it was well above their service ceiling and still accelerating. Ordinary ground radar couldn't find it, but NORAD *thinks* they might have caught a short glimpse with one of their satellite-watch systems, a hundred miles up and still going."

"So where did they go?"

"Well, chief, if we believe what those leftover scientists are telling us, I guess they went to the Moon."

* * * * *

Get "The Moon and Beyond" here:
https://www.amazon.com/dp/B097QMN7PJ.

Find out more about John E. Siers at:
https://chriskennedypublishing.com.

* * * * *

The following is an
Excerpt from Book One of Murphy's Lawless:

Shakes

Mike Massa

Available from Beyond Terra Press

eBook and Paperback

Excerpt from "Shakes:"

"My name is Volo of the House Zobulakos," the SpinDog announced haughtily. Harry watched as his slender ally found his feet and made a show of brushing imaginary dust from his shoulder where the lance had rested.

Volo was defiant even in the face of drawn weapons; Harry had to give him points for style.

"I am here representing the esteemed friend to all Sarmatchani, my father, Arko Primus Heraklis Zobulakos. This is a mission of great importance. What honorless prole names my brother a liar and interferes with the will of the Primus? Tell me, that I might inform your chief of this insolence."

Harry tensed as two of the newcomers surged forward in angry reaction to the word "honorless," but the tall man interposed his lance, barring their way.

"Father!" the shorter one objected, throwing back her hood, revealing a sharp featured young woman. She'd drawn her blade and balefully eyed the SpinDog. "Let me teach this arrogant weakling about honor!"

"Nay, Stella," the broad-shouldered man said grimly. "Even my daughter must cleave to the law. This is a clan matter. And as to the stripling's question…

"I, hight Yannis al-Caoimhip ex-huscarlo, Patrisero of the Herdbane, First among the Sarmatchani," he went on, fixing his eyes first on Volo and then each of the Terrans. "I name Stabilo of the Sky People a liar, a cheat, and a coward. I call his people to account. Blood or treasure. At dawn tomorrow either will suffice."

Harry didn't say a word but heard a deep sigh from Rodriguez. These were the allies he'd been sent to find, all right. Just like every other joint operation with indigs, it was SNAFU.

Murphy's Law was in still in effect.

* * * * *

Get "Shakes" now at: https://www.amazon.com/dp/B0861F23KH

Find out more about Myrphy's Lawless and Beyond Terra Press at: https://chriskennedypublishing.com/imprints-authors/beyond-terra-press/

* * * * *

Made in the USA
Monee, IL
16 January 2022